Ganja
BANANA

Alan Briggs

4p five o'clock press

This first edition published in Great Britain in 2009 by
Four O'Clock Press - a Discovered Authors' imprint
ISBN 978-1-907136-03-0

Available from Discovered Authors Online –
All major online retailers and available to order through all UK bookshops

Or contact:
Books
Discovered Authors
Roslin Road, London
W3 8DH

0844 800 5214
books@discoveredauthors.co.uk
www.discoveredauthors.co.uk

Printed in the UK by BookForce Distribution
BookForce Distribution policy is to use papers that are natural, renewable and
recyclable products and made from wood grown in sustainable forests wherever
possible

BookForce Distribution Ltd.
Roslin Road, London
W3 8DH
www.bookforce.co.uk

To my wife Jeanette
for her forbearance and help with the manuscript.

CHAPTER 1

PENTONVILLE
MAY, 1973

Brett Johnson emerged from the wicket gate of the prison with some trepidation, fearing - as far as he was able to feel fear - a hot reception from the racist groups. He fully expected that there would be some sort of retaliation for the exploits against them that had put him behind bars. His five years in Pentonville had been punctuated with threats and actual violence that had resulted more than once in spells of solitary confinement for his own protection from the thugs. Even sharing a cell with a feared Yardie enforcer had been no guarantee of safety.

'What better time to nail me than on my release, before I've time to disappear?' he wondered.

Sure enough, there they were. A crowd of skinheads was waiting for him, wearing Union-flagged tee shirts, their coarse

faces filled with hate; biceps etched with swastika tattoos. There were about twenty of them, massed in a solid group on his left. As the gate closed behind him, a familiar blood lust chorus started.

"Kill the commie swine." "String the black bastard up."

He attempted to step back, expecting an immediate attack, but the gate had closed behind him. The mob made as if to surge forward, but, to his relief, held back. He realised why they were keeping their distance when, from his right, came a counter chorus of,

"Down with Nazis. Out with fascists. Out, Out, Out."

The thugs were greatly outnumbered by his supporters from a motley collection of left wing and anti-fascist groups. Their numbers were not a deterrent for long. Whipped into a frenzied state by the bellows of an obese giant of a man wielding a pickaxe handle, the thugs charged forward. A protective cordon of men quickly surrounded their target, and produced their own weapons as if by magic. Knives appeared, and banner poles became lances. Casualties on both sides began to reel away from the fray, blood streaming from face and head wounds. Some fell and lay still. Only the belated deployment of a busload of riot police prevented a repeat of the pitched battle that had landed Brett Johnson in Pentonville in the first place. While the police tried to keep the factions apart with liberal use of their riot sticks, he was hustled into a waiting Cortina by two of his supporters and whisked away to safety.

With a puff-cheeked exhalation of pent up breath he settled down in the back between the two familiar members of the Cambridge Maoist cell, for the long trip back to headquarters. A compactly built black man in the passenger seat turned and

glanced at him, but said nothing. He was a stranger to Brett. His charcoal grey suit, white shirt and striped tie gave him the appearance of a successful businessman. The image was far removed from the truth. Although he had remained in the car, and played no part in the fracas, he had a presence that exuded physical power.

Clasping a hand each, Brett's companions welcomed him as if he was coming home.

"Great to see you again, Brett."

"How's my man?"

"Pretty good now, but better if the police had let you sort the fascists out."

As disappointed with the outcome as he was, they fell silent, thinking about what might have been. He closed his eyes, and was soon sleeping. He remained asleep until the car pulled up in the quiet Cambridge street where the group's headquarters was situated. Climbing awkwardly out of his position in the middle, Brett started up the street to walk off the stiffness in his cramped legs.

"No time for that," the driver insisted. "I'm pretty sure we were followed, at least as far as the outskirts. You don't get many black cabs out this way. Let's get him inside," he insisted to his colleagues.

They almost man-handled him through the wrought iron gate and up the short flight of steps, into the little terrace house, followed by the stranger. The driver accelerated away fast, to leave the car where it wouldn't be associated with that particular

house. Only when his passengers were inside was the man from the passenger seat introduced to Brett by one of his rescuers.

"Brett Johnson - meet Matt Maynard - a big wheel from the Kingston Left,"

With an attempt at a self-deprecating smile, Maynard took Brett's hand in a powerful grip, and while still shaking hands, said,

"I'm here for a reason. Your release date was picked up on the grape-vine. You're known about back home, and pretty well thought of. We reckon you're wasting your talents here, when Jamaica's crying out for an effective left wing. Manley's OK, but it'll take him years."

Brett shrugged, and led the way up the stairs. Over his shoulder he said to Maynard,

"Going back was something I considered in prison, but I rejected it as a non-starter. We've got a lot of support here, but if you're serious, and you think your organisation could be made as good as this one, it could be worth thinking about again. Give me time to get myself sorted out, and I'll consider it."

"Time's something we don't have. I need an answer," said Maynard, as they entered a second floor room.

Brett sat on the bed, and found Maynard staring hard at him, obviously expecting a quick response.

The room that Brett had used before he wound up in Pentonville hadn't been used since, and it gave that impression. It was shared with a dilapidated typewriter and copier, and was not much of a home, but it ought at least to be a safe house . Somehow, though, it looked as though even this place might be compromised if the Nazis had managed to follow him to Cambridge.

'Maybe they already know where I'm based' he thought. 'If so, a quick flit will be necessary, in which case a return to Jamaica could be a good move'.

The idea began to appeal more as he considered his options.

'As things stand, there's not much to keep me in England now, anyway, but there are bound to be problems. The press has probably identified me. That'll make a legitimate return difficult, or impossible. I'll need careful planning, and help on both sides of the Atlantic. Organising it all's going to take time'.

These thoughts occupied a matter of seconds, in which time Brett's mind was made up. He turned to Matt Maynard.

"I'm sold on the idea, but you do realise I can't go under my own name?"

Before Maynard could answer, one of the militant Maoists who had sat behind him in the car broke in.

"A new identity's no problem, just a matter of waiting a day or two. If you want, I can start setting it up straightaway."

Now that he'd made the decision, Brett was impatient at the thought of any hold up, but recognised that there was no way of speeding things up.

"Do it," he said.

The organisation took more than a day or two, because he needed to change his appearance. Waiting was made worse because he could do nothing himself. Brett had to stay in the room and leave everything to his friends. His days consisted of sleeping, eating and reading. The new identity and a forged

passport were the first requirements. A month's growth trimmed to a moustache and little goatee beard made an amazing difference. The acquisition of a passport was surprisingly simple. When the beard growth was sufficient, a booth photograph and a name taken to a professional forger, plus two hundred pounds up front, was all that was needed. Two days later, a document indistinguishable from a legitimate passport, even down to official entry and exit stamps for the UK and several European countries, was delivered to his hideout. Two days later he was on his way.

HEATHROW AIRPORT

To minimise the possibility of recognition by any of the security organisations that might have an interest in his movements, Brett's friends had avoided the scheduled airlines and booked him a return ticket on an Air Jamaica charter flight to Kingston. Once home he had no intention of returning, but they reasoned that a single ticket would arouse unwelcome interest. For extra insurance he was travelling as Ellery Masters, teacher, and was sporting the moustache and goatee beard shown in the passport photograph. He was now trying to mingle with a crowd of Jamaican athletes returning from an international athletics meeting. As they filed through the departure gate to await their flight call in the International Departure Lounge of Terminal 3, he made sure he was amongst the tallest of the athletes, but even so, had to stoop to disguise his own height.

Although, like himself, most of his fellow passengers were black, he was too tall and handsome to fade completely into the background. The fact that his dark blue blazer contrasted with the maroon of those of the athletes was no help.

'Maybe I'll be taken for an official', he hoped, without much confidence.

His proud bearing and good looks were characteristic of those West Indians whose Coromantin slave ancestors originated in the Gold Coast of West Africa. Somehow, over the generations, they had not mingled their genes with those of other black races. The piercing eyes, under thin brows, and the almost straight nose, gave him an aristocratic look, and there was no disguising his charisma.

'Thank whatever gods are looking over me', he thought, as he passed through passport control with no apparent problem.

The officer at the desk gave him only a cursory look, hardly glanced at his passport, and waved him through. What Brett could not know was that, as soon as he had moved on towards the departure lounge, the passport officer touched a button under his desktop. A red light flashed on a console in a glass-fronted cubicle in a corner. The two men there leaned forward to scrutinise the figure passing a few yards away. Brett was under surveillance by officers of DI6, the Secret Intelligence Service.

"Old Frank's on the ball today," said the slimmer one with the military officer's bearing. "I think we've got something special here."

"Another false alarm, more likely," his bored partner replied as he shifted his bulk to ease the pain in his knee, which every time he moved reminded him where he had stopped a sniper's

bullet in the Aden campaign. "I'll be glad when this shift's over."

"Worth a look," said his boss, Tom Sutherland, sometime major in army intelligence. "Pass that file", he snapped, "before I forget what he looks like."

He snatched the proffered black ring binder of mug shots provided by F Branch of MI5, and flicked over the pages.

"There," he said, with smug satisfaction. "Imagine this fellow with face fungus, and he's your man."

Taking the book, his colleague examined the page sceptically. Suddenly, with unusual animation, he said,

"OK, I'll buy it. That arrogant-looking bastard is Brett Johnson. What do we do about it?"

"Nothing, except warn Kingston and see him safely off our patch. Then he's their problem. Get on it straightaway."

Part of the DI6 mandate was to keep a watching brief on potential political troublemakers. In their assessment, Johnson fell into that category. He had come to the Department's notice a couple of years before his imprisonment. At Cambridge the tenuous ideas that his boyhood experiences had helped to formulate had crystallised in his mind. His political thought had moved inexorably towards the left of the spectrum, influenced by contacts with the activist societies of the University. The International Socialists, the Communists, the Maoists, had all attracted him in turn. He had taken part in violent demonstrations against police racial prejudice in South London. After Cambridge, he was involved in clashes with racists in the same area. It was during those that he had been arrested twice, the first time for affray. The second time, for GBH, when he smashed the jaw of a leading light in the recently formed National Front,

had cost him five years in jail. His potential as a black activist had been noted by Special Branch observers and passed on to the Domestic Subversion Branch of MI5. DI6 had opened a file on him at the same time.

Tom Sutherland's side-kick limped across to the TELEX machine in the corner. Minutes later a coded message appeared in the office of Chief Inspector John Anderson, of the Jamaican Special Branch. It was succinct. Decoded, it read:

BRETT JOHNSON ON FLIGHT JA 090 TODAY 9.5.1973
KNOWN LEFT WING ACTIVIST BUT NO NEW
ARRESTABLE FORM HERE.
TRAVELLING AS ELLORY MASTERS.
WORTH WATCHING. OVER TO YOU.
DSB. (LONDON HEATHROW)

At 08.45, flight 090 was called, and Brett made his way to Gate 3, where the Lovebird Flight was boarding. He smiled in amusement at the fanciful name given to the flight as he boarded the stretched Douglas DC-8L. Its startling livery was as fancy as its name. As he climbed the steps his amusement turned to keen interest as he was welcomed and shown to his seat by coffee-coloured hostesses in stunning lime-green and yellow uniforms. Feeling at ease for the first time since arriving at Heathrow he settled down in his seat near the tail of the aircraft, determined to enjoy the flight, unaware of the activity his presence at the airport had provoked.

After the 'plane had reached its ceiling at thirty five thousand feet, and breakfast had been served, Brett fell into a light sleep. He awoke when he became conscious of a figure standing nearby, opened an eye, and was amazed to find its

field of view filled by a light brown, naked female torso. A taut navel peering back at him swung into a smooth, side-to-side movement as the mannequin walked on, twirled, and swayed off back down the gangway. She completed her modelling of a brilliant white top and ankle-length slit-sheath skirt, which clung provocatively to her shapely body. She disappeared into a curtained recess. Immediately she was replaced by another model. This girl wore the briefest of yellow bikinis, clinging precariously onto chocolate-brown curves that she flaunted proudly as she swung her hips down the aisle. Her knowing smile reflected her awareness of the effect she was creating. The male passengers were goggle-eyed, and there was more than one female scrutinising her enviously.

Years of sexual deprivation in jail had not prepared Brett Johnson for such an assault on his libido. His initial astonishment now replaced by an awareness of an intense ache in his groin, he tried to ease his discomfort by surreptitious adjustments of his position and clothing, but to no avail. During the next hour he enjoyed, and suffered, a non-stop parade of clothed and partially clothed feminine beauty such as he had never before seen collected in one place.

'Well!' he thought, as the show ended with the writhing rear view of the last model disappearing behind the curtain, 'I didn't believe the pilot's announcement about the hostesses doubling as mannequins. They could be mannequins, but a pity the airline didn't think about passengers' discomfort'.

Following the show the hostesses, now back in their uniforms, served rum bamboozles. Brett caught the eye of the one with the cafe-au-lait skin, whose navel had earlier caught his eye. He came straight to the point with West Indian directness.

"Where you sleeping tonight, honey?"

With an air that spoke of much practice, Della Brook riposted,

"Man, I won't get much sleep tonight, but it won't be insomnia, or you, that keeps me awake," and passed on to bandy repartee with the other males who fancied their chances.

As she retreated towards the galley with a tray of empty glasses, he savoured again the sight of the flic-flac of her tight-skirted buttocks trying to occupy the same limited space. The uncomfortable feeling returned, and he longed for relief. He was only half-sorry that he found the woman so stimulating, aware that something more than raw sexual attraction was at work. His thoughts were interrupted by the captain's voice over the intercom, announcing,

"We will not be landing at Halifax, Nova Scotia, to refuel. There's a favourable wind for a safe, direct flight to Kingston. The estimated time of arrival is 13.10 Eastern Standard Time. Your watches should be put back six hours," he added.

This was welcome news to Brett. His immediate thought was, 'I can't be sure that I wasn't spotted at Heathrow. If I was, I'd surely be 'persona non grata' in Halifax, and a landing there could have been dangerous. Not that landing in Kingston will be any the less dangerous, but only one landing halves the risk'.

As the aircraft turned south and climbed to thirty nine thousand feet to take advantage of the following wind, he settled down again, adjusted his watch to 7.15, and wondered what kind of reception was in store for him in Kingston if he had been recognised. His reputation as an activist might have preceded him. Although he couldn't be sure, he was thinking,

'I've got to assume that any interest in me won't be benevolent. If they do know of my arrival, I won't get past immigration and they'll put me on the next flight back to England'.

Such thoughts preyed on his mind to the extent that over the next couple of hours he felt himself becoming paranoid over the kind of reception that might be waiting for him. Even if his charter flight ploy had been successful, and no advance warning had reached Kingston, there was always a chance that he might be recognised by some covert observer. In that case the danger would lie, not in open arrest at the airport, but in a more clandestine operation, to detain him out of public view. Local Maoist contacts he had been given would be useless in either of those situations.

'I've got to be on my guard against both possibilities', he thought.

His musings were interrupted by a bright,

"Lunch for you sir?"

He looked up to find the woman who had modelled the white sheath offering him a lunch tray. Taken by surprise, and slightly flustered by the presence of the vision in white who had been responsible for his previous discomfort, all he could manage to say was,

"Er, um, yes - please, and dry white wine."

"The driest we have is a Muscadet," responded Della Brook, producing a quarter litre bottle from her trolley, and a dazzling smile from Heaven which could have sold him anything.

"That'll do fine," he said, accepting the bottle and returning the smile with one of his own that sent a thrill through her.

She went off down the aisle, distributing lunch trays in a state of pleasant confusion, lecturing herself that she had more

important things to do than fall for handsome passengers. Two hours later Brett was roused from his after-lunch torpor by the Captain's announcement that they were passing over the strait between Cuba and Haiti. He craned his neck to see past his neighbour, marvelling that such different cultures, at opposite ends of the political spectrum, could exist side by side. He recalled with wry amusement the hours of argument with his fellow students around the topic of Cuba's status. Word for word he remembered his winding up summary in a Union debate.

'Well, my case is that socialism's nothing more nor less than applied Christianity. It believes in the importance of the individual, and it's democratic. Although communism also stems from Christian ideas, it's corrupted them, so that the individual is of less importance than the Party or the State. It suppresses democracy, and rules by dictatorship as totalitarian as any brand of fascism. For example, Cuba's a communist tyranny run by Fidel Castro, and Haiti's a fascist tyranny run by 'Papa Doc' Duvalier, but they're both dictatorships and police states. In that sense, there's nothing to choose between them. With regard to socialism, I'd go even further, and suggest that John the Baptist and Jesus of Nazareth were the first socialist activists. Even their socialism followed on from the Ten Commandments of Moses. I submit that you could roll the commandments into one that says 'do unto others as you would have them do unto you' and you have the basis for both Christianity and Socialism'.

BANANA

Now, as he reflected on his idealistic student days, with the benefit of hindsight, Brett realised that, although he didn't really want to see a socialist dictatorship in Jamaica, something along Cuban lines might be necessary in the short term. As the plane headed southwest for Jamaica his thoughts turned to the present political situation on the island.

'If I have anything to do with it, I'll make damn sure that if anyone gains absolute power in Jamaica, it won't be the extreme right'.

Brett knew that his aim would be opposed by many, including powerful foreign industrial interests. They had already demonstrated their strength by frustrating Jamaican attempts to control the proceeds from their bauxite mining operations. Most of the profits still went abroad, mainly to the USA.

The aircraft had begun its descent and was now passing over the north coast of the island. The transition in the colour of the sea, from deep blue to azure, from one side of the reef to the other, then to the pale green of the shallows, and its contrast with the opulent dark green of the vegetation, was breath-taking, even to him, a native. Beneath the plane now lay stretches of jungle, banana plantations, cane fields and bamboo forest, which gave way to coffee plantations as the Blue Mountain foothills appeared. Banking to turn westward, the plane began its circular approach to Norman Manley airport, coming in over West Kingston and the harbour. As it circled the airport to lose height it afforded a panoramic view of the whole of the Palisadoes; the long, serpentine strip of land protecting Kingston harbour. Brett knew the important part it had played in the chequered history of the island. At its tip he could see Port Royal, one-time buccaneer stronghold, now half-sunken since the earthquake of 1692.

The airport was about halfway along the strip, its single runway jutting into the harbour on a man-made promontory. Further east, towards Kingston, at the narrowest part of the Palisadoes, movement among the thorn bushes caught Brett's eye. Before his view was obscured by the starboard wing, he spotted cars moving into concealment in the bushes on both sides of the road.

'That looks like an unofficial reception committee, and it could be in my honour' he guessed, as the paranoia returned. 'So, was I spotted? Full marks to – whoever! What do we do now Johnson?'

The 'plane straightened for landing, and seconds later had touched down. It turned at the seaward end of the runway and taxied back towards the airport buildings. There wasn't much time. Brett's mind, working frantically, was already evolving the germ of an audacious plan of action.

NORMAN MANLEY AIRPORT
KINGSTON

When the aircraft halted, and the other passengers began to stand and collect their belongings, Brett Johnson remained seated. Then, as the cabin emptied, he grabbed his shoulder bag and moved along behind the last person until he reached the row next to the starboard wing emergency exit. He slid between the seats and ducked low out of sight of the stewardesses bidding goodbye to passengers at the forward door. When they were

occupied helping a woman with two small children out onto the steps, he wrenched down the handle of the emergency door. A moment later he was standing on the wing. Stepping quickly to the trailing edge, he dropped lightly to the ground. He moved rapidly into the cover of the deep shadow cast by the landing wheels and crouched there with eyes and ears straining for signs that he had been spotted. Everything seemed normal. Only yards away, on the opposite side of the fuselage, men were transferring luggage to a baggage train. Under the port wing others were manoeuvring a fuel bowser towards the tanks. In the intense shadow of the wheels he seemed, to his relief, to be invisible to all of them. Before the port tanks had been filled, the baggage train was on its way to the terminal. While the bowser men were occupied stowing their hose before moving to the starboard tanks, he managed to sprint across unseen to the shade of the port wheels. When re-fuelling was finished and the bowser started back to base, he was still unobserved as he ran across and sprang onto the coiled hoses at the back. Clinging there, he was carried across the tarmac to the Esso Aviation Service fuel depot. Once there, it was a simple matter to leave the back of the bowser as it turned into its parking bay, and disappear behind a storage tank. To make doubly sure he was safe, when the men had moved away he climbed the steps to an inspection landing halfway up the tank. Lying there, he took stock of his predicament.

'There's still a few hours of daylight left before it's safe to move', he reckoned, 'but at least I'll have time to think about what I do next'.

The few hours seemed interminable. As he became exposed to the glare of the late afternoon sun, his thirst became almost unbearable, but he realised that there was no other option to

staying where he was. It was so hot that he dared not touch the metal of the tank with his bare hands.

'I don't remember it being as hot as this' he thought. 'Maybe I've become too used to the UK climate'.

From time to time there was activity below as men with fuel bowsers came and went, but he was not discovered until one of them climbed the steps for the daily depth inspection. The man almost fell over the crouching Brett as he reached the landing.

"Who the —," were the only words he managed to utter before a well-aimed blow to the side of the neck dropped him unconscious on the staging.

"Sorry, Man," whispered his attacker. "Now I'll have to silence your mate."

The second bowser man, squatting in the shade to enjoy an illegal smoke, was alarmed by the commotion above.

"You OK Errol?" he called, and was rising to his feet as Brett bounded down the last six steps and hit him once, in the solar plexus.

As the man fell forward, fighting for breath, he was caught, hoisted on Brett's shoulders and carried up to the platform. Still unable to speak, he was nevertheless gagged with his own neckerchief. His partner was likewise gagged. The hands of the men were tied together, and to the rail, with their own belts. Adrenaline left Brett's bloodstream as fast as it had arrived. He felt totally exhausted as he sat by his prisoners and waited for darkness.

'How soon will they be missed?' he wondered. 'It won't take long to link their disappearance with mine'.

By sunset, Brett's thirst was raging, but at last he could move without detection. He offered a silent vote of thanks for the

early tropical dusk. The air was no cooler, but at least he was out of the scorching sun. In the parking bay he found a water carrier for topping up radiators, and drank deeply, ignoring the musty taste of the water. As though the long draught was a transfusion of fresh blood, he felt his strength return and his spirits rise. He was about to splash the rest of the water over his head when he thought of the plight of the two bound men. Climbing the steps again he, one after the other, told them to be quiet, or else, shifted their gags and poured water into their eager mouths.

"You'll soon be found," he assured them, as he moved to implement the next part of the plan he had been mulling over.

'The airport police are bound to be looking for me', he reasoned. 'And, whoever's been waiting along the Palisadoes road will be searching along the spit, certainly towards Kingston, and probably out towards Port Royal. My only chance of escape's by sea'.

He remembered from a school history trip to Port Royal that The Royal Jamaica Yacht Club basin was only a short distance away.

'I can probably reach it directly from the airport', he thought, but immediately rejected the idea of trying to steal a boat as too obvious. 'It's bound to be anticipated. I'll have to swim - but in which direction?' he asked himself. 'From what I remember of the map, I guess straight across the harbour to Kingston docks is about a mile and a half, but there are probably only a few places where I could land, and they'll be easily watched. I've got to choose an unexpected route and finish the swim before daylight. The search'll be widened then. My best bet, I'm sure, will be to cross the harbour mouth from Gallows Point to Fort Augusta,

where I can use the two light buoys for navigation. Great idea, Brett!' he thought – 'but there's a lot of swimming to do even before I get to Gallows Point. The Palisadoes is so narrow in places I'd be a fool to try to go by land - too dangerous. I'll avoid being seen by swimming parallel to the shore'.

First he ran to the seaward end of the runway. Then he took off everything but his underpants and shoes and made a neat bundle, held together by his belt, but with the shirtsleeves hanging free. The bundle was tied firmly onto his flight bag using the sleeves, and fixed to his back by looping the strap round his neck and under his arms. His shoes he kept on his feet until he had waded clear of the black-spine sea urchins crowding the rocks in the shallows. From childhood experience he knew how painful a prick from one of those spines could be. When the water was deep enough to swim, he took off the shoes, knotted the laces together, slung them from his bundle, and struck out westwards. His first target was the promontory that fingered out towards the chain of small offshore islands on the harbour side of the Palisadoes, which he knew ended at Gallows Point. His strong, steady crawl carried him to the isthmus in about thirty minutes. As soon as he saw the faint phosphorescence marking the water's edge, he put on his shoes to wade ashore. He walked along the beach to the end, where he took to the water again. Alternately swimming and walking, he progressed along the chain of cays. Two hours before midnight he reached the Point.

There was no sign of pursuit, so he lay down to rest for a while in the black velvet pool of night under a cluster of palms. As he watched the lights of cars passing to and from Port Royal on the distant Main Road, the thought came,

'Am I still being paranoid, or do some of those belong to my hunters?'

Gradually, lulled by the high-pitched buzz of crickets, and the whistling of tree frogs, Brett fell into a light sleep. He was awakened an hour later by the beams of a bright moon slanting through the leaves. In the distance, across the narrow channel separating the cay from the Palisadoes, he could hear voices and the barks of dogs. It was time to move.

Ahead of him lay the hardest and most dangerous part of his swim, across the shipping lanes, contending with tidal currents. As he had no idea of the state of the tide, it was impossible to make allowances for drift.

'Keep sighting on the light on Fort Augusta point', he told himself.

Following his now familiar routine, he waded out a short distance, removed his shoes, and began the long crossing. His powerful over-arm action took him quickly out into the channel, but as soon as he left the shelter of the shallows he could feel an ebb tide carrying him inexorably out to sea. Judging that it would be futile to pit his strength against the current, he accepted its dictation, but swam diagonally across it. After two hours of arm-wearying effort he had almost given up hope of reaching the opposite shore, which seemed as far away as ever. But a lessening of the strength of the current told him that slack tide was approaching.

'Now, with a bit of luck, the incoming tide will carry me back towards the harbour'.

Taking advantage of the twenty minutes or so of slack tide to make good headway parallel to his intended course, he coasted in towards the Point, carried forward by the flow tide. Relief at

conquering the currents was short-lived. A long, smooth shape brushing his thigh brought him to a terrified halt. He tried not to panic.

'Sharks have rough skins', he lectured himself, remembering the fishermen's catches he had touched on the harbour wall, 'and according to the fishermen they don't come into the harbour. But whatever that was, it was pretty big. Was it a barracuda? They're supposed to patrol the shipping lanes, scavenging the rubbish thrown overboard'.

Recalling the tales he had heard, of large tuna being hauled in on a line, sliced in half by the brutes, he lay still, struggling to control his breathing.

'I hope there's some truth in the legend that barracuda attack humans only by mistake - and this particular fish knows the legend'.

For long minutes he made no movement. No attack came, so he resumed swimming, now using a careful breaststroke. Occasional flashes of moonlight glinting on a flicking tail were his only indications that the deadly fish - if it was what he thought it was - was maintaining station a few yards to his right. Whenever it made a closer approach, he turned and thrashed vigorously at the water until it backed off. It was eventually distracted by what he assumed, from the twinkling flashes of reflected moonlight below, to be a large shoal of smaller fish. As the threat of the barracuda receded, and confidence returned, he began to make faster progress, but at any phosphorescent sign of disturbance around him, reverted to his careful breast-stroke.

Just four hours after leaving Gallows Point he reached the harbour wall at Fort Augusta. Although the straight-line

distance was a mere two miles, he reckoned he must have covered at least three. There was still two hours of darkness left as he swam along to find steps. At last he saw a steep flight and hauled himself onto them. Climbing the steps, for all the control he had of his legs they might well have belonged to someone else. Somehow, he staggered onto the quay, with his thigh muscles trembling with fatigue. The relief at finding no welcoming police presence overwhelmed him to the point of collapse. He had to discipline himself to don the sodden clothes.

'I need rest, time to think', he realised. 'My next move needs very careful consideration'.

He found a space between a wall and a workmen's hut where he could rest unseen and ponder. First he needed to get his bearings. He reached for the top of the wall and pulled himself up until his eyes just cleared the top. What he saw baffled him.

'The lights on my right must be in Kingston, but what about those on my left? I don't remember anything there but a shantytown. It looks as though there's been a lot of demolition and building since I left. Kingston's out of the question. The Hunt's Bay causeway will be too open and dangerous. I've no option but to go into this new development.'

He lowered himself and sat with his back to the wall to rest his tired limbs. He closed his eyes, but was obviously not destined to rest. Only minutes later he saw the glare of a car's headlights, approaching across the causeway. Realising that, so early in the morning, it could only be a police car he summoned energy reserves he didn't know he possessed, broke cover and ran for his life towards the lights on his left. He was not spotted

immediately by the policemen deploying along the South Causeway. They were all looking seawards. A constable left in charge of one of the cars was the one who raised the alarm.

"There's a man running along Dawkin's Drive, just passing the Skeet Club. Could be our man," he reported on his radio.

"Get after him, and pick me up on the way," responded his sergeant, "and inform the Chief Inspector."

By the time the car caught up with him, Brett had reached the junction with Portmore Parkway. As the two policemen leapt out with guns drawn, he held up his hands.

"Are you Brett Johnson?" asked the sergeant.

"No. Ellery Masters," replied Brett, not expecting to be believed.

He was not believed.

"Get in," he was told, and was given an unceremonious shove towards the rear seat.

As the sergeant bent to follow him in, Brett leaned across and slammed the door on his forearm, causing him to drop the gun. In an instant, he had the gun trained on the surprised constable, and was in control of the situation.

"Throw your gun into the bushes," he ordered the second policeman, "and both of you start walking. No, not that way - back along the causeway."

The two men headed back the way they came, just as a second police car sped along the causeway towards them. Brett tumbled over into the driving seat, put the still-running engine into gear and hurtled off with screeching tyres, following the signs to Independence City. His pursuers were not far behind. Before he reached Independence, he noticed a sign to Caymanas Park on his right. That rang a bell in his memory. Switching off

BANANA

the car lights, he took the racecourse turn, hoping the pursuit would assume he would head for the City. He abandoned the car in a cul-de-sac off Caymanas Boulevard and headed across the racecourse. The other police car tore past the turn on its wild goose chase into Independence.

On the far side of the racecourse Brett picked up the railway line.

'If I can get aboard a train heading for Montego Bay', he reasoned, 'I should be able to find the safe house there. But how do I do it? I need to find a spot where trains have to slow down. The big bend round Hunt's Bay's probably my best bet'.

To reach the bend he had to follow the line towards Kingston; towards greater danger. Where the railway crossed the River Cobre seemed a good spot. He climbed to a bridge girder spanning the track and settled down to wait for a slow goods train. The first to appear, soon after daylight, he recognised as a banana train.

'Not much good. Probably heading for Bog Walk,' he reasoned.

Shortly after, a goods train with a mixture of open and closed wagons came along, travelling slowly; ideal if it was going the right way.

'I'll only find out by riding it', he thought, 'but what's the best way to get aboard? The open wagons look empty, but I'd be taking too much of a chance by dropping into one of those, if it happened to have a load'.

Instead, he dropped onto the curved roof of a closed wagon. The forward speed of the train took his feet from under him. He staggered backwards, fell, and began to roll off the roof. In the nick of time he managed to hook an arm round a roof ventilator.

For what seemed an age he lay there, with his heart pounding and lungs labouring, as the accelerating train swayed along the uneven track. Only when it reached its cruising speed did he feel safe enough to rise on all fours and inch his way forward. Next in line was a low, tarpaulin-draped wagon which would provide good cover if he could find a way into it. Climbing carefully down onto the buffers, he inspected the ropes holding the cover in place. They had been carelessly tied. It was the work of seconds to free enough of the edge to worm his way inside. Cautiously feeling his way, he soon realised that he was sharing the wagon with a load of wooden furniture – 'for a school', he supposed, judging by its size. Easing into the space under a stack of tables, he prepared himself for an uncomfortable ride. In the cramped conditions, Brett was unable to sleep, but fell into a reverie which took him back twenty years to another, quite different, train journey.

CHAPTER 2
KINGSTON, JAMAICA
MARCH, 1953

"Well, Brett. This is your last day with us. You should do well at secondary school if you keep up the good work."

Miss Stevens, the Guyanan top class teacher, had taken a liking to this boy from the shanties who seemed to be a cut above his schoolmates in intelligence, and in spite of his background, to be more amenable to being taught. He had shone all through the primary school, but had really shown his brightness under her tuition. She fully expected him to carry on his schooling and go far. His response took her completely by surprise.

"I won't be goin' to secondary school, Miss," he said, with a tremor of the lip. "My Ma can't afford it. Why can't I stay with you?"

"I wish you could, but as well as having to pay for secondary education, you have to go to secondary school for it."

Fighting back the tears, and not wanting her to see how upset

he was, he turned and ran. He didn't stop until he reached what passed for home. He burst into the tiny timber and corrugated iron shack and threw himself down on his mattress. His mother, not long out of her own bed, asked,

"What's the matter wi' you Brett. You bin fightin' again?"

"I want to go to secondary school. Why won't you let me?"

"It ain't jus' a matter o' lettin' you. There's no money for it. Ah'm not made o' money."

At the mention of money a half-naked brute of a man, the latest in a long line of 'uncles' burst from his mother's room. He grabbed Brett by the shoulder, and with a vicious back-hander knocked him into a corner. His mother rushed to protect him from further blows, fully expecting to be struck herself, but the man contented himself with growling,

"Any money yo' Ma gets is mine. Jus' remember that – an' you remember," he added, scowling at Celia Johnson.

Brett crept back onto his bed, nursing his bruised face. He sobbed himself to sleep, wishing he had a father to protect him. His father, whose surname, Brett, was all that he had given the boy, and that as a Christian name, had left when Brett was three, leaving his mother to fend for both of them. She had become a 'hostess' in a Kingston night-club to make ends meet, and the brute currently sharing her bed was a hazard of the job.

Brett woke early with a feeling of despair.

'I've got to get away - get a job - earn money for school. But where can I find a job?' he wondered.

He had heard one of his mother's clients talk about the job situation. The man had said there were only seasonal jobs to be had in Kingston, but there might be regular ones up country, in the Bog Walk banana plantations. Long before

BANANA

dawn he had made up his mind. He was leaving. Creeping out of bed as soon as it was light, still wearing his school clothes, he stuffed his few belongings into an old duffel bag. They were followed by the remains of a loaf from the table, half a red snapper from the wire mesh meat safe, and two bottles of Red Stripe belonging to the man in his mother's bed. Moving stealthily outside, he paused only to steal a few mangoes from a neighbour's tree, then broke into a run. Through the maze of shanties he ran, past the more desirable residences of Skyline Drive, and down by the Botanical Gardens. On the Old Hope Road he hitched a lift with an early commuter who was accustomed to picking up kids on their way to school at that time of day. He was dropped at the corner of Victoria Park, from where it was only a short walk to the Victoria Crafts' Market and the docks.

The market was familiar territory, where he had shoplifted most of his possessions. He knew it well enough to know how to get from there over the fence onto the piers where banana trains unloaded. It had proved a useful route of escape from irate stall holders in the past. Today, though, he had no thieving in mind as he sauntered through the bustle of preparations for the day's business, trying to seem casual. When he thought he was unobserved, he shot through a dockside service entrance, and was over the fence in seconds, straight into the arms of a dock security guard. Holding him roughly by the scruff of the neck, the guard asked, in a voice that demanded an answer,

"Now, sonny. What yo'after?"

Thinking fast, and not wanting to reveal the real reason for his presence on the pier, Brett blurted out,

"I'm running from a man who thinks I stole from his stall."

"Let's see what's in yo' bag," the man growled, grabbing it from his shoulder.

He rummaged in the bag and turned out several items that he thought had obviously come from the market. There was a pearl-handled penknife, a woolly hat and the mangoes.

"You're a thief, alright," he decided. "Get in there, while I call the police."

Brett was pushed into a storeroom next to the security guard's office, and locked in. He heard the guard telephoning the police. There was no other door to the room - only a non-opening window. Incredibly, the man had not taken his bag away, but had he put the penknife back? The knife was still there. It was quickly put to good use, prizing the beading from around the windowpane. In five minutes he was able to lift the glass out and squirm through the small opening. Ducking out of sight of the office, he made a run for the banana train standing on Pier 1. Choosing a wagon halfway down the train, he hauled open the sliding door, and found to his relief that it was an empty one.

'Good, this'll be heading back to the plantations', he thought.

Climbing in and closing the door, he settled down in a corner where a knothole admitted a little daylight, and hungrily ate some of his bread and fish, washing it down with a bottle of Red Stripe. He finished off with one of the stolen-tasty mangoes. It was not long before activity and voices outside told him the train was being readied to pull out. There was the sound of shovelled coal, and much later the hissing of steam escaping from the boiler. With a series of loud clanks and jolts the train was underway.

The trip was uneventful, but after the train had left Kingston and was into new territory for Brett, it was full of interest. He kept his eye glued to the knothole in the planking. As the engine battled its way up the River Cobre gorge there were glimpses of the river through the lush vegetation. It was at its wet season high mark, fast flowing and turbulent where it plunged over rocky rapids.

At the top of the gorge the laboured sound of the engine changed as it pulled onto the plateau of Bog Walk. Brett peered out with renewed curiosity as the train passed first through cane fields and then mile after mile of banana plantations. Soon it was clanking over the level crossing at Bog Walk. It passed through the station and came to a jolting halt in a siding. Opposite the knothole a sun-faded board bore the legend:

THOMPSON ESTATE

Trespassers Will Be Prosecuted

In the act of sliding the door open, he froze in alarm at the sound of voices outside, fearing he was about to be discovered. His fear was unfounded. The engine crew was walking back down the line, discussing the merits of the new Antiguan opening-batsman, who was still at the crease in the match at Kingston that had started the previous day.

"He's making mincemeat of our quick bowlers."

"Yeah, Man. What we need's a good spinner. Valentine would have sorted him."

When the conversation had died away, Brett slowly opened the door, peered cautiously along the train, then dropped on

the line and made a dash for the plantation fence. He was over it in a jiffy. As soon as he was out of sight of the track, he sat down on a felled banana trunk to think about his next move. Immediately, his thoughts were distracted by the patter of what sounded like heavy rain drops on the thick carpet of dead banana leaves that covered the ground.

'I'm going to get soaked', he thought, and sprang to his feet to look for cover.

His eyes widened in amazement as he saw that the pattering sound was not caused by rain at all. Hundreds of tiny lizards were falling from the trees. Fascinated, he watched as they ran out to the ends of the banana leaves, fell off, ran back up the trees and out along the leaves, only to fall off again, and again, and again. Baffled by the futility of it all, he set off deeper into the plantation, hoping to find somewhere to spend the night.

At regular intervals the plantation was criss-crossed by straight, grassy tracks. Each looked so like the last that he was soon hopelessly lost. For all he knew, he might have been going around in circles. Soon, however, he found his progress barred by a narrow river. He turned to follow the bank, hoping it would lead to somewhere he could shelter. The water was very clear. In its sun-dappled shallows, sleepy perch were basking in the last warmth of the late afternoon sunshine. 'There won't be any problem about breakfast', he thought, beginning to feel hungry as an image of baked fish entered his mind.

No sooner had this thought occurred to him, than it was expelled by an explosive,

"Shit!" from somebody out of his sight, further upstream.

He sprinted into the plantation for cover. As there was no pursuit, he ventured a quick look round the mat of banana trunks

concealing him. To his relief, his presence and the expletive had no connection. On the bank was a young, blonde, bearded white man, his burly, bronzed body clad only in khaki drill shorts. His fishhook was caught in a leaf high up in a banana tree, and he was trying to free it, muttering to himself in a half-amused fashion,

"How stupid can you get, Andrews? All these fish and all you can catch is a flaming tree."

The hook remained stuck in the tree. No longer afraid, and even encouraged by some indefinable aura of goodwill emanating from the bearded man, Brett emerged from his hiding place, and offered,

"Can I get your hook back, White Man?"

The startled Steve Andrews gaped as the boy clambered up the tree. His gape turned into a guffaw as the leaf bearing his hook peeled away under the weight of the boy and deposited him heavily on the ground. When the breath returned to his gasping lungs, Brett sat up and the grinning white man said,

"Thanks. I'd never have thought of that," and began to chuckle as his imagination re-ran the comic episode. "That performance deserves a reward. What's your name?"

'Brett," replied the boy. "Brett Johnson."

"Well, my name's Steve. You can share my supper when I've caught it, Brett."

He flicked his line back into the river, more carefully this time. A fat perch was soon landed. Rapidly gutting and filleting the fish, he glanced up and said,

"While I'm frying this, see if you're any better at climbing coconut palms, and cut us a couple of nuts". Here, take my machete."

He handed over the long-bladed working machete, which Brett tucked into his belt. Using the two-footed hopping technique that was second nature to Jamaicans of his age, the boy shinned up the nearest palm with green nuts. When he reached the plume he hung there precariously with one hand and slashed away at the nuts with the other. After downing six, he hopped down and handed back the machete.

Taking one of the nuts, Steve lopped off the ends of the husk and the nut together with a single, practised blow of the machete, and offered it to the boy. Clapping his mouth to the hole and up-ending the nut, Brett greedily drank down its sweet, thirst-quenching contents. He had drunk nothing since the beginning of his journey in the train. Recalling the Red Stripe left in his bag, he decided to offer it to this friendly white man. He fished it out and handed it over.

"That's nice of you, son," said his host, "but your beer'll be warm and fizzy now. Let's put it in my cooler for later, and try some of mine."

Taking the bottle, he tied a loop of string round the neck and dangled it in the river from a wire coat hanger. Alongside it was a whole platoon of Red Stripe bottles. He selected two, knocked off the tops, and handed one to Brett.

"Cheers," he said, raising the other and draining it in one go.

"Cheers," copied Brett, and tried to emulate the man.

He spluttered as fizzy beer hit the back of his throat and came down his nose, and then settled for sipping it slowly. Dusk was falling by the time their meal was finished, so Steve Andrews built a shelter for Brett from dead banana leaves, forming a lean-to at the side of his tent.

BANANA

Steve had left Wallingford Grammar School at eighteen with low-grade science A-levels, not good enough for the university course he wanted, so he had to look for a job. The best he could find was as an assistant scientific officer at the Wallingford Institute of Hydrology. In his spare time from work at the Institute he had read geology with the Open University, and carried on to specialize in hydrology for an honours degree. With the backing of his new qualifications, and experience of several years of water surveys in the Welsh mountains, he had applied for a temporary post with the Jamaican Resources Board. Sponsored by the UK Overseas Development Administration, the job was to carry out surveys of soil moisture content and its effect on banana yields. Although the work was outside his direct experience, the fact that he was a bachelor prepared to rough it stood him in good stead. He got the job in preference to a dozen other applicants.

He had arrived in Kingston on a Friday, and made his way to the cheap digs recommended in his appointment letter. The only thing to commend the place was its closeness to the Geological Survey offices. On the following Monday he presented himself at the offices in Hope Gardens in a state of mounting anxiety. That was soon allayed by a warm welcome from the administrative staff and his new chief, Dr. Julius Grant. The smiling black face beneath the tight-curled grey hair immediately put him at ease.

"Come with me. I'll show you the office and laboratory you will use as your base, although I expect you to spend most of your time in the field," invited the cultured voice.

The principal scientist led the way to a sizeable, square office with white-painted walls and grey steel furniture. Across

the corridor was a small laboratory. It was equipped with the bare necessities for studying soils and their moisture contents. There was an old-fashioned chemical balance, a microscope, a pH meter, an oven and a range of glassware for wet chemical analysis. Steve concealed his dismay, telling himself,

'Remember, this is not Wallingford'.

As though reading his thoughts, Dr. Grant volunteered the information,

"We do have one of your Harwell/Wallingford fast neutron probes for soil moisture measurements in the field. All you have to do is calibrate it, and of course do the standard soil analyses."

Steve emitted a 'phew' at the welcome news.

"Thank God and physicists for that. I hadn't relished the thought of carting hundreds of samples back here. Now, what about bore hole drilling machinery?"

"There," replied Doctor Grant, pointing to a corner of the lab. Propped against the wall was a steel tube. It was about three inches in diameter and five feet long, with cross-handles welded to one end. Nearby was a sledgehammer.

"I'm afraid this project will involve a lot of hard labour, but I'll provide you with two assistants to help you with that. They can take turns out in the field and back in the lab."

Steve allowed himself a wry grin as he considered the mixed high-tech and primitive approach he was expected to cope with.

"Never mind," he countered. "I know the rudiments of the probe and the sledgehammer, and I've got a strong back. Playing prop forward in Berkshire second division rugby saw to that."

The half-smile showed Dr. Grant's appreciation of the humour.

"Now I'll introduce you to my water resources man," he said. "He can put you in touch with the right contacts at the Banana Board. Then perhaps you can start digging out some background information."

He led the way down the corridor to a similar office, where a wizened, grizzle-haired man of indeterminate age was poring over a large-scale relief map of the island.

"Jim, this is Steve Andrews, just out from England to start the six month study of banana water requirements I was telling you about."

"Hi, Man," Jim Bones greeted Steve with a wicked grin. "I suppose you'll be telling me before long what to do with my water. Would you believe there's a water shortage on this rain-soaked island?"

"How do," said Steve. "I'd gathered that's one of the reasons I'm here. In six months, though, I'll be a bit pushed for time to make any firm proposals, so any help I can get from you I'll appreciate."

"First I suggest you talk to Malcolm Bates at the Banana Board. He's got statistical data on crop yields from all the plantations. That should give you a starting point. Give me a few minutes to 'phone Bates, and I'll take you over there."

Ten minutes later they were climbing out of the laboratory van outside the Banana Board offices. Malcolm Bates was waiting for them at the entrance. Soon they were ensconced in his office, drinking Blue Mountain coffee out of big mugs, and discussing the merits of the plantations.

"The Thompson estate gets by far the highest yield on the island," said Bates. "About fifteen tons to the acre - three times the average. That should give you clues to the best practices.

Then there are other, smaller estates in the same area, with much smaller yields."

"Ideal," said Steve. "That should eliminate any geographical and soil quality factors, so I can concentrate on the water aspects. Thanks for your help."

"One more thing I can do," offered Bates, "and that's set up a meeting with Colonel Thompson."

"He's been alerted to the possibility of a study," chipped in Jim Bones. "Dr. Grant mentioned that he had talked to him at a reception in May. His first reaction was a flat 'No' to any work on his estate. 'Why should I help my competitors to improve their yields, and lose some of my market share?' was his argument. "The boss told him that he might even increase his own yield, and contribute to water conservation. I guess self-interest might make him a reluctant collaborator. In any case, you should meet him to discuss the details of what you propose to do, and what you expect to get out of it."

A meeting was arranged for the next day at 10 a.m. Colonel Thompson arrived at the Banana Board offices at precisely that time. Steve Andrews looked into the hard, sun-lined face, with its thin, grey, military moustache, and knew immediately that the man would brook no nonsense. Piercing blue eyes glared at him as the voice addressed him in clipped English Establishment tones.

"Well, young fellow, what airy-fairy rubbish are these water boys trying to foist on me now?"

"If you'll pardon my interruption, Colonel," broke in Jim Bones, sensing Steve Andrews' hackles rising. "You know that water shortages are developing because the water we have

isn't in the right places. We think the best way to make sure of adequate supplies in the short term is to conserve it. Mr. Andrews' job is to find out just how much irrigation the bananas need."

Hating the situation that forced him to speak on level terms with a despised black man, the Colonel snapped,

"I already know that. Why do you think my yield is the highest on the island?"

"An indication that you're using enough water, but not whether you're wasting it by over-watering," retorted the irritated Steve.

"Hrmmph," growled the Colonel, then changing tack, "What's all this going to cost me?"

"Nothing at all," replied Steve Andrews, except your co-operation. The ODA is paying my salary and the Board my expenses. They are also providing laboratory facilities. All I need from you is a map of your estate, and your permission to move around it, drilling small bore holes and making measurements. Oh, and I need to make small, controlled changes of irrigation rate in selected areas."

"There, I knew it was going to cost me, somehow!" the Colonel burst out. "If you change the irrigation rate, you'll change the growth rate. A slower growth rate's money lost."

"There's the same chance of increasing the growth rate. But in any case, such a small percentage of your output will be affected by the experiments it will make little difference to the total yield," said Steve persuasively.

Colonel Thompson studied the open, honest features of the big hydrologist and made a quick decision.

"Right," he said. "I'll warn my people that you'll be around.

Then perhaps you'll not be shot for trespassing. Just make sure
you keep me informed," he snapped, rose, turned on his heel
and stalked out.

THOMPSON PLANTATION
MARCH, 1953

The morning after Brett's arrival, Steve Andrews woke early and
plunged into the river to refresh his sweating body. Hearing
the splashing, the boy soon joined him, and they enjoyed some
pre-breakfast horseplay. Brett's natural swimming ability led
to more than one ducking for Steve, who was forced to retire
breathless. As they sat, naked, on the bank, drying off in the
sun, the boy was intrigued by his first sight of red pubic hair.
The size of the white man's equipment impressed him.

'So they're not as small as the black men say', he thought.

They breakfasted on bread, and bananas pulled from a
ripening bunch kept in the back of Steve's tent. Later they
drove to the workers' compound, where Brett was handed over
to the black foreman.

"Morning, George. This is Brett Johnson. I'm going to try
to get the Colonel to take him on as my assistant, so I want you
to find him a place to sleep."

"Sure, Boss," said old George. "There's an empty bunk in the
men's quarters. He can have that if the Colonel says OK, but
he's got it in for them village lads - keep pinchin' his fish."

"I ain't no village lad. I'm from Kingston," protested Brett proudly, adding defiantly, "and I got a hut in the plantation to sleep in."

"Colonel don't allow no sleepin', 'cept in the compound," said the old man sternly. "S'more than your hide's worth if he finds you campin' in the bananas. Come wi' me."

He took the boy over to a long, low, prefabricated building on the other side of the compound, and led him inside.

"That's your bunk," he said, pointing to a top bunk at the end furthest from the door. "It's the hottest, sweatiest bunk in the place, but it's the only one, and there you'll sleep. Leave your bag there - it's safe enough - Boss don't allow no thievin'."

Brett left his bag and went back to look for Steve. He was outside the compound gate, talking to two white men carrying rifles.

"Come here boy," barked the hard-faced one he guessed correctly was the Colonel. "Are you the Kingston brat who wants a job?"

"I'm not a brat, I'm —"

"When you address me, say 'Sir'," interrupted the man, in a voice that conveyed his contempt for the boy and his race. Then, as though he himself had not been interrupted, "Andrews here needs a boy who can work. If he's satisfied with you, I'll pay you four dollars a week. Take it or leave it."

"I'll take it - Sir," said the boy eagerly. To him the trifling sum was a fortune.

"Right," said the Colonel, turning to Steve. "He's yours. See that he does a good day's work, or send him packing."

With no more ado, he and his plantation manager climbed into their Land Rover and sped off towards the plantation house, a huge, white colonial place, with verandas on three sides, set

a discreet distance away from the compound, and half-hidden
behind a grove of Malaysian palms. Steve and Brett disappeared
in the opposite direction, towards the west plantation, where
Steve was setting up his latest experimental station.

"What are they going to shoot with the guns?" asked Brett.

"People," replied Steve, with a wry grin. "Black people,
when the revolution comes."

"Is there going to be a revolution?" asked the boy, excitement
in his voice.

"Maybe, but not the way he thinks," the hydrologist
muttered under his breath. "Power doesn't always come out of
the barrel of a gun." To Brett he went on, "Colonel Thompson
thinks that any day now the workers are going to rise, like
the slaves did many years ago. He's turned the house into a
fortress. At every corner there's a turret with a machinegun, all
the windows have steel shutters, and round the edge of the roof
he's built a walkway with rifle embrasures. In the middle of the
night, when he can't sleep, he's said to patrol it. He's really a
frightened man. It might have something to do with his army
experiences in Malaya, when the communists tried to take over.
A lot of white people were killed then. He got a reputation
for ruthless reprisals. His methods did succeed in driving the
communists out, though, and he thinks the same approach will
work here if the same sort of thing happens."

As he spoke, shots rang out behind them. Brett, his thoughts
still full of what he had just been told, hurled himself flat on
the ground, and crawled behind the nearest tree, thinking the
revolution had already started. Looking up, and seeing Steve
Andrews shaking with laughter, he got unsteadily to his feet.

"It's only turkey vultures this time," said Steve, chuckling.

CHAPTER 3

PALISADOES, KINGSTON
MAY, 1973

Staked out behind the bushes on either side of the Palisadoes Road, on the Kingston side of the airport, the waiting men were well hidden from anyone approaching from the airport direction. They became suddenly alert as the DC8 made its landing approach. Two were liaison men from the Jamaican Secret Service and four were from the Special Branch. All, except Chief Inspector Anderson, were black. He was a Scotland Yard-trained expatriate with twenty years' service in the Jamaican Special Branch and only five to go before retirement. His deeply tanned, square-jawed face still bore a keen look that belied the impression given by his startlingly white hair. A signal from London had warned him that Brett Johnson was on the way, even before his target had reached the

aircraft at Heathrow. The reception committee had taken up its position shortly before the plane's arrival. Immigration had been warned to allow Johnson through.

"The last thing I want is it to be general knowledge that he's on the island", Anderson had stressed in his briefing.

His intention was to hold Johnson temporarily, interrogate him about his contacts with the Jamaican ultra-left movement and then send him back to Britain. 'His chances for subversion will be more limited there, and my chances for a quiet life improved', was his private thought.

All cars leaving the airport were stopped and searched. When his quarry failed to appear the Chief Inspector took the precaution of notifying the city and airport police. His men then dispersed and began a systematic search of the Palisadoes strip and the airport environs. They failed to pick up Brett's trail until police arrived from the city with dogs, and then discovered that he had taken to the water. Assuming that Johnson was heading for the thickly populated area behind the docks, Chief Inspector Anderson alerted the harbour police. Also, anticipating a bluff, he detailed a party to search the rest of the Palisadoes, out to Port Royal. Soon, across the harbour, police were patrolling the whole waterfront from Springfield to the North Causeway. Of course, they, and the Palisadoes searchers, drew a blank. Brett was by this time battling against the currents across the harbour mouth.

Well before dawn the weary searchers were recalled, and a high level meeting was convened in Anderson's Kingston office to discuss the fugitive's most likely movements. The Chief Inspector's contribution was short and to the point. He stated his own view forcefully.

"I believe he'll go to ground in the capital. I suggest early morning raids on the homes of all known militants."

"Well," countered Tom King, senior of the Secret Service men, "since he's not been spotted by blanket coverage of the water front, he must have landed somewhere else. So he's more likely to be heading for some other part of the island. If so, what you're suggesting would be a complete waste of valuable time."

"You could be right, I suppose" retorted John Anderson, becoming irate, "but if he is in the city, he'll be found. If not, your view will be confirmed and we can plan accordingly."

At that moment a report came in over the radio about the capture and getaway of the man apprehended near the North Causeway.

"That clinches it," said the exultant Chief Inspector, clenching his fist. "Send this message to the Chief Constable: Brett Johnson heading for Kingston. Suggest you lean on all left-wing militants."

Later that morning every police station in Kingston saw its quota of left-wingers brought in, questioned at length, and released. Knowing, as yet, nothing of Brett's intentions, even of his arrival in Jamaica, they could reveal nothing. The only other left-wing activist group the Special Branch was aware of was at the other end of the island, a hundred and twenty miles away in Montego Bay. They were known to be a group of dissident, dropped out students. Little had been heard from them since the declaration of emergency, when political gang warfare had erupted in the capital. At that time, the CIA-backed Jamaican Labour Party opposition was making every effort to discredit the Manley government through violence in the streets. In

West Kingston, nightly pitched battles had raged between the criminal gangs supporting the two political parties. Often the police were caught in the crossfire. Their indiscriminate crackdown had driven some of the ultra-left out of the city, including the students.

As the negative reports continued to come in, anxious thoughts began to nag away at John Anderson.

'Suppose King's right, and Johnson is heading for Montego Bay. I'll look a complete fool'. Making up his mind suddenly, he radioed his opposite number in Montego Bay and warned him to keep a lookout for Brett Johnson. He also sent a signal to headquarters:

"Watch the bus and railway stations, and also the airport, in case our man doubles back and catches an internal flight."

Unknown to Brett, and quicker than he expected, the net was beginning to tighten.

MONTEGO BAY
MAY, 1973

Meanwhile, after an uncomfortable five hours, feeling the train beginning to slow down, Brett prepared to leave it before it reached Montego Bay. Crossing the Montego River Bridge, the train slowed to a crawl, and he saw his chance to get off the same way he had boarded, via a bridge girder. Quickly scrambling to the roof of the adjacent covered wagon, he reached up and braced himself for the shock as his hands slapped against the

bottom flange of the cross girder. Using the swing imparted by his momentum he managed to hook a foot over the top of the girder and haul himself up to sit astride it. Moving on all fours it was a simple matter to reach the maintenance walkway and climb down to the north bank of the river. In the shallows under the shelter of the bank he moved along until he reached a small plantation of cocoa bushes sufficiently close to the bank to give him cover. Leaving the river, he made his way into the plantation, selected a thick bush and crept under it. Lying there he waited for darkness.

Although he had not intended to sleep, the last two days and the jet lag had taken their toll. He slept soundly, undisturbed even by the clatter of passing trains. It was pitch dark when he woke. He had no idea of the time, but realised that after its long sea immersion his watch would tell him nothing, even if he could see it. All he had to go on was his urinary erection, which told him it was late. As he relieved himself, a gnawing sensation in his stomach reminded him that he had not eaten since lunch on the aeroplane.

'It's time I moved, while I've got the cover of darkness'.

Passing through the plantation, he emerged on the side away from the river into a residential street, just as a bank of cloud cleared the moon. There was sufficient light for him to see that he was entering Fustic Street, and the notice on a post-box on the corner informed him that he was in Jackson Town. Keeping his back to the railway, walking cautiously in the shadows, he made his way to the address of an alternative safe house he had memorised. The small house on Jarret Street appeared to be deserted. Not a chink of light could be seen but, in response to his coded knock, the door opened swiftly. Just as swiftly it closed behind him, leaving him in darkness in a narrow passageway. Immediately, a second door opened and he was ushered, by the one who had opened the doors, into a brightly-lit room full of activity. His guide was now revealed as a small, lithe black man with Chinese blood.

As they entered, all activity stopped. There was a tense silence as the occupants of the room regarded him with expressions ranging from frank interest to suspicion. The two young women present exhibited the greatest interest. One he recognised immediately as the hostess he had last seen when she served him a rum-bamboozle on the flight to Kingston. What was she doing here? Both women returned to packing polythene-wrapped supplies into rucksacks, but continued to dart glances at him as he introduced himself. He grinned broadly and said, simply,

"Hello, I'm Brett Johnson."

The suspicion on most of their faces faded as he came forward to shake their hands. Only one of the men showed reserve. He was a bright-looking young fellow, the obvious leader of the group. Brett went over and offered his hand, which he took but said, with obviously forced enthusiasm,

"Thank Christ you made it in time. We had word that the police were pulling in our people. It's just a matter of time before this place is raided, so we'll be moving out soon. I'm Wade Robinson. These fellows are George, Henry, Errol, John - better known as 'Moose', and the guy who let you in is 'Chinee'. The girl in the dress is Della. The other's Queenie. Looking hard at Brett, he said,

"You must be starving", then, turning to the girls, "Della, why not rustle up some of that rice and peas you packed?"

A minute later she had retrieved a container of the food, and was heating it over a small stove in the corner. Queenie placed a plate and a fork on the bamboo table, and Della served up the hot rice dish for Brett, who pulled up a chair and ate it ravenously. Plonking a couple of bottles of Red Stripe in front of him, Della watched him bolt the food and beer as though it might be his last. As he scraped up the last few grains of rice she could see that the food had not been enough. Without a word she rummaged again in the rucksack, pulled out another parcel, opened it and handed him the middle cut from a red snapper. As she leaned towards him, and the neckline of her simple cotton dress gaped to reveal the brown, bra-less cleavage, he felt a return of the uncomfortable symptoms he had experienced on the 'plane. She was not oblivious to the effect she was creating. The eyes riveted to the spectacle told the tale. Her actions were, in fact, calculated, although her thoughts were mixed.

'He is attractive, but get a hold on yourself Della, you can't afford to let your instincts take over'.

She turned away, and went back to packing the rucksacks. As she bent with her back towards him, he was uncomfortably aware, from their outline, that under the tight-fitting cotton dress, all she wore was the briefest of briefs. If anything, the dress enhanced her superb figure even more than the outfits she had modelled. His thoughts were no less mixed than hers.

'What a body! What a gorgeous girl! But who is she? Why is a beautiful air hostess mixed up with this bunch?'

Dismissing the thoughts for the moment, he switched his attention back to the food. With a heart-felt "thanks," he quickly devoured the fish, hardly pausing to remove the bones.

At last he sat back, replete. Only then did the full import of what Wade Robinson had said about pulling out strike him.

'With Kingston out of the running I thought perhaps I could make Montego Bay my base, but if there's no safety in a 'safe house', what chance is there?' Turning to Wade, he asked, "What plans have you got if you move out of this place?"

"Like every runaway in the history of the island, head for the Cockpit Country, and lie low 'til the heat goes off," replied the young leader. "We're all packed up and ready to go when you are."

Brett rose from the table and nodded his agreement.

"OK, let's go."

The group filed through the back door of the house and piled into the battered old Chevrolet standing in the lane outside. It was a tight squeeze. Brett was wedged into the rear seat with three of the men and with Della on his lap. Queenie sprawled across Wade in the other corner and, although she overflowed onto the next man, George, it was obvious that Wade was her man. Della's allegiance was more difficult to determine. She seemed quite happy to snuggle against him for the drive, so Brett accepted with pleasure the closeness of the soft body.

Chinee drove carefully through the back streets so as not to attract attention. Avoiding the main coast road, which he realised by now must be closely watched, he took the road out towards Maroon Town, on the fringe of the Cockpit Country. The well-made road soon gave way to a narrow, winding lane, still metalled, but badly maintained. Ordinarily, such a bumpy ride would not have been very enjoyable, but Brett had no complaints. Della, too, had no complaints as their bodies were joggled together by the lurching of the car. When it turned

northeast to skirt the Cockpit, the road became even worse, switch-backing crazily around and over the massive limestone outcrops. Chinee's driving skill was tested to the limit as he coaxed the big car round seemingly impossible hairpins.

Della, beginning to feel uncomfortable, stretched luxuriously on Brett's lap, and began to wriggle to ease the stiffness in her limbs. Her movements allowed life to return to his half-paralysed legs, but he hardly noticed the tingle of pins and needles. Her unintended provocation caused a more urgent column of life to attempt to spring to attention. Suddenly aware of the effect she was causing, Della moved her buttocks against him and nuzzled his neck. Her groin was suffused with heat. A thrill climbed her body, she could feel her nipples tingle and erect, and her face flushed. She felt that in different circumstances she would have surrendered without reserve.

'Watch it, Della', she admonished herself, not for the first time. 'Don't get carried away. Remember you have a job to do'.

Brett, equally affected, vowed that before long, he'd make a better acquaintance with this shapely body that had such a disturbing effect on him. For the time being, he was content with caressing her hip and thigh, and was gratified to feel the responding movement.

As the car slowed down for the Bunker's Hill junction with the Wakefield to Clarktown road, it was suddenly caught in the full glare of the headlights of cars converging on the junction from the other two roads. Armed uniformed police, and men in plain clothes, leapt out as the vehicles skidded to a halt, blocking the junction. The exit of the left wingers from Montego Bay had not gone unnoticed. An observant beat man had spotted

and recognised the ancient Chevrolet and raised the alarm. Its
initial route was reported, but it was soon lost in the maze of
back streets.

The head of the local police, Chief Constable Adam Brown,
had not been impressed.

"Jesus, how the hell do you manage to lose something as
big and ugly as a '61 Chevrolet? Never mind, they'll be found.
They're probably heading east, and that can only mean the
Cockpit Country. We know from our intelligence that they
must have some sort of hideout there. The question is, where?
The Cockpit's a pretty big area, and it's inaccessible."

A chastened Inspector Bennett pulled down a large-scale
map of the area on the wall of the operations room, and stuck
his finger on Bunker's Hill.

"If they're heading deep into the Cockpit, it doesn't matter
which road they take, they've got to pass through here," he
stated. "A car from Falmouth has time to get ahead of them and
cut off their escape. If we head for Bunker's Hill at the same
time, either we'll come up behind them or intercept them if
they've taken the Maroon Town direction."

"Good thinking," said the Chief Constable. "Get onto
Falmouth and fix it. If that team has lit out of town in a hurry,
they're up to something, and it's likely to have something to do
with this Johnson character that Kingston's getting its knickers
in a twist about."

COCKPIT COUNTRY

Chinee's adrenaline flow, after the initial shock of the roadblock, electrified him. He slowed the car as if about to stop and, as plain clothes and uniformed men rushed towards the doors, jabbed suddenly at the accelerator, at the same time yelling at his passengers,

"Get down, and keep down."

As the great car leapt forward, bodies hurled themselves aside, and he spun the wheel to bring the rear end of the Chevrolet round in a sideswiping blow which rocketed the right-hand police car off the road. Spinning the wheel the opposite way, he took off with a screech of smoking tyres through the gap created and sped away eastwards in a hail of bullets from handguns. Groans from the back seat testified to the fact that George and Errol had both been hit. George had a shattered upper arm, and a bullet had passed straight through Errol's right shoulder, causing a jagged wound on its way out before embedding itself in the driver's seat.

As the speeding car lurched along the winding road, with the second police car in hot pursuit, no words were spoken. Brett and the girls worked frantically to staunch the blood flowing from the wounds of the two men. Both were in great pain and suffering shock. Not much could be done for the shattered arm of George, except the application of a rough tourniquet. Della tore a strip from the bottom of her dress to make pads that she tied at the back and front of Errol's chest. Both men would require expert medical treatment.

Chinee let out a relieved "Ah" as he spotted a narrow track off to the right. His headlights illuminated a dilapidated sign with the legend 'Windsor Caves'. He switched off the lights, turned down the track, stopped, got out, wrenched the sign off its post, slid back into the car and drove blind until out of sight of the pursuit. Leaving the car where the track passed through a bamboo thicket, he went back far enough to see whether his ruse had worked. A few seconds later, round the last bend in the road, the lights of the police cars appeared. He held his breath as they approached the turn he had taken, and heaved a sigh of relief as they went by with undiminished speed. Back at the car he felt it safe to switch on the lights again to drive on towards their first destination - the Windsor Caves. There was no time to waste. The pursuing police would soon realise their error and guess which way they had gone.

Wade used their short time advantage to make an agonising decision. It was an inevitable one. The injured men would not be capable of the next stage of the journey into the Cockpit Country.

"Head for the caves," he told Chinee, "but turn off at the second farm track, and stop at the shack at the end. We can't leave George and Errol to the tender mercies of the Special Branch. They can lie low with old 'Pa' Roberts 'til we can get them a doctor."

The grassy, little-used track passed between fields of pineapple and tatty little banana plantations to peter out at a row of shabby wooden shacks. As the car pulled up at the last of them, a wizened old man came out on the veranda. He was followed by four young men in their twenties and thirties. All four carried machetes and were smoking their evening 'joints'.

They appeared aggressive and suspicious until the lantern light from the open door fell on Wade's face. Recognition dawned, and was followed by a whoop of welcome as the eldest of the sons slapped palms with his cousin.

"Waaaeeee. Wade, Man, how you doin'?"

"Great, Man, but can't say the same for these guys," Wade replied, gesturing towards the car. "We got shot up by the police. Two of my friends are so badly injured I need to leave them behind. Can you hide them, and see they get medical treatment? Oh, and if there's somewhere we can hide the Chev as well, that'll buy us some time."

Pa Roberts hesitated for only a moment. He had a soft spot for this nephew of his sister's.

"There's no sense in puttin' them in the shack," he said, half to himself. "They'd be found too easy. Hold on - I've got it! There's a shallow cave at the bottom of the cliff where we keep firewood. There's room for them and the car, and it's screened by bamboo. Let's go," he said, turning to his sons.

One drove the car round behind the grove of bamboo and under what was more a massive rock overhang than a cave. The others collected banana leaves and piled them to make thick beds for the wounded men. George and Errol were lifted carefully from the back seat and laid on the leaf couches. Both were by now semi-conscious, their pain numbed by natural reaction to their injuries. Wade touched each man on the shoulder and wished him 'good luck'. On the way out he left money with Pa Roberts for medical treatment, and gave him the name of a sympathetic doctor in Montego Bay.

"You can trust this man. He's one of us".

The remainder of the party shouldered the rucksacks from

the boot of the Chevrolet, and headed back to the track to the Windsor Caves, leaving Wade's second cousins doing their best to obliterate the car tracks. They soon came to the end of the track where it gave way to narrow footpaths branching in three directions. Just as they took the first path on the right, headlight beams appeared from the direction of the road. The chase was on again. Once in the shelter of thick undergrowth, Wade switched on a torch to light their way, and they could proceed at a jog. In a few hundred yards they came to the foot of a high limestone cliff. The path turned along the cliff's base, and soon began to climb its face. Above them they could just see, dimly, the wide, dark opening of the Windsor Caves.

In the twenties and thirties the caves had been a popular tourist attraction. The rotting remains of electric cables were still attached to the walls for the first few hundred feet near the entrance. No tourist, though, had penetrated as deeply as its present visitors, who pressed on with such purpose that it was obvious they had passed that way before. After travelling down an incline for what seemed like hours, and dropping through several tunnel levels, they came to a long chamber traversed by a fast-flowing stream. Turning to Brett with a wry smile, Wade asked,

"Are you a good swimmer?"

Brett nodded, but wondered at the point of the question. The stream seemed shallow enough. Without hesitation, all of the other members of the party except Wade and Della stepped into the water. They began to wade downstream. Brett was given a little push to urge him to follow suit, Della followed and Wade brought up the rear.

The coldness of the stream struck into their legs, and moved

BANANA

upwards as the chamber narrowed and the water deepened. Soon, only their heads were clear. A chill of horror that made the water seem warm sent a shudder through Brett. Twenty feet ahead, tunnel roof and water met. He and Della stopped dead in their tracks. Wade told them,

"Just ahead we have to pass through a siphon. For about thirty feet we'll be completely under water. Take a deep breath, turn on your back, let the current carry you, and use your hands and feet to keep you away from the roof. On the other side there's a big cavern, with a ledge on the left-hand side to climb onto. I'll see you there."

He handed Della his torch and disappeared under the surface. It was obvious from her hesitation that she had not been this way before, but there was no other option. She took a deep breath and followed. Brett Johnson's heart sank. In open water, no matter what the depth, he was happy, but he had a horror of small, enclosed spaces. Now he was expected to enter one full of water, but really had no choice. Obeying instructions to the letter, he dived, turned on his back, and allowed himself to be carried rapidly through the siphon. He was thankful that it was his hands and feet in contact with the roof as he bumped along the tunnel. Never had he felt so claustrophobic. Luckily the feeling was short-lived. With lungs and head seeming as though they would burst, he surfaced in a small lake, to find Della gasping for breath nearby. The torch in her shaking hand showed that the lake almost filled the floor of a cavern with the dimensions of a cathedral nave. He supported her with one hand and swam strongly for the ledge with the other. Wade and Moose helped her out. 'Now I understand why the decision to leave the wounded men behind was made so easily. They

would never have survived the passage through the siphon', Brett thought.

At the far end of the cavern, as his eyes accommodated to the dim light, he could see a wide cleft in the rock. He hauled himself out of the water and onto his feet in a single movement. Broad grins greeted his appearance. Wade, pausing only to slap him on the shoulder, led the group out of the opening and into a ravine with the stream exiting the lake running through it. After forty or fifty stumbling yards the boulder-strewn floor of the ravine gave way to a soft carpet of rotting jungle vegetation. They had emerged into a thickly forested valley. Wade spoke to Brett for the first time since before they entered the siphon.

"This is one of the cockpits. It's almost circular, completely surrounded by high cliffs, and there's no way in except the way we came, unless," he added, "you can abseil."

Walking in single file along a narrow path hewn through the thick undergrowth on the left bank of the stream, they were halted by a challenge.

"Stop! Identify yourselves."

An armed guard stepped out of the undergrowth, pointing a Kalashnikov at Wade in the lead.

"Wade Robinson, with the group from Montego Bay, and Brett Johnson," shot out his target, hurriedly.

"OK Wade, you can pass," replied the guard.

They filed on, into a large clearing near the centre of the valley. It was a clearing in only one sense of the word, in that the undergrowth below an extensive grove of giant fig trees had been cleared. Above, the spreading branches of the trees formed a canopy that provided complete cover from the air,

allowing only flashes of the brilliant moonlight to filter down to reveal the scene below. Tucked in amongst the twisted boles of the fig trees were stoutly built log cabins, mute testimony to the presence of a permanent camp. Turning to Wade, Brett remarked,

"This is no fly-by-night temporary camp."

"No" Wade replied. "Over the last few years we've gradually established it as a refuge for when things get too hot in the towns. Some of our people live here all the time. They can produce enough food for a large band to make a permanent base here if necessary."

"How did you find the way in?" asked Brett.

"Pure accident," replied Wade. "I trained as a scuba diver with the Montego Bay branch of the British Sub-Aqua Club. To make a change from reef diving we decided to try our hands at cave diving. The Windsor Caves were the nearest with an underground stream, so we started exploring there. It was a big disappointment when the first underwater bit turned out to be only a short siphon, but I'm pretty thankful now that it's no longer."

"Amen to that," said Brett, remembering his bursting lungs as he surfaced in the lake.

He felt a mounting sense of excitement as he recognised the potential of this place. His thoughts, which he realised would not be appreciated by Wade, were kept to himself. He was sufficiently perceptive to recognise that the young man would resent any threat to his own authority.

'This is the base I need - a secure place where I'll have time to think. Tomorrow I'll discuss the possibilities with Wade and his friends, but tonight all I want to do is sleep'.

His limbs were heavy with fatigue. He followed the others into the biggest cabin and was shown into a small cubicle, which he guessed belonged to Wade. It contained a single bed and rudimentary furniture, all built from rough-hewn timber.

"This'll be yours for the time being," Wade stated, and interrupted Brett's, "but —" by waving aside his protest. "I'll sleep in the dormitory with the others 'til we build more accommodation. Goodnight – what's left of it."

Closing the door, he left Brett to his own devices. Stripping off his wet clothes, Brett hung them over the solitary chair. He towelled his body with the cover from the bed until his skin tingled then, wrapping himself in the coarse sheet to keep off the mosquitoes, he slept.

CHAPTER 4

KINGSTON CENTRAL
POLICE STATION
MAY, 1973

After the futile search of the Palisadoes and the docks, and the fiasco on Dorkin's Drive, there was more depressing news; the negative results of interrogations of the Kingston Left. The chiefs of the security forces held an afternoon conference to discuss their next moves.

"Obviously," began John Anderson, "we're up against a very resourceful type who's going to be difficult to second guess. But we must head off his contacts with the local left-wingers. So far as Kingston's concerned we seem to have been successful, unless there are some pretty good actors among those we dragged out of their beds this morning. So, if Kingston's too hot for him, where will he go?"

Commander Thomas 'Tiger' King, his Secret Service opposite number, mulled over the problem for a few seconds only.

"If Kingston's out, the only other place big enough to have a sufficiently well-organised underground movement to engineer his disappearance is Montego Bay. He might have contacts there. If he can make it that far, he'll be able to go to ground with no problem."

"You could be right," agreed the Chief Inspector reluctantly, and in an aside to his aide, said, "Inspector, call up two cars, then warn Montego Bay we're on our way. I want you, your sergeant and two men, all armed."

When the cars arrived, the police, the Secret Service and Special Branch men piled in, and they were soon heading out of town. For maximum speed they took the road north to Ocho Rios before turning west along the north coast road for Montego Bay. Having reached Falmouth they had covered about two thirds of the journey when news of the Chevrolet leaving Montego Bay came over the radio. Pausing only to collect another carload of police reinforcements from the already-alerted Falmouth station, they headed for the Cockpit Country. So it was that they were able to set up an ambush near Bunker's Hill, resulting in two policemen being badly injured when the Chevrolet broke through the roadblock.

Momentarily shocked, but recovering quickly, Chief Inspector Anderson instructed two of his constables,

"Look after the injured men, and radio Montego Bay for more help. The rest of you get after them. Somebody with local knowledge go in the lead car with me."

The rest of the police and the Secret Service men crammed into the undamaged cars and set off in pursuit of the Chevrolet.

They followed its lights until they disappeared. The local sergeant voiced his opinion.

"If they're heading for the Cockpit Country, they'll want to drive in as far as possible. The Windsor Caves track's the deepest you can penetrate with a car, and it's sign-posted, so look out for the sign."

Chinee's ruse worked. The pursuing cars overshot the now unmarked turn, and had almost reached a point near Sherwood Content, where a second track led to the caves, before a trick was suspected. Although they took this track, the time lost in reaching the Caves area allowed Brett and his companions to disappear into their rocky fortress. The police cars followed the track to its end, but there was no sign of the Chevrolet or its occupants. Fanning out to search, the policemen looked for tell-tale tyre prints, but all they could find were the tracks of a mule-cart which had been dragged carefully up and down to obliterate all trace of the Chevrolet's passing. The Secret Service men stayed in their car. Chief Inspector Anderson pondered the situation for a moment.

"Obviously they got clean away, or we've missed them down some side track," he speculated. Turning to the local sergeant, he asked, "Are there any settlements nearby that might be sheltering them?"

"There are little subsistence farms scattered all over the area, some down the side tracks we passed on the way in," was the reply.

"Right, the men in this car take the first track. You and the rest of the men take the second. Search every shack and out-building and question everybody you find."

Only one shack showed any sign of life. Most of the others

had been abandoned by their owners, but Pa Robert's shack had a lighted window. The sergeant thumped on the door, and as soon as it opened, pushed his way in without ceremony. An open-mouthed woman stood by the door, but the scene inside looked normal. The old man and his sons were sitting round a table playing blackjack with a deck of scruffy-looking cards. In the middle of the table was a red rum bottle, only a third full. Each man had an almost empty glass in front of him. They were all smoking cigarettes.

"Who are these men?" the sergeant demanded truculently of the old man.

"My sons," replied Pa Roberts. "They help me to run the farm."

The roughly dressed young men looked as though they had never been near a town, and certainly didn't have the look of students. Obviously, they were not his quarry. The sergeant's suspicions, though, were not fully allayed.

"Have you seen any strangers or heard any cars heading this way in the last half hour?" he went on.

"Only you and yours, Man. We don't get no visitors down here since the caves closed - more's the pity," said old Pa Roberts wistfully. He had made a bit on the side as a cave guide in the old days.

"Well, they're wanted men, so if you do see them we want to know at the station in Falmouth. For now, we need to search your shack," said the sergeant.

"Be my guest," was the reply, as the old man resumed dealing the cards.

The search of the other rooms was as fruitless as the search of all the other shacks. As the searchers returned to the cars it

was obvious to Chief Inspector Anderson that they had drawn a blank. He consulted his Secret Service colleague.

"Well, Tom, we've lost 'em, and I don't think we have a snowball's chance in Hell of finding them in the dark, in this terrain. What's your opinion?"

"I agree John. Our friends have gone to ground, and it's going to take an army of men to winkle them out. In fact, we should call in the Army. This is a job for helicopters."

Tom nodded agreement. Immediately, he had a signal put through to army headquarters in Kingston. His request for Army assistance was shunted up the ranks until it reached Colonel Pearson. He took some convincing that Army involvement was justified, but as soon as he was convinced, moved rapidly. Soon after first light a solitary Bell 206 Kiowa helicopter arrived on the scene with a trio of tough-looking men on board, commanded by a lieutenant. It was hardly the response the Chief Inspector had hoped for.

Straight after the lieutenant had been briefed on the situation the helicopter took off and began quartering the scores of jungle-filled cockpits nearest the point of the fugitives' disappearance. Up and down, up and down - off to Montego Bay to refuel - up and down again. Each valley looked the same as the last and the same as the next. All day the search went on, without success. Out of sheer boredom the soldiers at the open doors poured occasional bursts of automatic fire into likely looking areas. There was no visible effect and no response. To the lieutenant, the fleeing left-wingers might just as well have been swallowed up by the earth, as in a sense they had.

Dusk was approaching when the lieutenant ordered the grounding of the helicopter and gave instructions for a bivouac to be set up, before radioing his report to headquarters. His call was put through to Colonel Pearson.

Yes?" the Colonel barked.

"Lieutenant Butler reporting sir," the young officer reported, diffidently.

"Good evening lieutenant, what news?"

"Not good, sir. Those people have disappeared into the Cockpit Country. We've made five sorties during the day, but my opinion is that an air search is quite futile. All the cockpit floors are covered by impenetrable jungle canopy that would hide an army. A ground operation wouldn't be much better. As far as we can see, there's no access except down the cliffs. We'd need a battalion with abseiling gear, and more helicopters to drop them on the cockpit rims."

There was silence on the other end of the line whilst the Colonel considered his options. His eventual response was,

"Mphm, there's no way I can justify that size of commitment for a job that's really a matter for the police. You can have one more helicopter and a platoon to go with it. And for God's sake, man, narrow your search! Look for valleys with clear spaces and water supplies, but don't forget to watch the approach roads."

"Yes, sir," said his subordinate in a chastened voice. "Lieutenant Butler signing off."

A truckload of men and equipment was despatched to the area overnight, and orders given for the Army's solitary old Bell 47 to fly in next morning. The lieutenant gave orders for pairs of observers to be stationed at all points of access, and at road junctions around the northern and western fringes of the Cockpit, with instructions to watch for signs of unusual activity. He turned to Chief Inspector Anderson.

BANANA

"Sir, I can spare only two men for each observation post, and I don't have enough radios for communication with all of them. Can you help?"

"I can put one man equipped with a handset with each pair, for communications and liaison, lieutenant. You will consult me if anything turns up - you heard what the colonel said about this being a police operation," said the inspector, in what was more of a statement than a question.

"Of course, sir," responded the lieutenant, with a note of reluctance.

About an hour after dawn the second helicopter arrived, with a couple of the promised platoon of men. Meanwhile, police reinforcements were arriving by squad car, and the lieutenant began using the first helicopter to ferry groups of three men to strategic spots. He assumed he was dealing with a small band of people, not very well armed, who would sooner or later have to venture out, and go to the town for supplies.

The Secret Service and police leaders met during the morning in Montego Bay police station to discuss the new problems posed by the developments of the previous night. They were in a better position than the army contingent to make an educated guess at the size of the band holed up in the Cockpit.

"We're almost certainly dealing with much more than the small group that escaped in the Chevrolet," was the opinion of Chief Constable Brown. "At least a dozen left-wingers have vanished from the Bay area in the last few months."

"You can add twenty or thirty more from Kingston," chipped in Chief Inspector Anderson. "They were thin on the ground when we made our raids yesterday. Now, if Johnson's managed to join them, they could have the effective leadership they've lacked so far."

He voiced a thought that had been troubling him ever since Brett Johnson had gone missing.

"Gentlemen, I'm afraid that we'll see an escalation of left-wing activity if we don't contain the group over there," waving in the general direction of the Cockpit, "or better, remove Johnson - or both. If we're not successful, we'll rue the day he was allowed to land."

His listeners nodded agreement, but there were no suggestions as to how the task could be accomplished.

"Short of saturation bombing or Vietnam style defoliation, I don't see any way of winkling them out," said Commander King.

"Infiltration," broke in the Special Branch Chief. "You might think that's a tall order, but we already have undercover people operating on the fringes of the organisation; a man and a woman. They've been penetrating the left-wing groups for a year and a half. The girl is now a trusted member of the local group. There's been no contact from her for several days or from him for more than three weeks. That makes me suspect that they've been discovered, or at best they're in a position where they can't communicate. Our man's scheduled to call in at midnight each night if he has something to report, and I have a duty officer on listening watch every night. Until he does call in, I'm afraid we have a blackout on inside information. The girl was probably in the car that broke through our roadblock, so it will be too dangerous for her to try to make contact."

"It does look as though we've no option but to wait, either for your contacts to come through or the resumption of the helicopter search tomorrow," opined Tom King. "I suggest we all catch up on the sleep we lost last night."

"I'll go along with that," put in the Chief Constable, but the best I can offer you here's a camp bed in the operations room. That's where I'll be sleeping, at least for tonight."

"Accepted." said the Special Branch Chief grudgingly, on behalf of himself and his Secret Service colleagues.

They all slept soundly, if uncomfortably, until roused next morning by the station sergeant with steaming cups of coffee.

IN THE COCKPIT

About nine-o-clock the morning after his arrival, Brett Johnson awoke to the bustling sounds of a camp already going about its chores. He was sweating profusely in the hot, humid confines of the cubicle. His uncovered head was surrounded by a cloud of vicious mosquitoes. Aiming to rid himself of sweat and insects, and waiting only to pull on a pair of shorts, he ran down to the stream and flung himself into its rock-cooled waters. He lay there for a few minutes, thinking about the new possibilities for the future created by the existence of this haven. He could see now, by the leaf-muted light of day, what could only be surmised last night. Here was a well organised, if small, base for the start of his Jamaican activities.

'There's room in the existing clearing for accommodation for three hundred men. If we cleared more undergrowth we could hide a small army in this cockpit', he speculated.

Where it was possible to glimpse the edges of the valley

through the trees he could see nothing but high, vertical cliffs.

'Wade was right', he thought. 'The place is virtually impregnable, and the only entrance is easily defended. It's vulnerable to air bombardment, but the jungle canopy will make a bomb-aimer's job difficult'.

With sudden decision he leapt to his feet and strode back to the main cabin. Over breakfast on some of the food they'd brought in he startled his companions by announcing,

"What I've seen here gives me new heart. With such a base we can take time to grow. In a few months we'll be strong enough to take control."

His listeners exchanged sceptical glances. Wade voiced their doubts. With an undisguised sneer he said,

"What can a few men, hiding in a remote hole in the ground, do against the army?"

Brett's thoughts went back to his modern political history, to the small, dedicated bands of men who had changed the political complexions of China and Cuba.

"Mao Tse Tung and Fidel Castro started with even fewer men. Look what they achieved. But all their power came out of the barrels of guns. What I've got in mind's more subtle than that. Of course we need guns, and we'll have to use them, but first we have to undermine the government by destroying its economic base."

"That's easier said than done," boomed the deep voice of Moose from the other end of the table. "In the days when we depended on sugar and banana exports it might have been a simple matter to disrupt the plantations and cut their output. They're widespread and easy to attack. Now we've got the multinationals and their bauxite interests - a much harder nut to crack."

"There's another angle to this," chipped in Chinee. "If you destroy the economy you put a lot of people out of work and alienate our potential support. I don't think much of that idea."

A grunt came from Henry. "Ugh, I suppose it would give us a pool of recruits, if nothing else, but we need money to survive and buy more weapons."

Brett began to think aloud.

"Of course we need weapons, and food, and we do need to weaken the government. Attacks on plantations and bauxite plants are not the only way though - not even the most efficient way. There's another force as strong as the army, and there's a crop that'll support the rural economy even if the plantations collapse."

They all knew which crop he meant. Ganja, the local cannabis product, which most of the country people smoked, was grown all round the fringes of the Cockpit Country and in every remote valley of the Blue Mountains. Small farmers supplemented their income by cultivating the tall green weed. They sold it to travelling middlemen, who passed it on to the processors who supplied the Kingston dealers.

"If we try to muscle-in on the ganja trade, we'll be taking on the gangs as well as the government," Wade said, morosely.

The others nodded agreement. It was common knowledge that most of the ganja sold in Kingston, and all the stuff that was shipped abroad, was controlled by one or other of two gangs. They were the offspring of the strong-arm groups that had fought the behind-the-scenes battles during the bitter political disputes of the Thirties, between Bustamante's Industrial Trade Union and Norman Manley's National Workers' Union. There was a widely-held belief that the parties that grew out of the two unions, the Labour Party and the National People's Party, still derived much of their income from the criminal activities of some of their past supporters, and still had the tacit support of the gangs. The amount of politically aimed violence that flared up around election times was a pretty good indication of the truth of this surmise.

There was a notable lack of enthusiasm around the table. Brett pointed out,

"If we short-circuit the ganja supply line at its source, and set up our own processing and export organisation, the gangs will be powerless to interfere. By the time they've finished blaming each other and realised the truth, we'll be in business and far too strong for them. We explain to the growers what we're about, offer them protection and a good price for their raw ganja. By cutting out the middlemen and the gangs we can offer such a good deal they'll be prepared to risk repercussions."

The faces around the table registered incredulity, hostility and doubt respectively as he looked directly at his hosts in turn.

"A pretty capitalist scheme coming from a committed Maoist," taunted Wade. "That's the sort of criminal activity we should be aiming to stamp out."

"I'll go along with that," said Chinee. "We didn't join this outfit to be drug pushers."

There were grunts of agreement from the others at the table. Brett could see that he had a rebellion on his hands. He set out to argue his case in his most forceful and persuasive manner.

"I'm no keener than any of you to get involved in the drug trade, but I see this as a means to an end, and the only way to

secure an economic base quickly. Hard drugs I'd never touch, but there's no evidence that cannabis is harmful."

"I read about an Egyptian study of long-term use that suggested it can cause genetic mutation," argued Wade.

"There's no evidence from anywhere else to back that up," was Brett's dismissive comment. "Look around you. Our people have been using ganja for generations. Is there any sign of damaged children?"

"We all know dudes who have moved on from ganja to heroin," put in a worried Henry. "Who wants to be responsible for increasing the junkie population?"

"Most of the heroin addicts would have ended up on the hard stuff anyway," replied Brett, beginning to show his exasperation. "Marijuana's just a bus-stop on the way for them."

"How come you know so much about cannabis?" asked the sceptical Wade.

"My final year dissertation at Cambridge was on the Jamaican economy - including the black economy. The biggest contribution to that's from cannabis exports, so naturally I studied the trade."

"There is just one more objection," - - - began Wade, but he stopped in mid-sentence as the clatter of a helicopter crossing the cockpit rim interrupted him. Dashing to the hut door, he ordered everyone outside under cover. "Movements outside might be spotted through gaps in the canopy," he explained as he turned back, but it's unlikely the camouflaged huts'll be seen."

For the first time Brett noticed that the roofs of the nearby huts were painted to resemble fig trees seen from above. The helicopter was meanwhile crossing and re-crossing the valley.

Occasional bursts of machinegun fire brought down leaves and twigs. Thuds of heavy calibre bullets twice came uncomfortably close, but it was obvious from the irregular pattern of firing that the gunner overhead had no idea they were there. He was just trying his luck. A few minutes later the pitch of the engine note changed as the machine lifted to clear the southern cliff and disappeared.

CHAPTER 5

A RIDGE
NEAR BUNKERS HILL
MAY, 1973

Chief Inspector Anderson groaned as he rose gingerly from the back seat of the police car and stretched his cramped limbs. It was years since he had slept in a car, and if it were up to him, never would he do so again. Dawn was breaking. Since he and his men had spent the day before and half the night combing the area for the Montego Bay fugitives, and half the previous night on that damned uncomfortable camp bed, he had had little sleep. He was tired and he was frustrated. That made him irritable.

'I saw a hail of bullets slam into the back of the Chevrolet. There must have been injuries, he reasoned. 'But we found no trace, either of injured or uninjured fugitives in the area. They

vanished like tree frogs in daylight, and must have escaped into
the Cockpit, but where, and how?'

Although he failed to understand how it was possible to
enter the area on foot, there must be some such explanation for
his quarry's disappearance. The whereabouts of Brett Johnson
was not the only question worrying the Chief Inspector. There
had been no contact from his two undercover agents. Wayne
Daniels had not reported in for weeks, and Della Brook's last
contact had been three days ago.

'Della, I guess, is with the fleeing group, he supposed. She
could have stopped one of the bullets that hit the Chevrolet. I
can only assume that Wayne's dead or a prisoner. There was
still nothing except static on his frequency at midnight'.

He went over to the other car, in which the two Secret
Service men were still dozing, and opened the rear door.

"Morning gentlemen," he said, putting on a cheery voice.
"Pleasant dreams?

"Go away," replied the squarely built figure who occupied
the seat nearest the open door. But a grin creased the black
face as he eased himself out and stretched. "Nice accommodation you've got here."

'Tiger' King had specialised in Cuban affairs, and had spent
much of his professional life tracking down Cuban links with
the Jamaican far left. He headed the small Secret Service unit,
and had worked closely with Anderson before, in the days when
Castro had been trying to foment unrest by shipping arms to the
left-wingers in Kingston.

"We well and truly blew it the other night," he said. "What
a fiasco! Two badly injured men, and a car written off. How do
you reckon we ought to play this now John?"

"It's a new situation," replied John Anderson, "and we need a new approach. The difficulty is that until we know where they are, we don't know how to tackle the problem."

"They must be somewhere in the Cockpit, said 'Tiger', thinking aloud, "but unless they've learned to fly, they must be on foot. The terrain's so impossible in there they can't be very far in. So we should concentrate on the fringes of the area and carry on air-spotting."

"The chopper crews have spent two days searching and seen no sign of life, but there's such a jumble of crags and valleys, you could hide an army," Anderson replied gloomily.

"Maybe we should take a look ourselves," suggested Tom King. "If they do have a bolt-hole in there, surely it shouldn't be too difficult to locate. There must be clues."

"Right," responded John Anderson, glad of some positive action to rouse him out of his early morning lethargy. "Lieutenant," he called to the young officer in charge of the army contingent, who was just emerging from his tent, "we want to take a look at the problem ourselves. Can you fit us on one of your sorties today - the earlier the better?"

"Certainly, gentlemen. How about the first flight? The chopper's tanked up and ready to go."

With alacrity that belied their age, the two men joined the crew of the first helicopter to leave. The self-starter fired first time, the pilot engaged the rotor and the craft rose smoothly to fifty feet, before banking away from the cliff. It then climbed to about five hundred feet before passing over the rim of the nearest cockpit. From this altitude the sheer magnitude of the task was brought home to them. A great profusion of greenery-filled rocky cauldrons extended as far south and east as they

could see. All looked quite impenetrable, and it was evident why the area always appeared on maps as a featureless white patch. It was a surveyor's nightmare. There were no passes from the outside to the interior, and none from valley to valley. It was inconceivable that anyone could enter or leave except by scaling the cliffs and abseiling down the other side.

"We can narrow the search down a bit," shouted John Anderson, in a voice audible only to the man next to him above the sound of the rotors. His policeman's mind was at last beginning to emerge from hibernation and move with more accustomed speed. "It's not likely that they've penetrated this lot very far, so we only need to look at valleys near the edge of the Cockpit Country. They need water, so we can rule out any cockpits without streams, and there's a chance that we can pick up the smoke from cooking fires."

"Don't forget," his Secret Service colleague yelled in his ear, "wherever there's human waste, the Jim Crows'll collect."

"That's for sure," agreed the Chief Inspector, who had already made a mental note to keep an eye open for the scavenging turkey vultures, which would be a tell-tale sign of food waste.

They cruised up and down a strip of terrain about two miles long and half a mile wide, in which they picked out four cockpits that looked tenable according to their criteria. There was no sign of life in any of them. In one, the stream crossing the valley seemed to enter it from a gorge on the western side, and leave it through a cave in the base of the cliff on the southern side. All four cockpits merited a closer look, but as fuel was running low, they had to abandon the search and return to base. The chopper dropped its passengers temporarily on the ridge and whirred off to Montego Bay to refuel.

For the rest of the day the helicopters made low-level passes over the four promising valleys, but to no avail. They made no attempt to land. There was no clear space big enough. During the last sortie of the afternoon, they were crossing the cockpit containing the gorge and a stream, when Tiger shouted in the ear of John Anderson,

"Maybe they're not out in the open at all, but holed up in a cave like that," and pointed to the dark gash at the end of the gorge ahead.

Chief Inspector Anderson was hardly listening. His gaze was fixed on the top of a flat rock overlooking a natural pool in the stream behind them. In the middle of the rock lay a white towel, carelessly left behind - or was it deliberately? He mentally complimented his undercover team, and nudged his Secret Service colleague. Tiger's gaze followed his own, and he stiffened in excitement as he realised the implications of the discovery. John Anderson motioned the pilot to carry on as though nothing had happened, so as not to alert their quarry. His mind raced as he tried to formulate a strategy for prising them out of their natural fortress. Not knowing the numbers of the opposition was a problem almost as big as that of the cliff barrier. He was convinced that far more than those in the fugitive group in the Chevrolet were involved, but how many more?

As the helicopter rose over the western rim of the valley, they had their first good view of the cavernous opening at the end of the gorge at the foot of the cliff face. Tom King broke a long, thoughtful silence at the sight, and his face broke into a wide grin.

"My God," he said. "That's it. That must be it. The only way they could have made it into the Cockpit on foot so quickly

is underground. There must be a cave system connecting with the outside."

"Very likely," put in Anderson, with a marked lack of enthusiasm, "but the area's riddled with caves. Windsor Caves themselves are supposed to be very extensive, and they're only partly explored. There are many others. It might take years to find a way through."

"Then we'll have to think of a different approach," replied the Secret Service man.

When they landed he began to discuss with the lieutenant the pros and cons of a helicopter assault on the valley.

BACK IN THE COCKPIT
EARLIER

After the helicopter ended its low-level search earlier in the day and had lifted over the cockpit rim to try further afield, Brett caught a glimpse of Della Brook leaving the next cabin, nonchalantly swinging a towel. She disappeared down a path through the undergrowth on the opposite side of the clearing, towards the southern edge of the valley. Brett, remembering the implied promise of her closeness in the car, followed at a distance that allowed him to hear her progress without being seen. Once she stopped and turned her head from side to side as though listening. He froze. He could not see the knowing smile that curled her lips in amusement as she went on. About fifty yards from the cliff she stopped again. Creeping closer,

he saw that she stood in a small, sunlit clearing in which the stream fell about fifteen feet into a rocky pool before plunging, eventually, into a sizeable cave at the cliff's foot. Climbing the easy slope that led to the top of a flat rock jutting out by the side of the short waterfall, she laid out her towel and unhurriedly stripped off her clothes. Facing the sun, she stretched her arms high, luxuriating in the feel of its hot rays on her naked body. Revelling in the freedom, she cupped and lifted her breasts, and ran her hands over her hips and thighs, as though celebrating satisfaction with what they explored. Then she turned and stood poised on the edge of the rock, the sun highlighting the contours of her sleek, brown body.

Brett caught his breath at the sight of her profile. Della had that type of body, rare amongst even the most beautiful of women, on which each curve ran smoothly into the next. Following the curves, his eyes were led from small, pert breasts needing no support, to a slightly rounded belly above a carefully trimmed black bush, and round to high, firm buttocks merging into long, slim thighs. His arousal was instantaneous. Suddenly, the sculpture sprang into glorious life, as she dived cleanly into the pool. There was the merest ripple as she entered the water. Della swam to-and-fro across the small pool, first with an easy crawl, then sculling on her back, as Brett watched entranced. Before she left the water he made his way round through the trees and, whilst her back was turned, hauled himself up the other side of the rock. Having no public modesty considerations now, he saw no reason to suffer the clothing constriction he had during the mannequin display. Quickly, he undressed, and lay back beside her towel, propped on his elbows, gazing at the autonomous cause of his discomfort.

Becoming bored with swimming, and now thoroughly refreshed, Della climbed out of the pool and sauntered back, her long legs stepping easily back up the slope. She was wringing out her hair as she walked. The glistening rivulets of water cascaded from her nipples in a side-to-side spray. As she came within sight of Brett, the sway of her hips produced fascinating rocking movements of her pubis that riveted his gaze to the tight curls of the black triangle. Then his attention switched to the firm jiggle of her breasts, the nipples standing proud after their immersion in the cool water. Faced with the eternal male problem of a visual feast and not knowing where to look next, he tried to widen his view to take in the whole spectacle, but failed as his eyes insisted on flitting from part to delectable part. His dilemma was resolved as she suddenly realised he was lying there. She halted in her tracks, and her hands flew to her mouth to stifle a startled gasp, and not to cover herself as he might have expected. His gaze was finally trapped as their eyes met. The quizzical expression in his remained unchanged, but the surprise in hers turned to pleasure as her guess was confirmed and she recognised her handsome travelling companion. Her gaze was distracted by his obvious arousal. A thrill of delight coursed through her as she watched the member with its own agenda unveil itself. Impulsively, she darted forward and, kneeling astride his legs, brushed the tip with what she intended to be a delicate kiss. The silky feel inflamed her, and before she knew it, her lips had enveloped the tip, and were working over and around it.

It was almost more than Brett could stand, but he didn't want the sensation to end. He reached for her breasts, and made a more leisurely exploration of the contours his eyes

had so recently skated over. He cradled both breasts and squeezed the nipples gently as they slid between his splayed fingers. Under the gentle massage she felt a surging message from her nipples travel to her groin. She began to ache with an intense desire to be entered, but he continued to tantalise her. Moving her gently forward, he raised his mouth to her breasts, taking her nipples one after the other between his lips, and manipulating them with his tongue. At the same time he slid his hands down and over her belly, caressing it with feather-light circling movements, slowly approaching the tangle of wet hair. An electric thrill shot through her entire body as a finger passed lightly over her most sensitive part. Her whole being focussed on the sensation produced by the exploring finger. She was on the point of losing the last vestiges of prudence and surrendering herself, when common sense returned. Appalled by what she had come close to doing in the heat of the moment, she pulled away from him, saying,

"No, Brett. Please. I can't do this", ashamed that she had almost betrayed Steve.

"Why", demanded Brett, angry at the rejection.

She tried to placate him by saying, "Not now Brett. We'll be expected back at the cabin soon, for Wade's mid-day meeting."

Disappointment was plain in his eyes, and it was obvious that he didn't believe her excuse, but he supposed she had her reasons. He said, off-handedly,

"OK, another time. Let's head back. I have a job of persuasion to do."

They dressed quickly, and walked back separately, Della going to the women's hut and Brett to the main cabin, where

the leading lights of the group were already gathering. The seat at the head of the table was vacant.

'Ah,' he thought, 'It looks as though they're accepting me as leader at last'.

No sooner had the thought entered his mind, though, than Wade Robinson came in and took the place. He motioned Brett to sit beside him. Sounding oddly formal, he started the meeting by saying,

"Welcome to our humble hideout, Brett. It's a bit basic, but pretty impregnable, except from the air. I don't think we've been found yet, but it's only a matter of time before we're spotted, with those whirly birds going to-and-fro. Somehow we have to get rid of them."

"The sooner, the better," agreed Brett. "Before daylight tomorrow, or we're going to be like sitting ducks here. Give me a few men and a guide, and I'll take a raiding party back through the caves."

He felt a lot less confident than he sounded, but realised that, if he couldn't overcome the claustrophobia, he might as well give up now. Wade was reluctant to risk part of his small band, but recognised the weight of the threat posed by the helicopters. He was also concerned about the welfare of his injured friends. This concern, more than anything else, persuaded him to go along with the suggested course of action.

"I'll guide you myself," he offered, "but I'll leave the rough stuff to you. I want to be sure that George and Errol are being looked after."

He went to the dormitory hut, briefed the men there on what was intended, and asked for volunteers. They were all prepared to go. Wade selected six men.

Shortly after the briefing, the helicopter made its second pass of the day over the valley, making the need for action even more urgent. That evening, as darkness approached, the party mustered at the entrance to the gorge. In single file with Wade, carrying a torch, in the lead, they entered the lake-filled cavern. Again they passed through the siphon, this time struggling against the flow of the stream. Instead of simply fending themselves off the roof of the tunnel, they now had to scrabble along it with hands and feet to make progress against the current.

Brett's claustrophobia was, if anything, worse. With bursting lungs he emerged in the rocky cleft that connected with the Windsor Caves. The others were also gasping as they popped up after him. In silence they filed through the cave system to its huge mouth, then along the ledge that carried the path down along the cliff face. A family of parakeets squawked their alarm as they took off in panic from a giant fig ahead of them. The party stopped as though at an order, and waited to see whether their presence had been betrayed. The birds settled again across the valley. No other sound rose above the usual background hum of insects and the piping of tree frogs.

Reassured, they moved off again towards their first objective, Pa Robert's shack. While the rest of the band remained under cover, Wade went in to learn what he could about the police and army dispositions in the area. His 'uncle' was jumpy, and not particularly pleased to see him again so soon.

"What do you want, Wade? Haven't I done enough?" he asked truculently. "Your friends have been moved into the wagon shed up on my top pineapple field. They'll be much safer there because the police checked it out before. They seem to be holding their own, but there's no way of getting a doctor up here - too risky with so much police activity."

"I'm grateful Pa, but I need to see them - check what they need. Where is this shed?"

Pa led him through his two small pineapple fields to the shed near the base of the cliff. The two men were on makeshift mattresses behind the wagon. Errol was asleep. Slapping palms with George, Wade asked,

"Hey, Man, how goes it?"

"Could be worse, I s'pose," George replied philosophically. "When do we get out of here, Wade?"

"When the heat goes off, we'll be back for you," promised Wade.

George's heavily bandaged arm had been set in a crude splint made from split bamboo, and was supported in a sling made from sacking. Errol's shoulder was patched back and front with clean cotton pads, and his right arm was bound to his body with bandages passing round his chest. Pa had not done a bad job, but Errol was obviously in a worse condition than when he was left.

"It looks as though you've done all you can Pa, and they should be very grateful," Wade said. "But we must get them to a doctor, whatever the consequences for them. They'll be better off prisoners than dead. In any case, for now, they should go back to the cave where you put the Chevrolet. There'll be more police searches after we've finished tonight."

"What yo' up to, Wade?" the old man asked, in a frightened, suspicious voice.

"The less you know, the better for you", replied his 'nephew'.

BANANA

The old man was still scared, but said no more. Wade stayed around to supervise the move of his injured friends by his second cousins. Pa rejoined the raiding party at the shack, where he explained what he knew about the army dispositions. Brett asked him for rope and a can of paraffin, which Pa went off to find. The group unwrapped their weapons. Brett held his hand out for one of the empty bags. He poured paraffin into it and followed that with two coiled fifteen-foot lengths of rope, which he swished about to saturate with paraffin. Carrying the bag in one hand and a pistol in the other, he said,

"Right, let's go," and set off down the track towards Bunker's Hill at a quick jogging pace.

They loped after him, their footsteps muffled by the grass underfoot, the silence broken only by their heavy breathing. About halfway to the village, over to the left, was the flat-topped ridge, where two helicopters and two tents could be seen silhouetted against the stars. There was no sign of guards.

Under cover of the bushes, they crept closer until they could hear low voices. Two soldiers could just be made out, sitting with their backs to a low rock between the tents and the helicopters. They were conversing in such low tones that what they were saying couldn't be distinguished. In a whisper, Brett issued instructions,

"One man to each guard, two to each tent, and leave the choppers to me. No killing if possible. No shots. Use your gun butts."

In a matter of seconds, both guards had been felled with blows to the head. The two off-duty guards suffered the same fate as their attackers entered their tent through a knife slit at the back. In the other tent the lieutenant, a light sleeper, was

disturbed by the scuffle. He was sitting up and reaching for his pistol as his two attackers entered. He found himself looking into the barrels of two Kalashnikovs, and decided on discretion. He and his men were trussed up and gagged, then carried to a safe distance from the helicopters.

One end of a length of paraffin-saturated rope was inserted into the fuel tank of each helicopter and a cigarette lighter applied to the other end. The ropes behaved like lamp wicks, and a minute later, as the raiders raced back along the Windsor Cave track, they heard a 'whoof', followed closely by another as the aircraft burst into flames. Looking back they could see flames rising fifty feet, and exchanged satisfied grins at the sight.

"That'll keep 'em off our backs for a day or two," chortled Chinee, who had enjoyed the exploit immensely. So had Brett, but he expected instant repercussions.

"OK, quiet from now on," he cautioned them.

They fell silent, but maintained a steady pace for the remainder of the trip to the cave entrance. At the scene of the fire, the trussed soldiers were being freed by police. Chief Inspector Anderson viewed the burning wreckage with dismay.

"What a shambles," he muttered to himself. Then, to the lieutenant, he put a question to which he was sure he knew the answer. "How long to get replacements up here?"

"I doubt whether there'll be any replacement," replied the lieutenant, shaky after what had happened. "The colonel's lost a third of his chopper force, and he'll be reluctant to risk more."

He went back to his tent to make his radio report to base, and returned looking chastened.

"The colonel was not very pleased," he reported, wryly. "In fact, he's told me to withdraw half my men. He'll not send out any more helicopters 'til we have the lefties pinned down."

Chief Inspector Anderson had no intention of allowing the opposition to profit for very long from the setback. He organised pursuit along the track, but his men were non-plussed when it divided three ways, and there was no knowing which way the raiders had taken. One led to a pineapple field and another to a small banana plantation, both of them backed by thickets of giant bamboo that could have concealed hundreds of men in ambush. The third path ended at the mouth of the Windsor Caves. When this was reported back to John Anderson, he immediately recalled the cave he had seen in the nearer wall of the valley that he was convinced held the hideout of the Montego Bay left.

'Perhaps there's an underground connection to the cockpit', ran his thoughts. "Send for lamps," he shouted to his sergeant, and made his way gingerly along the precipitous path to the cave entrance, where he waited for the lamps.

When the powerful hand-lamps arrived from the police station at Falmouth, he ordered a small group of constables to follow him, and started into the black recesses of the cave. Four tunnels petered out in solid rock. The fifth led them eventually to the stream that further on filled the tunnel - another dead end. The disappointed inspector ruefully ordered a return to the entrance, and the party stumbled its way back to the open air. Dawn was breaking as they left the cave, but Anderson was not surprised to see 'Tiger' King on his way up the path.

"Drew a blank, again," the Inspector announced, as the Secret Service man gave him a questioning look. "Any luck at your end?"

"Not a peep from the radio," replied King. "I'm beginning to think our undercover pair has been rumbled. If not, the only possible explanation I can think of is a problem with transmission out of that valley. "How in hell do they get in there," he ejaculated, with a vicious swipe at a cloud of persistent mosquitoes. "It must be underground, and if not through Windsor, through some other nearby cave system."

"You're probably right," agreed Anderson, "but it could take forever to find the way in. We need a different approach. I'm sure the stream that runs through the valley is the key. We need to find the source of that, and follow it."

"Maybe the Water Resources Board could help," suggested Tiger King. If anybody knows about the water courses, they will."

"Leave it to me," responded John Anderson. "I know the Chairman, from meetings of the school governors. I'll contact him."

He called off the search for the time being, and told his men to get some sleep. Tired of sleeping in cars, he and Tiger decided to go back to Montego Bay for a more comfortable bed in a hotel.

The raiding party was meanwhile popping up one-by-one in the lake in the cavern, after passing through the siphon once more. 'There's got to be a better way than this', thought Brett, as he gasped for air and rubbed his grazed hands.

"Has anybody made a serious search for another way through to the valley?" he asked the others, as he hauled himself onto the ledge.

"Not in detail," replied Wade. "You only have to look at the height of the cliffs and realise how sheer they are to know it's

a waste of time even to think about it. Besides, if you get up these cliffs, that's only the first obstacle. Then there's the next cockpit, and the next, all filled with jungle, and with jungle on top of the cliffs between them." Brett resolved to find out for himself. It struck him that, as well as making the valley an impregnable hideout, the sole means of entry also turned it into a trap.

CHAPTER 6
IN THE COCKPIT

After the raiding party had slept off the tiredness from their exertions of the night, Brett asked for, being careful not to demand, a meeting to talk about finding another route in and out of the valley.

"The army, and the police, are looking for us. It's only a matter of time before they cotton on to this valley. When they do, we'll be like rats in a trap if we don't have another way out. Any suggestions?"

"Well, of course we've thought about this before," Wade burst out, with unconcealed hostility. "There's no other way. You can forget about the stream outlet. The sub-aqua club found that, a few hundred feet from where it goes out of the cockpit, it falls down some pretty hairy underground rapids. The cliffs are as bad. I haven't seen anywhere they're climbable."

"There's bound to be some way up," countered Brett, with an edge to his voice. "I suggest we each take a section of the north side of the valley and look for a way."

Wade was still not convinced, but a glance around the table told him he had little support. He agreed with Brett with a shrug of his shoulders. They spent the next few exhausting hours forcing their way through the thick undergrowth at the foot of the cliff. Chinee was the only one to find anything remotely like a route up it. He came across a narrow crevice that split the rock face from top to bottom, with enough foot- and handholds for someone with his agility to climb to the top. Back at the camp he reported this, but the enthusiasm aroused was quickly dampened by his next words.

"When you get to the top," he warned, "there's rough ground, covered with thick jungle. No way through."

"Then we'll cut a way," said Wade Robinson, determined to maintain his authority, and not be outdone by anything Brett might say.

For the next few days, relays of men climbed up and hacked their way with machetes along the ridges between cockpits, cutting a snaking path to the outside world half a mile away. A dried-up waterfall gully provided a way down the outer cliff, well away from the Windsor Caves entrance. A young man who was unlikely to be known to the police was sent into Falmouth to buy ropes, and they were fixed in place to make the climb out easier. As well as a second way out, they now had an easier supply route.

Wayne Daniels involved himself in the path-cutting activity, hoping for a chance to make radio contact. He was desperate to call in, but found no opportunity. In any case, he reasoned,

it was unlikely that there would be any monitoring during daytime. He would have to find some other way to get the height he needed, and it would have to be at midnight. After all day slashing at undergrowth, when the rest of the men were settling down to sleep, Wayne sat with his back to a fig buttress, turning over ideas how he might get sufficient height, avoiding the cliff climb, which he knew would guarded. He had a sudden inspiration.

'These fig trees are nearly as high as the cliffs. Maybe if I can climb high enough I'll be able to make contact'.

Looking at the figs shielding the campsite, though, he realised that climbing a tree with such great flying buttresses would be difficult, especially in the dark.

'I'll need a special technique', he concluded.

He remembered a film showing Canadian lumberjacks shinning up trees using straps looped round the trunk. He got up and searched around for something suitable. Spotting an off-cut from the rope used on the cliff, he casually picked it up, and returned to his tree, where he waited until it was close to midnight.

Glancing quickly around the now-still camp to ensure that he was unobserved, he slipped into the bamboo thicket, retrieved his hidden radio, and forced his way through the undergrowth until he found a suitable giant tree. Its soaring branches reached at least as high as the top of the cliff.

'If I can reach them, they should give me the height I need'.

He cut the rope into two unequal lengths. After tying the ends of the shorter piece to his ankles, he hauled himself up onto a prominent buttress. Swinging the longer piece round the tree, he caught it, then wrapped the ends several times round his wrists until he held just enough free loop to allow him to jerk it up the trunk. That gave him enough purchase to allow him to inch his feet higher. Using the two loops, he hoisted himself to the first fork, and sat there to rest and take off the ankle rope. The rest of the climb was comparatively easy, needing only one hand-held rope for safety. Clinging precariously, high in the canopy, with one elbow hooked over a fork, he fished out his radio. At one minute to midnight, very quietly, he began to broadcast his call sign.

"Mongoose One to Mother. Mongoose One to Mother. Come in Mother."

He switched to 'receive'. There was silence except for static. He tried again.

"Mongoose One to Mother. Are you receiving me? Come in Mother."

Still there was no response. For ten minutes he tried, but there was nothing on his frequency except the loud static that confirmed poor communication conditions.

'Either I'm not high enough, or nobody's listening', he concluded. 'Not surprising, the length of time I've been out of contact.'

Returning the radio to its pouch, he shinned down to the main fork, attached the ropes again, and was quickly down on the ground. For security, he buried the ropes and the radio at the foot of the tree and then made his way back to camp by a different route, encircling it and approaching from the opposite side.

The day after the destruction of the helicopters, Chief Inspector Anderson woke from his first deep sleep for days, wondering why he had not chosen a hotel from the outset. After a quick breakfast, his first action was to ring the Water Resources Board. Joel Green's only previous contact with the inspector had been in the context of Saint Jago School governors' meetings. His immediate assumption was that there must be some problem at his beloved school.

"No, no, Mr. Green. I'm not ringing about school matters at all. I need information about watercourses in the Cockpit Country. Is there anybody in your organisation I can talk to?"

"Not really, Inspector," replied Green. "We're mainly concerned with accessible water resources. There's only one man who knows anything about water in the Cockpit Country. Many years ago he worked for us at the Geological Survey, but he moved to the University Geological Department. He still does some consultancy work for us from time to time. I forget his name, but I'm sure that if you ring the Department, they'll put you in touch."

"Thanks for your help," said John Anderson, and rang off.

Everything seemed to be conspiring to frustrate him. Straightaway, he rang the University of the West Indies, and was put through to the Geological Department Secretary.

"The person you want is Doctor Andrews," she told him, in response to his enquiry, "but I'm afraid he's out on a field trip in the Blue Mountains now, and for the next two weeks."

The Chief Inspector's impatience showed in his voice. He let out a 'damn' of frustration before moderating his tone somewhat.

"I need to speak to him urgently. Where in the mountains is he, and how can I contact him?"

"Well, I know roughly where he is. He's doing water surveys for a new reservoir up in the Mount James area," replied the secretary, with an icy edge to her voice, "but contacting him is a different matter. He stays out of touch with the Department for weeks on his field trips. Your only hope is to go up there and find him. If you can wait till the weekend, your best bet is to catch him on Saturday night or Sunday morning. I usually book him into the Casa Monte Hotel for Saturday night - he likes the special Sunday breakfast and barbecue lunch - gives him a change from camp cooking."

"Is that the place in the foothills, up on Stony Hill Road, where they train hotel staff?"

"That's the one Inspector. He reckons that if they're training, they'll be out to give good service, and it's cheap.

"Thanks very much," said John Anderson, dryly, and replaced the receiver.

The last thing he wanted was another search on his hands. Waiting for the weekend was not an appealing option, but he knew that in the rough, trackless mountain terrain it might take days to find the water expert. He decided to wait. Meanwhile he stood down most of his men in the Windsor Caves area, leaving only a sergeant and two constables to liaise with the Secret Service men and the small army unit that was all that had been left to the lieutenant after his loss of the helicopters. He made arrangements with Tiger King to keep him informed of any developments, then headed back to Kingston with one of the cars and the rest of the non-local men.

BLUE MOUNTAINS
EARLY MAY 1973

The object of the Chief Inspector's latest quest was lugging equipment round the site of the proposed new reservoir, cursing under his breath his lazy assistant's penchant for carrying the lightest gear. This would be his fourth three-week spell in the area in the last six months, measuring the flow rate of streams into the valley to be flooded, and surveying the estimated fill line. He was filthy and sweaty, and looking forward eagerly to his regular weekend visit to the Casa Monte. He put down his load and pulled out his working machete to hack a path through particularly dense undergrowth. This surveying work was very labour intensive, he thought.

'It shouldn't be my job at all, but I suppose it's one of the penalties of showing willing'.

He had agreed to do a preliminary survey to estimate the approximate capacity of the reservoir and its fill rate. When the go-ahead on the project was finally given, the pros. would be brought in. While he was methodically chopping a path to his next survey point, Steve's thoughts went back to his first meeting with Della Brook. At the end of his first week's work at the reservoir site he had hurried back to his flat to shower and change, ready to go with the Prof. to some Jamaican Airways reception, to be held at the Casa Monte Hotel, wherever that was. Steve drove, and they arrived to find the car park almost full of the most expensive cars in Kingston. His Mini looked totally out of place.

Inside the hotel, the elite of the city was gathered. The business people, the lawyers, the accountants, and the

academics were all there. The din of the chatter was incredible, as everybody shouted to be heard above the noise. As was his wont, Steve sat keeping himself company, watching the complex interactions of people around him, and listening to the polite small talk. Suddenly a champagne flute appeared under his nose. Holding it was a light brown vision in white, smiling at him with genuine concern at his loneliness in the crowd. She offered him the glass and sat by him on the small sofa.

"You don't enjoy crowds, do you," she began, stating the obvious.

"No," he admitted, "I enjoy inconsequential chit-chat even less, but I wouldn't mind talking to you all night."

Flattered, and warming instantly to the big awkward-looking man beside her, she told him,

"There's nothing I'd like better than to take a rest and keep you company".

"Well, why don't you? What's to stop you staying right here and brightening up my day?"

"I'm afraid I have to work. You see, I'm a hostess with the airline, and my only reason for being here is to promote our charter flights to the UK."

"If they have hostesses like you, I'm sorry I came out by British Airways. They have some fine-looking women, but nothing to compare with you."

Recognising the chemistry developing between them, but anxious to be seen to be doing a good PR job at the reception, Della suggested, with the slightest of sideways tilts of her head that turned what she said into a question,

"Meet me later, at the pool-side bar?"

Steve agreed, nodding vigorously. He was too smitten to risk talking.

'The evening's certainly looking up' he thought, and his spirits rose at the prospect ahead.

Della picked up a tray, recharged it with champagne, and began to circulate again among the guests, bestowing a smile here, exchanging a glass there, and generally raising the tone of the function. Steve, bored with listening to trivia, took himself off to sit by the pool, armed with a couple of Red Stripes. The night was balmy. There was no moon but perhaps for that reason, the stars were as bright as he'd ever seen them. He amused himself picking out the constellations. There was Ursa Major, pointing to the Pole Star; Ursa Minor, anchored to the Pole Star; Orion the hunter. The Pleiades were so brilliant he fancied he could see more than the traditional seven. Jupiter, high in the sky, was a bright disc and Mars was a distinctive red. Over all arched the band of the Milky Way, its myriad stars forming a belt across the heavens. Lost in wonder at the magnitude of it all, he was startled by the appearance of Della beside him.

"I've heard of people being star-struck," she teased him," but I object to taking second place to them."

"Oh, hello - er - I'm glad you came. I wasn't sure you would."

"My name's Della – Della Brook." She held out her hand. "Of course I came. I promised to."

"I'm sorry. I'm a bit awkward with women, especially so when they're as good-looking as you. Steven Andrews is the name. I answer to Steve"

"With a line like that, Steve, what have you got to be awkward about?" she asked.

Blushing with embarrassment, he hastily changed the subject.

"Have you a car here, or can I offer you a lift home?"

"I would like you to take me home - later if you wouldn't mind. But I can't ask you in. There are more sisters in my home than in a convent, so I'd rather stay here for a while and talk."

She didn't mention why her home was full of sisters; that her mother had died giving birth to her seventh child, all daughters, and that she, the eldest, had for the last ten years been the main breadwinner and responsible for bringing up the rest because her father had given up on the never-ending struggle and taken solace in a diet of rum and ganja. Her need for a second job stemmed from his demands for money, but she had no intention of revealing to Steve or anyone else the nature of the second job.

"Suits me," he said, delighted by the turn of events. "I'd like to get to know you better. The first thing I want to know is whether I can see you again."

"I would like that," she replied, "but it's difficult to make plans and stick to them. I can be called out for a trip to London at very short notice."

"Sounds a very glamorous life to me, compared with mine," he commented.

"Oh, it can be a bit boring," she said. "It's not quite as glamorous as it seems. I'm really an airborne skivvy. The only thing that keeps it interesting for me is the in-flight modelling we do on the side."

"You mean, clothes modelling?" he asked, with genuine interest.

"Yes, all kinds of clothes, from swimwear to ball gowns. But that's enough about me. What are you doing in Jamaica?" she asked, recognising from his accent that he was an expatriate.

He explained his involvement with the banana irrigation project, twenty years before, and how it had led to a post at the University.

"Twenty years is a long time. Are you saying you haven't been home in all those years? There must be pretty strong reasons for you to stick it out here for so long."

"Well, there's nothing much for me back there. No family and no promotion prospects. The offer of a lecturing post here was the icing on the cake that swung a decision I was close to making anyway. This climate appeals to me, and the warmth of the sea lets me indulge my favourite hobby - fish watching. I spend hours out on the reef whenever I can get away from work."

"I like swimming, but I don't go in the sea much. The thought of all the nasties, like sharks and jelly fish puts me off," she confessed.

"No problem," he pronounced. "In all the hours I've spent snorkelling on the reef, I've never seen a shark. A few barracuda, yes, but they keep their distance. The incredible thing for me is that, out there, every time you turn your head you see something you've never seen before. The colours and variety of the fish and the coral are amazing."

"If your enthusiasm's anything to go by, it looks as though I'm missing out on something special," she conceded. "One of these days you must take me out there."

"That's a pleasure I'll look forward to. I'm sure you'll be so fascinated that you'll forget all about the nasties. There's a very good place for beginners near Port Maria, where the reef's only about fifty yards offshore. It also happens to be the best place

for coral varieties. American universities send parties of marine biology students there because of that. But, forget about the reef! Tell me more about yourself and the hostessing."

"There's not a lot to tell. We fly to-and-fro across the Atlantic, getting jet-lagged in both directions, and feeling too tired to do very much when we arrive," she said, dismissively.

"That's hard to believe," was his sceptical rejoinder. "I can't imagine someone as attractive as you being left alone by the aircrew."

"Of course," she told him, with a mischievous smile, "we go out for a meal together, and if there's a good concert or opera on in London, we'll try to get tickets for that."

"And afterwards?" he asked, raising a suggestive eyebrow, and already feeling pangs of jealousy over this beautiful woman he hardly knew.

"None of your business," she said lightly, passing off his implication with a toss of her head. "There's some hanky-panky, of course, but the goings-on between air-crew and cabin crew are mostly pure myth, and the idea of the Mile High Club is laughable."

"Mile High Club?" repeated the ingenuous Steve, who was unsophisticated in such matters.

"Sex at high altitude," she told him, with laughter in her voice. "There's neither time nor place for it in the air, even if the inclination's there."

"If that's a myth, it's one I haven't heard, though I suppose there's no smoke without fire," he responded with a quizzical look.

He was about to make some amusing comment when, from the front of the hotel, came the sound of car doors slamming, as the last guests began to leave. Those standing talking by the entrance from the pool area started to move through to the main entrance, or to their rooms if they were staying overnight. Waiters cleared the empty glasses from the poolside tables, and very soon Della and Steve were alone on the pool terrace. When the lights went out they appeared to each other only as disembodied voices. It was an eerie experience.

Suddenly, Steve was conscious of being plagued by mosquitoes. Whether they had been there before, and he had been too preoccupied to notice, or whether it had anything to do with the lights being switched off, he couldn't say. Della had no such problem.

"Maybe," she suggested, "it has something to do with my perfume."

"Well, I don't think much of the mosquitoes' taste," he said. "I think it's very attractive."

"Why, thank you, kind sir," she replied, pleased with the compliment, but passing it off lightly.

She watched him swatting away ineffectually at the hungry swarm for a while, then suggested a remedy.

"Why don't you go for a swim. That's the quickest way to get rid of them."

"If I do, it'll have to be in my underpants," he replied, embarrassed.

"Well, go ahead. Don't mind me," she encouraged him.

Itching all over by now, he needed little prompting. Stripping down to his Y-fronts, he plunged into the deep end of the pool. The relief was instantaneous. Up and down he ploughed with his strong crawl stroke, dived to thoroughly wet his hair, and came up blowing hard, close to Della's chair.

"Come on in. It's terrific," he invited her.

The idea of midnight bathing had always had erotic connotations for Della, although she had never actually done it. The thought thrilled her. Quickly, she unbuttoned her dress, let it fall to the ground and stepped out of it. She kept her panties on. She didn't wear bras. Kicking off her shoes, she slipped into the water beside Steve. After swimming once up and down the pool she returned to his side. Steve tentatively kissed her on the lips. What began as a light, brief contact turned into a long, lingering embrace as she responded. Her nipples, already stimulated by the sensual caress of her movement through the water, hardened perceptibly as she reached up to clasp her hands behind his neck. He could feel them thrusting against his chest. He tightened his embrace. She pressed against him. Then, suddenly, she twisted away, confused by mixed feelings. An insistent question entered her mind.

'Is it simple sexual attraction, or is love at first sight really possible?'

Disturbed by the apparent cold-shoulder treatment, Steve slipped his hands around her waist from behind, and held her to him. Sensing his feelings, she turned her face towards him and, over her shoulder, kissed him again, this time gently on the cheek.

"It's alright," she said. "It's just that I'm not sure of myself, or of my feelings."

Still standing behind her, Steve moved his hands to caress her breasts, hoping she wouldn't be offended. Her nipples were still erect. 'So, she's not turned off me'.

Della relished the massaging hands, and felt the urgency of his desire behind her. 'Isn't this what I'd anticipated? What I wanted? Or is it not what I wanted? Still confused, she ducked out of his arms, and slipped away from him. Steve swam after her, caught her in the deep end, and took her in his arms again, supporting her by treading water. She clasped him to her, and was close to succumbing when the reality of the situation struck her with such force, she gasped. The thought surfaced through an erotic haze,

'What am I doing? In a swimming pool - a hotel pool at that!'

"No, Steve. Not here," she whispered. "And please, not now. I have to think."

She didn't really have to think. What was happening with this man was all she could ever want. But she was in no position to make a commitment, not yet. First, her job was very important to her, and second, it was dangerous. How could she commit herself?

"I'm sorry Steve," she managed to get out. "I have to leave. I'm on duty early in the morning and need to get some sleep first. Will you take me home, please?"

"Yes, if I can see you again," answered Steve, half-disappointed, but half-approving of her decision. "If I can't come to your home, I suppose the best place is here. I'm always here at the weekend when I'm doing field work, and from now on I'll make a point of being here on other weekends."

They said little on the way into Kingston; both immersed in their own thoughts. When they reached the mean little house where she lived, Steve got out to say goodnight. With a quick kiss on the cheek, she thanked him for his company and disappeared inside. Her thoughts were racing. Never had she felt such an instant rapport with a man. She tried to convince herself that she didn't believe in love at first sight, but this was ridiculously close.

'How can I feel like this after less than an hour talking to a man? He isn't particularly handsome or witty. Perhaps it's his enthusiasm and his air of dependability'.

Steve returned to his flat with his thoughts in a whirl. 'What am I, a confirmed bachelor, with a fly-by-night attitude to women, doing?' He could not get Della Brook out of his mind. Her beautiful face and gorgeous figure kept thrusting itself forward for attention. Sleep was out of the question.

'If I keep this up, I'll be a wreck by the weekend, and even then I can't be sure she'll turn up.'

By daylight he had fallen into a fitful doze, but was wakened by the shrilling of his alarm clock what seemed like seconds later. After a quick fruit and cereal breakfast he headed back to the reservoir site in the hills. Perhaps some hard physical work would switch his mind away from the delectable Della. His poor assistant took the brunt of his frustration. The lad was worked harder than he'd ever worked before.

Della failed to turn up that weekend or the following weekend. There was no message either. Steve Andrews became more and more morose. He tried to forget the vision in white.

'Perhaps I imagined her interest in me. Maybe she was just a good actress, still doing her PR job that night. No, surely she wouldn't have stayed on to talk to me if that was the case'.

It was several weeks later, when he had still not seen nor heard anything of her, that Chief Inspector Anderson approached Steve and set in motion the events that would involve him more deeply in her fate than he had ever imagined possible.

IN THE COCKPIT

Later the same morning that Steve returned to the reservoir site, Brett Johnson was discussing the arms situation with Wade, Chinee, Moose, Della and Queenie.

"We don't have enough weapons for everybody. If any more people join us, we'll be very short. We need more people and guns. Who supplied those you have already?"

"They were shipped in from Cuba," replied Wade, "but they're expensive, and we haven't got the funds for more."

"OK, the first thing we need to do is raise funds and we need to do it in a big way."

"How do you propose to do that?" asked the sceptical Moose.

"Quite simply, we take over the ganja trade."

The open mouths of the rest of the group were testimony to how simple they thought that idea was.

"The ganja trade's run by the biggest gangs in Kingston," protested Wade. "There's no way we could muscle in on them. Do you want to commit suicide?"

"I know a lot about the trade," said Brett quietly. "I shared a prison cell with a Yardie drug dealer. He ran the Southampton end of an operation smuggling ganja on Fyffes banana boats. They were shipping the stuff in the false walls of containers. It was very lucrative 'til Customs and Excise latched on to it. Now the gangs have to rely on couriers - airline personnel and tourists. I've got a better idea."

He went on to explain how the idea had come to him while watching one of the men in the camp carving a face on the skin of a banana with a sharp knife.

"To make a nose, he cut the shape, leaving a hinge at the bridge, then lifted the hinged part of the skin with the tip of his knife until it stood proud. This seemed so trivial that at first I thought nothing of it. Then an idea struck me, and it was so simple and apparently foolproof that I thought it through, and I've done a few experiments. I'll show you".

Brett reached down by his feet and mystified the group by producing a green banana, a short, cylindrical plug of wood; a longer, hollow length of bamboo, sharpened at one end like an apple-corer, and a new, single-edged razor blade. Without explanation, he carefully cut almost through the banana close to the end opposite its stalk, leaving only a hinge of skin. Gently folding back the end of the fruit, he used the bamboo tube to remove a core of flesh about two inches long. He inserted the wooden plug in the hole and replaced the hinged end of the fruit. Within seconds the sticky juice exuding from the cut skin had healed the cut so that only very close examination would reveal its existence.

"Imagine that the plug of wood is ganja resin, and there we have our method of shipment in bulk. We insert a plug in one banana in one hand in each box of a shipment. When the fruit's unloaded at the distribution depot in England it will be inspected, and rotten or discoloured bananas thrown out. The ones that have been doctored will be amongst them. They'll be prematurely yellow, and arouse no suspicion amongst the rest of the rejects."

"A great theory," scoffed Wade. "There are just a few minor practical problems like, we know nothing about how bananas are shipped, or how they're handled at the other end, or even this end, for that matter. The ganja trade's been in the hands of

the big gangs for the last twenty years, and they've got the whole business, from collection to distribution, sewn up. They're as well organised as the Mafia."

"Of course, we'll have to set up an organisation here and in England, and we need to know the details of how the bananas are handled and shipped, so that we can work out the best place to doctor them. I can get that information from old friends on the Thompson estate. They hate the colonel, and I think they'd revel in the idea of using his business to help us. I spent months on that estate, sinking boreholes for an English hydrologist. I'm sure I can get Thomson's overseers to turn a blind eye to what his loaders are doing. In fact, when they know what's afoot, they'll probably want to join us. When the time's right, I'll make the approach myself, but we have a long way to go before we can break into the ganja trade."

"You're telling me," said Wade, with heavy sarcasm. "We don't even know where to start. Apart from not being able to process the stuff, how do we break the hold of the gangs?"

"Their weak link's in the first stage of their operation - collection," countered Brett. "Production's in the hands of subsistence farmers, and that's where we have to break into the cycle."

"Easier said than done," chipped in Moose. "Apart from being trapped in the Cockpit, here we are, a bunch of amateurs, talking about taking over a lucrative racket from Mafia-style outfits with powerful front men. No farmer's gonna supply us without some pretty effective protection. How you gonna protect a thousand little farmers?" he asked.

"Only by being stronger, better trained and better organised than the gangs," replied Brett.

"In a year I'd aim to have an elite force of five hundred men and women, armed by Cuba. We'll wipe the gangs out."

"What about refining?" asked Queenie, who knew enough to realise that you don't simply smoke the weed as it comes. "That needs equipment and expertise we haven't got. You seem to have an answer for everything else", she said, with a truculent stare. "What's your answer to that?"

"When we control the suppliers, the processors will have no option. Either they co-operate or they go under."

Looks of dawning belief appeared on the faces around the table as his new comrades began to appreciate the possibilities. Brett looked around to see whether the approval spread to Della, as he suddenly remembered the episode on the rock, and realised that her approval mattered to him. She wasn't there, and now he wasn't even sure that she had been in the room when the discussion started.

"Where's Della?" he asked.

The other men signalled their ignorance by shrugs. Queenie shook her head and spread her hands.

"For the last couple of days she's been goin' for a swim about noon, then for a siesta," she volunteered, adding cattily, with a pointed look at Brett, "and not always alone."

Brett's eyes narrowed at the gibe. Furious at the possibility that Della was not what she seemed, he pushed back his chair violently, leapt to his feet, and was out of the door so quickly, the others sat staring at each other in amazement. Brett knocked on the door of the women's cabin, but there was no response. He sprinted down the path to the pool. Della was at that moment well hidden in the forest of bamboo behind the camp, fiddling in exasperation with the controls of a small, two-way radio. All she could elicit from the set was crackles and buzzes. With a groan of despair she realised that the surrounding cliffs were blocking all chances of radio communication. Her time for reporting was long past. For days now she had failed to make contact, and understood at last why her colleague had been in-communicado for so long.

'I've got to find a way out of this valley if I'm going to alert Inspector Anderson to the plans being hatched. By way of the cave, or the new cliff route's too risky. They're both too well guarded. I'd have to be pretty desperate. But how desperate do you need to be Della?' she asked herself, with the thought that she was already in fairly desperate straits, trapped with a bunch of militant left-wingers, and out of contact with base. 'You got yourself into a pretty pass this time', she chided herself, with a wry smile.

As an airhostess she had been a natural Special Branch recruitment target. The lure of the extra money had a big influence on her acceptance of the role. It was difficult supporting her sisters and her drunken father on a hostess's salary. The airline job made surveillance of travellers easy, and over the last few months she had developed a knack for identifying the drug couriers. There were always nuances of behaviour that betrayed them. Many had been picked up at Heathrow following her tip-off.

Surveillance of political subversives was a different matter. The only job-related factor was the frequent extended breaks of a hostess, which gave her time to cultivate contacts. For eighteen months she had been spending most of her time off in Montego Bay, listening to boring Maoist lectures and attending protest rallies. Almost without effort on her part she had infiltrated

the fringes of the left-wing culture, and been accepted as part of it. Thinking about how her contacts had developed, and how they had led to her intimacy with Brett Johnson reminded her of the towel she had left on the rock. The memory gave her a severe jolt.

'My God, I left my towel on the rock too long. If it's found, I'm sunk'.

In her haste to retrieve the towel, Della ran to the pool. Breathless, she climbed to the top of the rock. The towel was still there, but it was around the neck of Brett Johnson. Thinking fast, she cried out,

"Brett, I'm so glad you found it. You must have addled my brain to make me forget it. None of the others would have understood if they knew I'd left it here."

Giving her a quizzical look, Brett thought,

'I'll have to keep a close eye on you, my girl. You might be genuine, but you might be a very good actress'.

Reserving judgement for the moment, he suggested,

"Let's have a quick swim before I go back to finish discussions about tactics."

At that moment Queenie emerged from the path, dressed in a bikini and carrying a towel to give the impression of being intent on swimming herself, but more interested in keeping a jealous eye on Brett. Her presence deterred him from his swim and the post-bathing pursuits he had in mind. Nodding to her, he stood in one graceful movement, bounded down to the foot of the rock, and disappeared along the path, still carrying Della's towel.

"Enjoy your swim, but be careful not to leave any evidence around," he called.

The two girls splashed about in the pool for a few minutes, dressed without bothering to dry off, and headed back to the camp. Queenie's talk, all the way back along the path, was of the 'gorgeous' Brett Johnson, who had evidently made a lasting impression. Lecture herself as she might about love and duty, and objectivity, Della could not suppress pangs of jealousy. As they emerged into the cleared space around the huts, leading members of the band were converging on the main building. Another meeting was about to start. When the women attempted to enter the hut, the door was blocked by the massive frame of Moose. He waved them away, saying, half apologetically,

"Brett Johnson's orders! Top security meeting going on," and closed the door in their faces.

Queenie bridled, stamped her foot in frustration, and stormed off to their quarters, where she paced up and down furiously before flinging herself down on her bed.

"I was never treated this way in Montego Bay," she spat out to nobody in particular.

Although never a central figure in the left wing group, she had always been an accepted fringe member, and been party to any discussions and activities. Now she felt torn between admiration for the new leading light and resentment at her treatment by him. Soon her futile rage was spent. As she calmed down, her thoughts turned to Wade Robinson, and suddenly, she slept.

Della's thoughts and emotions were different. She, too, admired the man. There were more intimate reasons for doing

BANANA

so, but she had other reasons for wanting to be part of the central group. She desperately needed to know what was being planned, but could think of no convincing ruse that would allow her to get within earshot. However, finding herself excluded from the continued discussions, she resigned herself to playing a waiting game. Going back to the small room she shared with Queenie, she stripped off the dress and briefs that were all she ever wore in Jamaica, and kicked her sandals into a corner. By then, her body was almost dry, so she splashed herself all over with water from a gourd on the rough table, and lay down to think over her position. Enjoying the cooling effect of the water evaporating from her body, she drifted off to sleep. She was still asleep, lying on her back, when Queenie woke. Hearing the measured breathing from the other bed, she sat up noiselessly and studied the naked form of the other woman with the analytical interest of one female in another. She noted enviously the perfect breasts, still provocative, though slumped, the flattened belly between rounded hip bones, the long, slim legs, slightly parted to reveal the pale coffee-coloured contours of her inner thighs. In spite of her heterosexual preferences, she thrilled at the sight. Never had feminine charms prompted such an effect before.

Queenie also stripped, and lay on her bed, propped on her elbows, looking down critically at her own, darker body.

'Not bad, she thought, but stared across with envy at her companion's lighter skin.

She sat up, and the creases in her belly appeared even darker, with a blue-black sheen. Dissatisfied, she looked again at the sleeping Della. The breasts were so perfect she wanted to kiss them, to feel rising nipples on her lips. She could

understand the fascination they would have for men. Even in the recumbent position they moved and jiggled attractively in time with the girl's breathing. Resisting the temptation, she made do by massaging her own breasts, imagining that a man was performing the service. Then, with a sigh, she turned her back on the sleeping Della and let half-awake fantasies take over.

CHAPTER 7

CASA MONTE HOTEL
KINGSTON
EARLY JUNE, 1973

On Saturday night Steve Andrews was sitting by the pool bar at the Casa Monte, sipping a red rum and orange and enjoying his weekly sample of civilisation, when he was startled by a low voice beside him saying,

"Dr Andrews? I'm Chief Inspector Anderson, of the Special Branch. There's something important I want to discuss with you. Is there somewhere more private than this?" nodding towards the pool area.

When he had recovered his equilibrium, Steve said,

"Well, yes, my room. But what have I done to interest the Special Branch?" he asked, apprehensively.

Steve was not accustomed to being accosted by big police officers.

"Nothing, yet.   It's a matter of what you might be able to do," the Inspector replied.

This only served to intensify Steve's puzzlement, but he was intrigued. As they walked through to Steve's ground floor room they exchanged pleasantries, but as soon as the door closed behind them, the Chief Inspector explained the problem of the vanished fugitive.

"We've got a pretty good idea that Brett Johnson's gone to ground in the Cockpit Country, and we think information on the water courses there will help to pinpoint his position".

At the mention of the name, Steve did a classic double take.

"Why, he's an old fr - - - - acquaintance of mine," he hastened to correct himself, "who helped me with my work in the plantations when he was a boy."

"Well, now he's up to no good; stirring up left wing trouble for the country. He's got to be found and stopped. I hope your knowledge of the water courses in the Cockpit Country will help us to stop him."

Steve motioned the Chief Inspector into the solitary armchair, and sat himself on the edge of the bed. He was interested, and at the same time baffled.

'What possible interest can the Special Branch have in rivers? No doubt I'm about to find out'. "Have you any idea what a tall order that is?" he asked the Chief Inspector, rhetorically.   "Part of my Ph.D. work on water resources was to estimate the flow rates of the rivers, including those with their sources in the Cockpit. It was well nigh impossible because the area was so inaccessible, and because so many of the tributaries run underground. I couldn't even be certain which tributaries fed which rivers. What I really needed was a system of dye

release experiments and aerial spotting by helicopter, but funds wouldn't run to that. Added to that, it would take months."

"How would you go about it, if I could arrange for a helicopter, and said you could confine the observations to a small area?" asked John Anderson.

Steve cast his mind back to his project ideas.

"I'd need two teams," he replied, "one to go into the cave systems and release a dye into whatever underground streams they found; the other to fly the helicopter and look for emergence of the dye above ground".

"I suppose you need large quantities of dye for that?" guessed the Inspector, hinting at his disappointment.

"No, not at all. If you use fluorecein you can dilute it two million times, and it will still give a bright green fluorescence in sunlight."

John Anderson's face brightened at that. He asked, with some excitement,

"Will you help us and, if so, when can you start?"

His companion considered for a while before answering.

"Of course, I'm willing to help, but I need the permission of my Department and the sponsor of the project I'm working on here. The Water Resources Board won't be very pleased if I'm diverted from their pet project, and I'm sure the University will make a charge for my time."

"This is a question of national security. There'll be no problem," stated the Chief Inspector in a matter-of-fact tone. "Leave the arrangements to me. I'll set everything up and get back to you. It would help if you could check in here every day for messages."

Steve agreed to collaborate, and the Chief Inspector left to

make his arrangements with the Army, the Water Resources
Board and the University. The hydrologist remained in his
room. He lay on his bed pondering the turn of events that had
brought him full circle to impinge again on the career of Brett
Johnson, this time not as his mentor. His thoughts went back to
the eager, willing helper of his carefree days on the Thompson
plantation. The boy's thirst for knowledge had impressed him
deeply. Even while slogging away with the sledgehammer,
sinking boreholes, he wanted to know what the holes were for,
what the instruments did, and how they worked. Although he
doubted how much of the technicalities Brett would understand,
Steve had tried to answer his questions in terms that might be
understood by a twelve-year-old. In his mind he was now back
on the Estate.

THOMPSON ESTATE
MARCH, 1953

"This is bloody hard work," panted Brett, as he hammered the
drill tube into the ground to finish his third hole of the day,
his body gleaming as the sweat streamed off him. "Why do we
have to do this?"

He extracted the tube from that hole for the last time and
poked out the plug of earth from the end.

"Take a rest," ordered Steve, "and I'll tell you. We want
to find out how much water banana trees need to produce the
best crop, so that we can tell all the growers how much water

to use. One of the things we don't understand is how the need for water varies from one part of the tree's life cycle to another. Because the cycle's so complicated it's going to be very difficult to find the answers."

Brett sat in rapt attention, knees drawn up, elbows on knees and chin in hands.

"A banana tree grows from a corm just like a lily. In fact, it's a member of the lily family. It fruits about fifteen months after planting, one bunch to each tree, and then it's cut down. When the tree's about six months old, it produces two new corms from its roots. One of them is allowed to grow as an offshoot of the tree, and the other's taken away to be planted somewhere else. So you see that in some parts of the plantation there are rows of mature trees with off-shoots, in others just off-shoots, and in others just freshly planted corms. That's why we need boreholes in different places."

"That's easy enough to understand," Brett scoffed, but what I don't understand is what you do with the thing you stick down the hole," gesturing towards the neutron probe and its black box.

"It's an instrument for measuring the amount of water in the soil," explained Steve Andrews.

Trying hard to suppress a look of amusement, he launched into a simplified explanation.

"In the end of the probe there's some radioactive americium and some beryllium. The americium shoots out alpha particles. When they're absorbed by the beryllium it shoots out fast neutrons that are then slowed down by hydrogen atoms in the water in the soil. The black box counts the number of neutrons slowed down, and that tells us the amount of water."

The boy's eyes glazed over. "And you think bananas are complicated?"

"Never mind," said Steve. "You have to study for years to understand all this guff. Let's get back to work. One more hole, then I'll show you how to make the measurements."

All that winter and spring they toiled, mostly on the Thompson estate, but also on the nearby plantation with poor yields. They irrigated with known amounts of water, and measured the amount taken up by the trees, the amount lost by evaporation and the amount added by rainfall. At the end of it all Steve had a mass of data, some conflicting, which would take months to analyse. He also had a very useful assistant, who had shown his intelligence time and again. Now he had the problem of what to do with the boy at the end of his time. The estate had employed the lad only for the duration of the project. There was no other work for him on the plantation. Steve remembered the original reason for his being there - he wanted to go back to school, but had no money to pay.

'There must be schools on the island with free places for bright boys', he thought. 'I'll make enquiries'.

The next day Steve had to drive down to Kingston to present his preliminary results at the Banana Board. He decided to kill two birds with one stone and dig out some information on schools at the public library. He called there on his way to the Board. The desk had information on all the schools and, sure enough, there were free places at most of them, funded by the government since 1950. Candidates for the free places had to pass entrance examinations, held in July for entry in October. Brett would be just in time.

Following his seminar, which went very well considering the preliminary nature of his findings, he was approached to apply for an assistant lecturer post in the University geology department. Since he had already decided that he wanted to stay in Jamaica if possible, it sounded like a capital idea.

'At least I'll be able to keep an eye on Brett's schooling. No doubt I'll have to provide for things like uniform and books out of my own pocket, but I don't mind that. It seems a good cause'.

His next stop was at the Education Office, to find out what subjects had to be presented for examination to enter Jamaica College. There was some self-interest in the choice of school. It had a good reputation, but it also happened to be in Hope, where he should be able to get a University flat.

The subjects for the examinations were English, history, geography and mathematics. They would all have to be brushed up by Brett, who had been out of school for six months. On his way back through town, Steve stopped and bought schoolbooks on all four subjects, a ream of writing paper and pencils. Back at camp, he told Brett what he had done, and presented him with an armful of educational materials.

The boy was overcome with a mixture of gratitude, excitement and apprehension. His primary school had set tests, but he had never sat an exam before.

"How can I be ready in time?" he wanted to know.

"You've got three months," Steve told him. "Study these books, and ask me if there's something you don't understand. I'm tipping that you'll pass without any problem."

The tears welling up in Brett's eyes were enough testimony to his feelings.

Brett Johnson moved into Steve's digs. He spent most of his time over the next three months devouring the information in his books, and duly passed the entrance examination near the top of the entry. He attended Jamaica College as a day boy. His progress through the school appeared almost effortless. Academically and athletically he proved to be amongst the best in his year, and that remained the case through to the sixth form. Throughout Brett's time at the school, Steve Andrews kept an avuncular eye on him, when his own Ph.D. research and frequent field trips allowed. He attended sports days and other school functions to provide support. Then the time to choose sixth form subjects arrived, and with it University preferences. Steve hoped that Brett would have a scientific bent - he was competent in science - but the boy insisted on economics, history and English. It transpired that his choice was coloured by a desire to read Philosophy, Politics and Economics at Cambridge; a desire fostered by his expatriate economics teacher, who continually sang the praises of the University.

The fact that three A-grades and also an outstanding pass in an entry examination would be necessary proved no deterrent. Brett was adamant. The issue caused the first real rift between them. Brett gave up all his sporting activities to concentrate on study, and by the end of his second year in the sixth, had his three A-grades, and had also won a government-sponsored grant for study abroad. This took him to England, where his performance in the entry examination won him an Exhibition and a PPE place at Cambridge, which he took up in 1960.

Ganja
BANANA

CAMBRIDGE, 1960

The culture shock of Cambridge was enormous. Brett had a room of his own in Churchill College, could do pretty much as he liked, whenever he liked, and was a black alien in a largely white bastion. He was surrounded by the English wealthy classes, braying at each other in accents he had never heard before. Nor had he experienced racial prejudice before. Only one group of people treated him at all decently. The International Socialists all had working class backgrounds. They despised the cultivated, tired-of-life drawl of the Hooray Henrys as much as he did. Soon he was being invited to their meetings and distributing pamphlets with the best of them. On the fringes of the group was a pale girl with intense dark eyes and long, straight, black hair. She attended meetings but said nothing. One evening she left at the same time as Brett, and spoke to him for the first time.

"I've been to every meeting this year," she complained, "and haven't heard anything constructive yet. The Communist Society meetings are much more interesting - cut and thrust debate, and ideas for discrediting the government. You should come along sometime. I'm sure you'll enjoy it."

This intense English girl, with her milk-white skin, held a strange fascination for Brett. There was sexual chemistry on both sides, and she intrigued him.

"If that's an invitation, I'll take you up on it," he said, feigning enthusiasm. "When do you suggest?"

"Saturday night. Meet me in the Royal Oak about eight."

She was sitting in the public bar, keeping an eye open for him. He bought two beers, and straightaway was led to a back room. There was a long table with a dozen people round it, mostly male, but a couple of females. One fellow was on his feet, denouncing what he saw as the British Communist Party's backsliding from true Marxism-Leninism. He acknowledged the presence of the girl and Brett, and waved them to seats by the wall. After the meeting he asked to see Brett's Party credentials. When he admitted having no card he was told he would be banned from future meetings unless he joined.

"Jessie, get him enrolled before he leaves," he instructed the girl, who it emerged was the Society secretary.

Brett endured the meetings for most of his second year, mainly to maintain the steamy relationship that seemed to be a quid pro quo for becoming a member. He was a sexual novice. She was a nymphomaniac with an insatiable appetite. On her back in The Backs; sat astride him in his chair; over his table; in the bath; even in bed! The relentless pursuit by this sexual athlete, in her attempt to satiate her desires on him, drove him to participate in some of the Party's demonstrations just to escape her attentions.

The group's activities were limited to ban-the-bomb marches and counter-demonstrations against right wing rallies. Apart from that, he was convinced that the Society was just a talking shop. It was at one such demonstration in London that he saw some real action for the first time, not from the communists, but from the Maoist contingent. About two hundred fascist thugs were marching through Whitechapel, escorted by files of policemen. A motley crowd from the left of the political spectrum blocked their way. There were communists, socialists,

BANANA

peace campaigners, and ban-the-bombers, and the Maoists were prominent in the front ranks.

The police were brushed aside as the hate-filled mobs clashed. A bewildering array of weapons was produced as they tore into each other. Knives, chains and knuckle-dusters appeared, and banner poles became spears and clubs. Brett Johnson joined in, and was soon in the thick of it. He grabbed a banner, ripped away one of the poles, and laid about him furiously. When a police riot squad moved in to separate the combatants, he was snatched as a ringleader and charged with riotous assembly. As a first offender he was placed on probation. His exploits had not gone unnoticed, however. He was invited to join the Maoists and quickly became a member of the Cambridge group. They were dedicated to smashing the Nazis wherever they raised their ugly shaved heads. Where there was action, he was in it. His second arrest, seven years later, followed a provocative march in the East End by the skinheads. A picture of him, wielding a baseball bat, and aiming a blow at the head of a Nazi marcher, made the national newspapers. This time he was sent down for five years, for grievous bodily harm, which he served in Pentonville. Although his exploits had not been very effective, they had succeeded in getting his name onto official files.

CHAPTER 8

KINGSTON
JUNE, 1973

It was ten days after Chief Inspector Anderson's first meeting with Steve Andrews that he managed to get all the interested parties to agree to his plans. He had found the army particularly difficult, following its helicopter losses, but after a great deal of argument and cajoling, and an appeal to the Prime Minister, he had finally been promised the services of a helicopter and crew. The Water Resources Board had been dead against the idea of releasing dye into the rivers. They had been brought to supporting it only by the University's insistence that, at the dilutions proposed, the dye would be a negligible pollutant. This was not the only way the University had turned up trumps. The Chemistry Department, through its contacts with chemical companies, had obtained a five-gallon drum of fluorecein

dissolved in sodium hydroxide solution. The flourishing speliological society in the students' union had agreed to provide a
team of experienced pot-holers to find the underground streams
and release the dye.

A note in his pigeonhole at the Casa Monte informed Steve
that everything was ready to go. Next morning he drove down
to Kingston for a planning meeting with Anderson, Lieutenant
Butler and a Speliological Society representative. They went
over the difficulties of the exercise.

"As I see it, communication between the underground
team and the helicopter will be the main problem," said the
lieutenant, "but there is a solution. If the cavemen don't get
too far underground they can pay out a cable behind them and
contact the surface by field telephone. Messages can then be
relayed through our usual radio link."

"That's one problem solved," put in Steve Andrews, "but
there is a more difficult one. To give the helicopter any chance
of being in the right place to spot dye releases, the underground
team has to know roughly where it is when it makes the release,
and also the flow direction of the stream. There's not enough
time for proper surveying methods underground, so we'll have
to resort to simple dead reckoning, using a compass for direction
and measuring tapes for distance."

"My navigator would be capable of the dead reckoning,"
replied the lieutenant, "but he's needed in the air. Somebody
with surveying experience should be underground," he said,
looking hard at Steve, who was about to respond when the
Chief Inspector broke in.

"That settles it. I had hoped that Dr. Andrews would be
doing the dye spotting from the air, but it looks as though his

talents will be more useful underground. Come to think of it, he can also supervise release of the dye in the right quantities."

The logic of the approach couldn't be faulted, much to Steve's regret. They dispersed to prepare for their agreed roles; the lieutenant to order the helicopter to be readied, Steve Andrews back to the University to pick up his basic surveying gear and alert the cavers, and the Chief Inspector to contact his Montego Bay colleagues. That afternoon they all, except the cavers, who were travelling by pickup truck, assembled at the University cricket ground to be picked up by the helicopter for the flight to the Cockpit Country.

A thrill of mixed anticipation and apprehension ran through Steve. Potholing had never appealed to him. He didn't even know whether he would feel claustrophobic underground, but the appearance of the cavers was reassuring. They looked a competent bunch with their helmets and cap lamps, ropes and harnesses.

IN THE COCKPIT
THE SAME DAY

When the surface route out of the cockpit had been well established, Brett decided it was time to start to attempt the take-over of the ganja trade. He sent spies out to the local growing areas to identify the middlemen collecting the crop from the farmers. They were followed around to their suppliers and back to the places where the raw cannabis was processed.

Each processing shed was tucked away in some remote position where the only access was by track. 'So far, so good', he thought. Up to the processing stage it was necessary to maintain the system as it stood, and he had no intention of intervening. The processing, and what happened to the ganja after it was processed, was a different matter.

Brett, leading an armed group, visited each of the processors in turn. He told them that in future they would have new customers. If they co-operated they would be paid double for their services. If not, their supplies would be cut off, and their sheds burnt down. In spite of fear of their gangland customers, faced with offers they couldn't refuse, most of them agreed to co-operate, even to the extent of producing the resin in the form of cylindrical plugs with the right dimensions for insertion into bananas.

That was the easy part of the operation. Dealing with the gangs was to prove a problem of a different order, both difficult and hazardous. When the heavies from the Denham Town Super Studs arrived at one of their processors on their monthly pick-up run, they ran into a hot reception from Wade Robinson's men. The left-wingers took up positions in the undergrowth on both sides of the track. As the old Bedford van slowed to turn into the space beside the processing shed, Wade stepped out and signalled the driver to stop. Suspecting a police trap, the man attempted to run him down. A hail of bullets from the bushes missed the driver, but killed his two companions on the front bench instantly. Two other men holding handguns leapt from the back of the van, but they were cut down before they could fire a shot. The terrified driver made a rapid three-point turn, and with tyres spinning in the mud, hurtled back down the track. Motioning his men to stop firing, Wade told them,

"Let him go. He'll take a message back that we want his boss to hear."

Head honcho of the Super Studs, 'Machete' Morgan, so-called because of his exploits with the wickedly sharpened weapon around the South Kingston backstreets, almost exploded at the news.

"Those Hannah Street bastards," he spat out, swinging his favourite toy. "They're responsible for this. So the East of the island's not enough for 'Screw' Spencer and his clowns. Well, they're not going to take over my territory as easy as that. Tonight we hit them on their own patch."

After midnight, a dozen of the Super Studs made their way in ones and twos to the bar in Hannah Street where the Tel Aviv mob hung out. At a signal, four heavily armed men burst into the bar and sprayed automatic fire indiscriminately around. Taken completely unawares, young men who had been sitting drinking and playing blackjack fell where they sat. A few who had escaped the carnage by running through the rear entrance were mown down as they left. In a matter of seconds the Denham Town gang was effectively wiped out. Only a terrified youth remained alive. He had gone down when a bullet creased his temple. He was not badly hurt, but was shaking like a leaf. Morgan handed him a tumbler of rum.

"Get this down, and tell me whether you know the ganja collectors and processors out East."

The fellow gulped at the rum and began to calm down. He was a snappily dressed, young blood-about-town type, a tearaway. His loyalty was to whoever paid him well. There was not much left of the JLP-sponsored Studs. If he played his cards right, maybe this gang leader from the PNP territory would take him on.

"Yeah, Man. What yo' want, and what's it worth?"

"It's worth your miserable life, and maybe a place on my payroll if the info's good. If not - - - he left the rest unsaid, but tested the edge of his machete with a thumb as he glared at the youth.

His meaning was unmistakable, and the point taken.

Gunfights in the South and West Kingston slums had been regular occurrences since the political gang battles between the Norman Manley and Alexander Bustamante supporters in the thirties and forties had first established their fiefdoms. Fights usually arose over territory. One gang or the other was trying to extend its 'protection' into an area claimed by the rival gang. The police, having been caught in the crossfire too often, had a tendency to ignore these inter-gang squabbles. After all, the victims were usually the criminals on one side or the other. They wouldn't be missed, except by their mothers! This occasion was no exception. Since there was no election at stake, the police kept out of it. Tomorrow's body count would reveal who had been involved, and who had come off worse.

Next day the young survivor of the bar massacre took a vanload of his new masters on a guided tour of the ganja processors in the Anotto Bay, Port Antonio, Bath and Newcastle areas. They now had a new wholesaler, but not for long. Once again the collection operation was under surveillance by the left wingers. Once again the deliveries were intercepted. Another vanload of low life was removed from the scene, and the processors intimidated into supplying yet another customer.

THOMPSON ESTATE
EARLY JUNE, 1973

With supplies of ganja ensured, the way was open to forge the next link in the chain. Brett paid a clandestine visit to the workers' compound on the Thompson estate after work had stopped for the day. In the foreman's hut old George was busy cooking his peas and rice. There was no sign of recognition as he opened the door to his tall, good-looking visitor.

"Hello George. Remember me?" Brett asked, as the old man peered into his face. "I'm Brett Johnson, who you set on drilling holes for the Englishman, all those years ago"

Alarm was mixed with the dawning recognition on the old man's face. He had heard on the radio about the hunt for this man, but had not made the connection with the boy he had helped so long ago. He said, in a fearful voice,

"What yo' want here? It's not safe for you or me if you're found. Colonel'd shoot you on the spot, and I'd be out of a job."

In a matter-of fact voice, Brett told him,

"What I want is to get rid of the colonel and all the others like him, but first I need funds for men and weapons. I'm taking over the ganja trade to get the funds, and I'm going to ship the ganja abroad hidden in bananas. That's where you and your people come in."

The certainty in his voice, and the force with which he said it brooked no argument. George was resentful of the years of demeaning treatment at the hands of Colonel Thompson and his estate manager. When Brett explained in detail how he

BANANA

proposed to hide ganja resin in the bananas he was close to being convinced that the operation would work.

"Yo' might get away wi' it," he conceded. "Few years back, stuff was shipped on banana boats, in the linin's of containers. It was found. Folks 'ere and England were jailed. But they'se not goin' be lookin' for ganja inside bananas," he concluded, cackling with glee.

Brett didn't enlighten him about his own experience of sharing a cell with part of the British end of the organisation.

"Ah don't know if there'll be time to do what yo' want wi' the bananas," George said. "After cuttin', bunches are on'y racked overnight, ready for cuttin' into hands, boxin', and loadin' in wagons next day."

"Show me," demanded Brett.

The old man took him across to the open, bamboo roofed shelters, where hundreds of bunches of bananas were laid carefully on racks. The set-up looked ideal for what he had in mind. All the bunches were within easy reach, and well separated to prevent bruising.

"What time do the carriers finish loading the racks, and what time do they start loading the wagons?" Brett asked.

"They stop work at five, and start loadin' at six next mornin'. Only loadin's supervised."

"Good, that gives us thirteen hours - twelve hours of darkness - to get the ganja into the bananas," Brett mused aloud. Turning to George, he said, "with enough people to do the cutting and stuffing, that's plenty of time."

"That's your problem - people," replied George. "Yo' can't s'pect them all to go 'long with somethin' that dangerous. Wi' tree fellers and bunch cutters - no problem. They all tough guys.

Loaders is different. They're mostly women, and more interested in keepin' jobs than politics. They'd be too 'fraid to do it."

"Then we'll have to find something they're more afraid of," said Brett, in no mood to have his plans thwarted at this stage. "Is there an Obeah man on the estate?"

"Not likely. Wouldn't last ten minutes if Colonel got wind of 'im. Obeah Lady's over at Lucky Valley. She'll cast a spell for a few dollars."

LUCKY VALLEY
EARLY JUNE, 1973

Brett walked the few miles to Lucky Valley, and went into the only bar, fount of local knowledge. The room was filled with a haze of acrid-smelling marijuana smoke. Reggae blasted from a transistor radio. Its only occupants, apart from the barman, were four Rastafarians, smoking joints and playing poker. Suspicious looks were cast in his direction through the dreadlocks, but the men carried on their game. Brett ordered five topped Red Stripes and took them over to the table.

"Have one on me," he invited, taking a swig from the neck of his own bottle.

The men accepted their bottles without comment, but raised them to him before taking their own long pulls of beer.

"What yo' want, Man?" asked the first to surface.

"Info," said Brett, "fixing him with an intense, no nonsense stare, "on where to find the Obeah Lady."

They exchanged alarmed glances that silently asked the question, 'What's this big stranger after?' They felt jumpy enough about that night's ceremony, and he could spell danger. Men usually gave Obeah a wide berth unless some dire misfortune demanded magical intervention.

"He don't look in need of any sort o' magical help - arrogant looking bastard!" the spokesman of the four whispered to the others. "He needs watchin', but if he wants to mess with Obeah, it's his funeral".

Their shoulders shook with mirthless laughs in response to his remark, and four grinning faces turned to Brett.

"Shack - top o' the valley," said one, gesturing with his thumb.

Brett nodded his thanks and left. Dusk was approaching, but he had come too far to turn back now. He headed up the dirt track that led out of the village. It soon petered out, to be replaced by a narrow path through thick foliage. In a clearing so small that the jungle seemed to encroach on all sides stood a wooden shack. The place was deserted. Behind it the path continued higher up the valley, from where he could hear the rhythmic throbbing of a big drum. He hesitated, but overcoming a slight apprehension, decided to investigate. Half a mile further up the valley the path broke suddenly into a broad, flat, open space, edged by a circle of guttering torches. In the middle he had just time to observe a massive sawn-off tree stump before his vision became a kaleidoscope of flashing lights and he lost consciousness. He had been felled by a well-aimed blow to the nape of his neck. The last sound he heard before blacking out was a half-heard comment from his attacker.

"He'll make a good subject for —"

The next sound that penetrated the depths of Brett's unconsciousness was the heavy, hypnotic beat of the drum, seemingly from far away. As his swimming senses returned, the beat became louder, and more insistent, until it throbbed in his pain-racked head. He couldn't move his arms or legs. 'Whatever hit me must have paralysed me', was his first panic-stricken thought. With an effort he raised his head, and through badly focussed eyes discovered that he was spread-eagled, with his wrists and ankles tied to two palm trees. He had been stripped naked.

Around the clearing, figures in demonic masks, decked out in the Obeah paraphernalia of feathers, bones, human teeth and chicken feet, gyrated in a monotonous dance to a loud, equally monotonous drum beat. The powerful vibrations of the Maman drum struck at the base of his spine and rose like an electric current into his skull, where his brain seemed to pulsate with the same rhythm. As the beat accelerated it was joined by the penetrating staccato of smaller drums. It was impossible to count the whirling and leaping figures as they spun faster and faster, but his guess was that there must be twenty of them, mostly male, but some female.

'There must be every Obeah man and lady on the island here', he supposed. 'I got more than I bargained for. It looks as though I've stumbled on some important ceremony'. As Brett's wits began to return, he became more and more conscious of the excruciating pain in his shoulders and hips. He also felt extremely vulnerable in his spread-eagled position.

'What in Hell's name have they got in store for me', was his next thought, and he shuddered in horrified anticipation.

At that moment the small drums took on a more urgent beat, which accelerated in a crescendo, then stopped. There

was a profound silence in which even the jungle noises were stilled. So suddenly that Brett felt a physical jolt, the silence was broken by blood-curdling screams from the dancers. The screams were followed by low moans as they flung themselves flat on the ground, facing the stump.

Thump, thump, thump, thump, the big drum began again, this time with the rhythm of Brett's own heartbeat. From the far side of the clearing, stepping in time to the same beat, came the four Rastafarians he recognised from the bar, carrying a rough timber coffin. They laid it down near the stump, removed the lid, and took up position behind Brett. He tried to twist his head round to see what they intended.

'This is it', he told himself. 'Brett Johnson's going to wind up as an Obeah sacrifice'.

That thought, and any other, was suddenly banished from his mind by an ear-splitting screech. A horrific figure bounded into the clearing and onto the stump, where it stood with widespread feet and flexed knees, holding a snake above its head with out-stretched arms. Its devil mask was even more terrible than the rest. Round its neck was a double necklace of vulture claws and shark's teeth. From its elbows and knees hung mongoose tail fringes, and from its waist dangled a vampire-skin pouch, complete with head. Otherwise the figure was naked - she was naked - for it was unmistakably a statuesque female figure that now began to move sensuously to the primitive rhythm begun by the drums. In a dance that was evidently dedicated to the snake deity of Obeah, without moving her feet she gyrated her pelvis and swayed her torso like an anchored belly dancer. The oiled, jet-black body gleamed in the torchlight. She began, pro-vocatively, to slide the snake's length over her body, between her breasts, around her thighs, between her buttocks. Brett, in spite of his predicament, was erect as a flagpole. Then she thrust the head of the snake inside her. The drumbeat reached fever pitch as the speed of her gyrations increased, and the frantic creature thrashed about obscenely. As the drum beat slowed again, she extracted the snake with a flourish, and leapt from the stump. With her feet wide apart and bent knees, she moved menacingly towards Brett in a series of pelvis-thrusting hops, brandishing the snake in front of her. Holding the reptile just behind its head, she offered it towards his genitals, tantalising him by moving it closer, then snatching it away. He struggled against his bonds as he strained in vain to move away from the exposed fangs in the gaping mouth. His erection subsided as quickly as it arose. An evil chuckle came from behind the mask, followed by,

"I have much more interesting plans for such a snake as can rise to the occasion in your position."

'So', thought Brett, as relief flooded his mind, 'I'm not going to be sacrificed, at least, not yet.'

"No," she hissed, as though reading his mind. "You're not going to die. Nothing so simple as that," she whispered. "You will seem to die and be brought back to life. I must demonstrate my power over life and death before these fools will elect me Obeah Queen."

Slowly she extracted a vulture foot from her pouch, and with muttered incantations ending in a shriek, raked it diagonally across his chest. She had carefully coated each talon with a minute amount of tetrodotoxin, extracted from the liver and ovaries of the puffer fish, diodon hystrix. There was enough to cause profound paralysis without killing. As the drug entered

BANANA

his bloodstream, Brett first lost control of his eye muscles. He couldn't close his eyes, even to blink. Then paralysis crept into his limbs, starting at his toes. His neck muscles were the last to succumb, and his head drooped. To the onlookers he appeared to be dead as his body sagged against the restraint of the ropes.

The Rastafarians cut him down, laid him in the coffin and replaced the lid. The Obeah 'Queen-in-waiting' took up a position sitting cross-legged on the stump, staring at the coffin. Her minions continued their dance of ecstasy, to the now subdued, but insistent drumbeat.

In the coffin, Brett had the disturbing sensation of floating above himself, aware of all that was going on, but separate from his totally immobile body. Even his breathing had almost stopped. He had no awareness of time passing but, what must have been hours later, his body returned to painful life as the effects of the toxin wore off gradually, and began to release his muscles from their paralysis. Finding himself in the confines of what he could only assume was the coffin, he tried to push off the lid. He was so weakened by the drug he succeeded in moving it only a fraction of an inch. That was enough for his tormentor though, waiting for the first signs of life from the coffin. She rose majestically to her feet, uttering a shrill, spine-chilling ululation. Moving round the coffin in a slow, foot-stamping dance, she invoked the dead to rise with encouraging upward motions of her hands and loud calls in some obscure African dialect.

The coffin lid slid aside and fell to the ground. Brett sat up slowly and stiffly, his eyes staring before him under still-paralysed lids. The drumming and the dancing stopped abruptly. A low moaning came from the dancers as they flung themselves down and crawled forward to prostrate themselves before the new Queen. Brett climbed out of the coffin with jerky, unco-ordinated movements, looking and feeling like a zombie. That was, no doubt, the intention. At a nod from the Queen, two of the Rastas held his arms while the other two lashed him all over with sisal whips soaked in salt solution. As the cortisone from the sisal entered his blood stream the last traces of the toxin disappeared and a feeling of normality began to return. It was accompanied by a stinging sensation all over his body as the salt got to work on the whiplash weals.

The Rastas holding Brett's arms slow-marched him out of the clearing and down a concealed path to a circular hut; not the one he had seen before. The Queen waved her arms in dismissal and the clearing was deserted as if by magic. Brett was shoved unceremoniously through the single door of the hut. In the dim light from two candles on an altar built from tiers of skulls, he could see that the place was crammed with Obeah paraphernalia, except for a semi-circular area of beaten earth nearest the door. He was made to lie down on his back on this area. Four wooden pegs were hammered into the ground, and his limbs tied to them. Leaving him there, the Rastafarians took up positions on guard outside.

Unable to move anything but his head and eyes, Brett was assailed, not by the raw terror of his previous predicament in the clearing, but by an icy feeling of dread, which spread shivers from his bowels to every extremity. 'What's she got in store for me now?' He had to force himself to examine his surroundings in detail. Centrally on the altar sat the polished skull of a child. Its jaws were bound together with black ribbon, and a small, dead snake threaded its eye sockets. In

front of the altar were carefully positioned piles of human and animal bones, topped with skulls of humans and dogs, interspersed with crude pots of - who knows what? On the walls hung hideous masks, bundles of feathers, chicken feet, and the dried skins of puffer fish.

Sounds from outside drew his attention to the door. As the 'Queen' entered, the guards followed, bent almost double in their obeisance, their dreadlocks hiding their faces. She was still in full regalia. Crossing her feet, she sank slowly down to sit cross-legged in front of the altar, facing Brett. She waved the guards away and they took up their positions outside.

"So you are the notorious Brett Johnson" he was startled to hear her say, in an incongruously normal voice, "and you want the help of Obeah."

"Yes" he replied, "but how did you know?"

He could not help thinking how ludicrous a position he was in, making what amounted to polite conversation whilst pinned down, naked, in front of this demonic figure.

"I make it my business to know everything that goes on," she said, with a half-suppressed chuckle.

Brett thought, 'There's more to old George than meets the eye.' Aloud, he explained his political aims and the plan for shipping ganja, stressing the need for co-operation of the loaders, who would probably prove difficult.

"A simple enough task for Obeah," she responded in her cultured tones, "but I'm interested in your attitude to the cult. Seaga's government tried to stamp out Obeah. They backed off only after 'mysterious' accidents caused big projects to fail, like the Rio Cobre hydroelectric scheme. Just a rumour that Obeah was involved in the tunnel drowning was enough to make the workers abandon it. I'll help if I have your assurance that Obeah will have a free hand when you are in power, but without that assurance —."

She made no direct threat, but the implication was plain.

"You have my agreement," promised Brett, recognising the implied threat, and wishing, for the moment at least, to placate the 'Queen'.

"Good. Then consider your loaders co-operative," she replied. "Now - to unfinished business." She knelt between Brett's legs and proceeded to stroke his genitals with a bunch of rooster tail feathers, tickling and teasing. His response was half-hearted, not least because he was so apprehensive about her intentions. Disappointed, but determined to reproduce the effect her ceremonial dance had elicited, she chose a stoppered gourd from the collection in front of the altar. Pouring a little of the potion onto her hand, she sprinkled a few grains of powder strategically. A few moments later he felt heat spread from his tip to his groin. With horrified fascination, he watched as his over-heated member grew to massive proportions. At last satisfied with the appearance of the distended object, she straddled it, placed it, and bore down vigorously. Slowly and powerfully she worked at her task, producing orgasm after orgasm - for herself. Brett was kept at a height of intensity bordering on agony, but without release. At last she slid off him, her limbs trembling. Brett looked down his body in dismayed wonder. Was this an erection for life? The 'Queen' quickly regained her composure.

"Guards", she called, and as two of the Rastas ran in, with machetes at the ready, "cut him loose, give him his clothes and escort him back to the village."

When the bonds had been cut, Brett grasped his now-burning member and looked at the 'Queen' with desperation in his eyes.

"You built this. At least do something to demolish it," he implored her.

Taking the contents of another gourd, she dissolved a handful in water, and bathed the suffering flesh. Behind her the Rastafarians looked on with broad grins. Under the influence of the solution the erection at last began to subside, to Brett's great relief. Her ministrations went on too long, however, and he felt the return of faint stirrings.

'No, no. Please, no more', he silently pleaded, and attempted to spring to his feet, knocking aside the hand of the 'Queen' and her bowl of soothing fluid. The grins of the guards faded as they stepped forward menacingly and held him down.

"No. Let him get up," she ordered, and handed over his clothes.

Brett dressed quickly. He was escorted back to Lucky Valley, where his guards left him to his own devices. Groggily, he set off on the way back to Bog Walk, feeling already the heat of the early morning sun.

THOMPSON ESTATE
SAME DAY

Back at the estate, Brett found an unsurprised George and a queue of fearful women volunteering for banana stuffing. Obeah had spoken. Not one who valued her wellbeing would disobey the order. Needing to keep out of sight during the day, for fear of discovery by the colonel and his armed manager, he lay low in George's shack until nightfall. He slept well. When George returned they discussed the logistics of the operation. The old man was a mine of information about the bananas shipped out from the estate. About 1,500 tons a year, with an average bunch weight of 50 pounds, he reckoned. A quick mental calculation told Brett that represented roughly 70,000 bunches.

'If we put only one ounce of cannabis in only one banana in every bunch, we can handle about 4,200 pounds of resin a year', he thought. 'Landed in England, that would fetch, wholesale, according to my cellmate, about £700,000; more than enough to finance my plans, pay off the workers here, and keep the English connections sweet.'

Brett arranged to supply George with the necessary razor blades and coring tools, and demonstrated his banana stuffing technique. Confident that the supply side of the enterprise was well in hand, he set off to return to the Cockpit. Hitching lifts first to Ocho Rios, then to Falmouth, he made his way on foot to the new surface path into the valley.

CHAPTER 9

COCKPIT COUNTRY
JUNE 1973

The Bell 206 army helicopter, with Chief Inspector Anderson and Lieutenant Butler on board, picked up Steve Andrews and the leader of the cavers on the University campus grounds. The machine took little more than an hour to reach the eastern edge of the Cockpit Country. As they flew over the craggy, inhospitable territory, they could gauge the size of the problem. Scores of streams appeared and disappeared in the jumble of valleys and cliffs. They landed on the flat-topped ridge near the Windsor Caves where the twisted metal shells of burnt-out helicopters bore testimony to the resourcefulness of the fugitives. The bulk of the army contingent, along with the rest of the caving group, had been despatched earlier by truck. Leaving nothing to chance, the lieutenant placed all his men on a guard rota, with strict instructions that whenever the machine was on the ground it was to be watched by three men, in four-hour shifts.

"Any man caught resting on duty will be court-martialled," he threatened.

As soon as they arrived, two signalmen began testing their field telephones, and the cavers checked over their gear before donning it. Two of them had spent a summer vacation exploring some of the many cave systems emerging on the northern edge of the Cockpit Country. They knew which caves had streams, and which were impassable without diving gear. On their advice the ones with flooded sections, including Windsor Caves, were ignored. The investigation of each cave followed a pattern. Its entrance was spotted from the air, and its co-ordinates marked on the map. Cavers, together with signalmen and Steve Andrews, were dropped as near as possible. They moved slowly into the cave, making careful measurements of direction and distance and paying out telephone line as they went. A continuous flow of positional information was sent back to the signaller at the entrance, who relayed it by transmitter to the helicopter. When a stream was found underground, the machine took off and hovered over any stream that was in about the right place on the surface, and flowed in the general direction indicated by the cavers. When the helicopter was in position a signal was sent to Steve, who tipped a bottle of dye into the underground stream. At the Chief Inspector's insistence they paid particular attention to the cockpit where the towel had been seen.

It was a slow process. In the next few days the sources of several streams were traced, but none of them led to the one in the suspect cockpit. They all fed ultimately into the Martha

Brae or Main Gully rivers, which flowed to the north coast. The Chief Inspector's frustration came to a head as the teams met in camp on the fourth night. Deafened by hours spent in the helicopter, he shouted,

"Damn it. That stream must come from somewhere. Tomorrow we start looking at caves with flooded sections, and the Windsor Caves are first on the list."

Stamping off to his tent, he flopped down, and was asleep within seconds of hitting the bed, exhausted by constant concentration.

Next morning the army camp was astir early. By daylight the underground team was ready to leave. Two signallers joined them, carrying between them a reel with a thousand yards of telephone wire. Steve filled his dye bottles, and the familiar routine began. They made their way through the Windsor Cave system to the point where the stream disappeared into the rock face. Information was relayed back to the surface that the flow direction was roughly south. It was the right direction.

'If this is the way in', Steve wondered, 'how do they get through?'

The helicopter took off and headed for the suspect cockpit, where it hovered over the end of the gorge where a stream entered the valley. For about thirty minutes after the signal for the dye to be released, nothing happened.

"According to the positional data," John Anderson yelled at the lieutenant above the clatter of the blades, "the release was no more than a few hundred feet away from us. It looks as though we've failed again. Let's move on".

"No we haven't", the lieutenant, who was just about to issue the order, shouted. "Look."

He pointed towards the gorge. The water emerging from the cave had a faint yellow tinge. When it emerged from the shade into bright sunlight it turned a brilliant, shimmering yellow-green.

"Great stuff," shouted the Chief Inspector. "Head for base, and we'll decide the next step. Tell the underground team to stand down."

As the helicopter lifted over the cockpit rim and headed northwest, Steve Andrews received the news of success with quiet satisfaction.

"It looks as though this is the way in," he said to the cavers, "but I don't fancy trying it myself."

"Nor me," replied the leader of the team. "Leave that to the divers."

They returned to the surface to find John Anderson already back at base, discussing the next move with Lieutenant Butler. The Chief Inspector turned to Steve as he joined them.

"There's something puzzling us Steve. It took the dye a long time to come through the underground part of the stream. What does that suggest to you?"

"For it to take so long over such a short distance, either the passage is very tortuous, or there's a big hold-up of water.

IN THE COCKPIT

Wayne Daniels was obliged to take cover with the rest when they heard the helicopter approaching. He had so far failed

to make contact but was heartened to see it hovering over the stream inlet.

'They must be suspicious', he thought, 'but I wish I knew what they're doing'.

When he saw the stream turn yellow he guessed the reason. It was a good sign that the way into the cockpit had been discovered. He reasoned that he must make contact with base before anybody tried to come through the siphon, which would be too dangerous because the cave exit was so well guarded. If they came in that way they'd be picked off. Even the alternative, over the cliffs, wasn't much better, but at least they'd have an even chance if he could get a warning through.

'Somehow I've got to get to the top of the cliff where my radio works, but I could be too late. I've got to wait 'til my call-in time. I'm not rostered for guard duty, so I need to take the place of somebody who is; somebody on night duty'.

He went into the hut where off-duty men were playing cards or just lounging around. Choosing a small group of loungers, he threw himself down, and gasped,

"Phew. It's hot. I'm bored stiff. It's OK for guys who've been out on the ganja runs and seen some action. I've not even been on guard duty."

"What makes you think guard duty's not borin'?" asked one. "I know where I'd rather be tonight - in bed."

"Well, I wouldn't mind givin' you a spell," said Wayne, trying not to appear too enthusiastic. "Anythin' for a change."

"You're on," said the man. "In fact, you're on at ten-o-clock. Be my guest."

Just before ten, Wayne and the other relief guard turned up at the foot of the crack in the cliff and changed places with the

men coming off duty. Somehow he had to be at the top of the cliff before midnight to make his call.

"Do you want top or bottom spot?" he asked his companion.

"Usually we both stay at the bottom," he replied. "You won't catch me goin' up there in the dark," he said, looking up at the precarious ropes fixed along the line of the crack.

"OK. I'll go up an' take a look around," offered Wayne, who had expected just such a response. "See you later."

He set off on the hair-raising climb up the cliff, thinking as he did how much easier shinning up the fig tree had been. By the time he reached the top he was sweating from exertion and fear, but settled down near the cliff edge until he felt calmer. A few minutes before twelve he unwrapped the radio from the bundle tucked inside his shirt and on the hour, started transmitting his call sign. There was an instant response, not from his base, but from behind him. A sharp knife drawn across his throat ended his words, and his life, in an obscene gurgle. His fellow guard, suspicious of his motives in volunteering to climb the cliff in the dark, had followed. He took the radio as evidence and reported back to Wade Robinson that they'd had a mole in their ranks for the last few months. Wade's first question was,

"Did he get through?"

"I heard his call sign, but no reply. If he did make contact, no information was passed."

"Good work. At least, if they find our underground way in, we've still got an unknown way in and out," he said, thankful that it had not been discovered. 'That really would have caught us like rats in a trap', he thought.

A RIDGE
NEAR WINDSOR CAVES

The call sign had been heard, and also the death gurgle, by the ever-alert operator who had at that moment tuned in to Wayne Daniel's frequency in case of the midnight contact which had been missing for so many weeks. Immediately, he reported his suspicion of the agent's death to Chief Inspector Anderson.

"Shit and corruption."

The Chief looked as though he was about to explode, and proceeded to curse Brett Johnson and his ilk in terms so violent that the operator removed his headphones to protect his ears.

"That does it. One of my agents is probably dead, and there's no news from the other. Lieutenant, we've got to get in there."

He called Steve Andrews over to discuss the possibilities.

"Steve, I think one of my men's been killed in the cockpit. I'm concerned now for his colleague, Della. She hasn't been heard from for days. Have you any ideas how we might get through that flooded cave system?"

Startled at hearing the name Della, but ignoring the question, Steve became suddenly animated.

"Did you say Della? Not Della Brook?"

"Yes, that's right. It's not her real name, but how do you know it?" asked the puzzled Chief.

Steve explained the events of a few weeks before, leaving out the intimate details. Then he fell into a brooding silence.

'No wonder she didn't turn up', he thought. So she's a good actress. Has she made a complete fool of me'?

Breaking into his thoughts, the Chief Inspector said,

"Did you hear my question, Steve? How do we get through the cave? Obviously, we're going to need divers, but I can't risk the civilians, and getting army divers here will take time.

Steve's concern for Della overcame his better judgement and for the moment allowed his bravado to overcome his claustrophobic fears. He said,

"I've got a lot of snorkel diving experience. I can borrow a snorkel and mask from one of the cavers, and if the underwater stretch isn't too long, I can get through. If your girl is in there, I'd like to have a go at getting her out. I've got some questions for her."

The Chief Inspector gave him an old-fashioned look on learning that he knew Della, but said nothing. Loath to risk Steve's life, though, he hesitated. He considered that Della was in danger only if she had been discovered. There was a good chance that, having unearthed and disposed of Wayne Daniels, the left-wingers were unlikely to suspect the presence of another mole. If she laid low she could be safe. On the other hand, she could already be dead or a prisoner. He made up his mind.

"OK Steve, but we need to take some precautions. I suggest you tie a rope round your waist so we can haul you out if you get into trouble. The rope will also be your means of contact."

Turning to his sergeant, he ordered,

"Take a constable and commandeer one of the cavers' ropes, then go with me and Dr. Andrews into the Windsor Caves."

Lieutenant Butler and two of his men joined the party for the trek down to the flooded section of the Caves. There, Steve tied a running noose round his waist.

"Ready," he said, feeling anything but ready, and entered the water.

The lieutenant offered him a pistol for protection, but he refused it. He had a horror of the things. He made the excuse,

"I'd have no idea how to use it".

"When you reach the other side, give two tugs on the rope," the Chief Inspector instructed. "If you get into trouble, tug three times and we'll haul you out. Good luck."

Talk of the other side was not what Steve wanted to hear at the moment.

"Thanks very much," he said wryly, then, "OK, start paying out the rope."

Taking a deep breath he ducked into the water-filled cave opening and disappeared. Moving cautiously, swimming with one hand and fending off the roof with the other, he made his way along the tunnel. The darkness, such as he'd never experienced, seemed to press in on him as though he was being wrapped in wet black velvet. Claustrophobia, never far away from him in caves, gripped him. His chest tightened and his head seemed about to burst. There was still no sign of the end. Panicking, he gave three frantic tugs on the rope. Instantly he was hauled backwards through the cave, bumping and banging against the walls and roof. He emerged coughing and spluttering into the welcome lamplight.

"Sorry," he gasped, "I don't know how far I got, but I was still in the cave when I ran out of breath. Maybe, if I try again, I'll make quicker progress now I know there are no obstructions in the first bit. Give me a few minutes to get my breath back."

When he felt rested he re-entered the water, which struck even colder into his chilled body. This time he swam quickly through the cave, thrusting himself along with a double-handed

motion, ignoring the fact that he was bouncing off the roof. After about twenty seconds he was no longer scraping against rock, so guessed he must be clear. Surfacing from the blackness of the siphon, he found his eyes accommodating slowly to the dim light coming from a cleft at the far side of a small lake. He gave a double tug on the rope. As he untied it from his waist he gave himself a mental pat on the back.

'So this is the reason for the hold-up of the dye. There's an underground lake'. Swimming across the lake took only a few strokes. He was careful to avoid splashing. Staying in the water, he cautiously propelled himself through the gorge with only the top of his head and his eyes clear of the surface. The stream was shallow enough for him to scrabble along the bottom with his hands. Where it exited from the gorge he heard voices coming from the direction of a brushwood shelter, tucked away under the trees. Without the voices he would never have spotted it. Closer examination showed it to be built like a bird-watching hide, with slits commanding a view of the stream and the gorge entrance. Feeling lucky not to have been seen, he back-pedalled into the gorge, where he sat thinking and shivering. Something had to be done, and quickly.

Steve crawled out of the stream and collected a pile of rotting vegetation from the floor of the gorge. He slid silently back into the water, and arranged the vegetation around his head. Thus camouflaged, he drifted past the observation post unseen. He almost drifted too far, but saw the camp just in time. The stream broadened in front of it, which suggested to him that it was probably too shallow for concealment. He left the water and crept into the undergrowth. Circling the camp clearing, Steve took stock of the situation.

'This camp's much bigger than I'd imagined. There must be accommodation for at least fifty people, so we should assume at least that many. I wonder which is Della's hut'?

He felt that he had to believe the woman he loved was still alive, and reasoned,

'If she's a prisoner, she's most likely to be held in one of the smaller huts'.

He set about examining them in turn, approaching them from the back. Peering cautiously through a window of the second hut, he was relieved to see Della, and was overjoyed that she was still alive. She was sitting on her bunk, gazing into space. Another, darker-skinned girl, who was fast asleep, occupied a second bunk.

'So she's not a prisoner, unless they both are'.

"Pssst," he hissed, as quietly as he could.

The startled Della looked up, and caught her breath in amazement at the sight of him. She opened her mouth to speak, but thought better of it. Nodding towards the sleeping Queenie, she put her finger to her lips. Before he could move or speak, though, rough hands grasped Steve from behind, and he was a prisoner himself.

With great presence of mind, Della let out a stifled scream and ran to the window, where Moose and another of the Montego Bay contingent were holding Steve Andrews.

"Who the Hell is he?" she demanded, looking angrily at the intruder. "Can't we get any privacy around here, without white Peeping Toms peering in at our window?"

"We don't know," said Moose, ominously, "but we'll soon find out. Move," he said to Steve, giving him a shove towards the main hut. Inside, Steve was made to sit on a chair. His wrists were tied together behind it, and his ankles were tied to the back legs. In this uncomfortable position he was left while they decided what to do with him. The killer of Wayne Daniels wanted to get out of him what information they could, then get rid of him.

"He's obviously a spy, or the advance guard of a raiding party," he insisted.

Turning to Steve, he hit him hard across the mouth with the back of his hand. Blood oozed from his split upper lip.

"Well," prompted the killer. "You can make this hard or easy for yourself."

He hit Steve again, on the other side of his face, with his clenched fist. Glaring at his torturer, Steve spat out a mouthful of blood, and mumbled through swelling lips,

"It's quite simple. I'm a hydrologist, studying the water resources of the Cockpit Country. I was intrigued to find people living in here, in what I thought was an inaccessible valley."

"You're lying. You couldn't get in here by accident. How did you get in?"

Steve, whose sopping wet clothes were a give-away, saw no point in lying about his way in, but was not about to confess his reasons

"Through the Windsor Caves. I was wading along an underground stream when I lost my footing and got swept into an underwater tunnel. I lost consciousness, and found myself in the stream outside your camp when I came to."

He had never lied so convincingly in his life, but the sceptical looks exchanged by the group around him registered their disbelief. At that moment, Brett Johnson burst into the room. He had just returned over the cliffs from his encounter

with Obeah, and had almost fallen over the dead body of Wayne Daniels. His immediate assumption had been that the valley must be under attack from the cliff route, and that the attackers had killed Wayne. This white man tied to the chair must be one of them. Striding across the room he grasped Steve's shirtfront and almost lifted him and the chair off the ground.

"So you're the killer," he growled, in a voice full of menace. "Where are the rest of you?"

He thrust his face closer. Then he recognised something in the swollen face of the captive, and he gaped in disbelief.

"Steve? Steve Andrews? My God, this is an old friend of mine," he shouted. "Cut him loose."

Moose sprang forward and cut the ropes with a few swift slashes of his knife. Steve tried to stand, but pitched forward when the stiffened muscles of his legs failed to support him. He was caught by Brett Johnson and helped back onto the chair. Brett looked at the bruised mouth of his mentor and wondered, if he was the killer, whether the beating might have been justified.

"Well, did you kill Wayne Daniels?" he asked.

"I don't know any Wayne Daniels, and I don't know what you're talking about," mumbled Steve through puffy lips, but with spirit nevertheless.

"I killed him," volunteered the true killer. "I caught him on the cliff top, trying to transmit a radio message, when he was supposed to be my partner guarding the cliff path."

"Then why are you here, Steve," demanded Brett. "Was it you he was trying to contact?"

'So one of the Chief's agents is dead', thought Steve. 'How do I play this? Maybe it's best to come clean, and rely on Brett Johnson for protection from his thugs'.

His reply to the question was this time a little more informative.

"I repeat - I don't know any Wayne Daniels. He wasn't contacting me. I was brought in as a hydrologist to find the source of the stream that runs through this cockpit. I found it and followed it. I'm here by accident."

"And here you'll have to stay. I'm afraid we have to keep you prisoner for the time being," Brett told him, with a hint of apology in his voice. "Lock him up, but treat him well," he instructed. "He's responsible for me being here in the first place."

Steve Andrews was taken to a small, windowless store cabin, given food, and left to ponder his situation. He could hear a heavy bar being fixed outside the door. Brett Johnson was meanwhile recounting his Obeah experience to a group including the Haitian exile, Moose. When he was describing being brought back to life after apparent death, Moose broke in.

"You're lucky not to have been zombified. Back in Haiti I've seen people taken by the Tonton Macoutes houngans come back as walking vegetables."

"Houngans?" queried Brett.

"Voodoo priests," explained Moose. "Most of the top Tontons are houngans. They keep the people under control through fear of torture or zombification for slavery in the canefields. My father was an academic who studied voodoo. He found out too much, and was killed for his pains. That's why I left."

"What did he find out?" asked Wade Robinson, keen to know what was so important a man had been killed and his son had fled because of it.

"The ingredients of the potions they use to make people appear dead, and the antidote to bring them back to life. The active ingredient that causes paralysis is an extract of puffer fish liver. A lot of other stuff that goes into it's mumbo-jumbo. The antidote they use isn't really an antidote. If the right dose of puffer fish toxin is used, the victim recovers spontaneously, with very few ill effects, but that's not usually what the houngan wants. He's interested in producing stupid robots. He force-feeds them with a paste made from the calabar bean, to counteract any toxin overdose. Then he rubs their skins with a concoction of dried and ground leaves of six exotic tropical plants and trees, shavings from a variety of human and animal bones, made into a paste with sea water and a special alcohol. All a lot of mumbo-jumbo, according to my father. Even that's not really an antidote, but it helps to prevent eventual poisoning. At the same time it maintains the zombie state."

They all looked at him with amazement and a new respect. Now embarrassed, he shrugged, and passed it off with,

"Well, I was a medical student."

'That accounts for the puffer fish hanging in the Obeah Queen's hut', Brett thought. 'She didn't rub anything on me, but maybe the lashing did the trick. She must have got the dose exactly right'.

His thoughts took him back to the horrific experiences in the jungle clearing, and he fingered the scars on his chest left by the vulture talons. To the group he said,

"That's enough of Voodoo. What matters now is that they know we're here. That helicopter must be an army one. If they've called the army in we need to make contingency plans for defence and escape. It's only a matter of time before they assault the cockpit."

"Considering how easily your friend got in through the cave, I'm going to double the watch on this end of it," said Wade Robinson in a firm voice, attempting to re-assert his authority, "and have a round-the-clock guard at the top of the cliff path. That's our only escape route, as well as the only way in on the ground."

"On the ground - they're the operative words," put in Chinee. If they've any sense they'll come in by helicopter."

"If they do, there's only one possible landing place," pointed out Brett, "on the flat rock down by the fall. That's another place we need strong defences."

"OK, I'll get that organised," said Wade.

"Before you go, there's another important matter to be dealt with," said Brett, laying a hand on his arm as he was about to leave. "Once we get our ganja exports moving, we need to liaise with the distributors in England. That means somebody has to go over - somebody who's not known to the police."

Wade thought for a long moment, looking around the group, and his eyes alighted on Chinee. 'He's probably known on the island as a left-winger, but he's never been pulled in for questioning. He might have been spotted driving the Chevrolet, but it's unlikely, given the circumstances'.

"Chinee," he asked, "how about you?"

Chinee's reply made his reluctance clear. "Well, I've got a passport, but I've never been to England. I don't know anybody on the drug scene, here or there."

"That doesn't matter," interjected Brett. "We'll soon have the handling at this end sewn up. What you have to do is make contact with the distributors at the other end - my Yardie cellmate will be your best bet there – and find out the details of

the handling system at Southampton docks for bananas shipped from here. We need to know exactly what happens to the fruit from the Thompson estate when it's landed there."

"Is that all?" Chinee was bitingly sarcastic. "Finding your cell-mate would be hard enough, without the rest."

"I know his name, and the street in London where he lives, so that shouldn't be too difficult. He should be out of jail by now, even if he served his full term. If he doesn't know the set-up at Southampton, he'll know people who do."

Chinee considered carefully before committing himself, thinking, 'It can't be any more dangerous than if I stayed here, probably less. I don't relish contacts with criminals, but if it's all in a good cause, what the Hell'!

"OK," he agreed. "I'll do it. What's the best way over?"

"Book a charter flight for a holiday in England. Air Jamaica does one with a three-week turn around. That should give you long enough there to do what you have to," suggested Brett.

"What about money?" asked Chinee, ever practical.

"Contact Kingston," chipped in Wade. "We've had no contribution from them for months."

KINGSTON
JUNE, 1973

Taking the cliff route out, Chinee easily avoided the observers still posted at strategic points around the northern edge of the Cockpit Country, and made his way to Montego Bay, where he booked a flight from Kingston leaving two days later. He then took a train to Kingston, where he reported the latest events to Gad Marshall, the leader of the capital's Maoists, and asked for funds for his trip. Brett would have been interested to see who lounged in a chair next to Marshall's desk. It was the front seat passenger who had been responsible for inviting Brett Johnson to Kingston. He was Marshall's lieutenant and leg-man. He nodded in reply to Chinee's nod, but said nothing. Gad was enthusiastic about the ganja-banana idea. He went into another room, and emerged with a wad of money from his Cuban slush fund.

"So, you're the lot behind the latest ghetto gun battles. I liked the way the gangs were played off against each other. Very effective - for a few days - but I doubt whether it'll last very long," he said pessimistically. "In fact, I've heard that the Rasta gunmen from the Matthews Lane and Back O'Wall gangs are already moving in."

"I thought Rastafarians were supposed to be peaceful. Only interested in their god, Haile Selassie, and smoking ganja," said the puzzled Chinee. "First there's what happened to Brett Johnson" he said, then seeing the looks of incomprehension on the others' faces, told them about the Queening ceremony. "Now this. Where do the gunmen come in?"

"I think it's something to do with the way Bustamante hammered them a few years back. If you remember, he had the Rasta areas in Trench Town and Back O'Wall flattened by bulldozers. Since then, they've rebuilt and armed themselves. After the ghettos were flattened, Michael Manley was sympathetic, and the true Rastafarians put their support behind him. Gangsters masquerading as Rastas lined up behind the government party,

and there's been political gang warfare ever since. There's no way the Rastafarians are going to stand by and let any outsiders control their ganja supplies. The weed's got religious significance for them - brings them close to Ras Tafari, and raises their consciousness, they claim. Their religion's got a natural affinity with Obeah", but the ganja connection's probably spurious".

"One other thing you ought to know about," Chinee told him. "Our people are holed up in a valley in the Cockpit Country, and they expect an assault by the army at any time. They're goin' to need as much help as they can get."

"There's not a lot I can do about that," replied Marshall, "but Wade Robinson knows about our training camp up near Nanny Town, in the Blue Mountains. They can use that if it gets too hot in the Cockpit. There's plenty of room."

How spurious the ganja connection was, Chinee was soon to learn. Since Brett Johnson's encounter with the Obeah Queen, a network of Rastamen had kept a lookout for known members of the Montego Bay left. A yellow-black face was not hard to spot. His progress had been monitored all the way to Gad Marshall's house. As he left, he was surrounded by Dreadlocks, and 'invited' to accompany them to The Citadel. High above Bull Bay, a few miles east of Kingston, The Citadel, the foundation house of the Rastafarian Prince Emmanuel, the self-styled Black Jesus Christ, looked out on the sea. It was isolated from the outside world by high walls decked out with the Rastafarian colours, red, gold, black and green.

Chinee was escorted in, and after a few minute's 'reasoning' of his escort with the guardians outside a large, carved wooden door, was admitted to the presence of 'Father' Good. The Rastafarian priest greeted him politely and invited him to sit.

"Now, Mister, I am Father Good, leading disciple of His Excellency, Prince Emmanuel. I am instructed to question you about the intentions of your group with respect to the supply of ganja on the island. It is an integral part of the religious ceremonial of our black consciousness movement. Without it, our leader would be unable to take I and I out of the bondage of Babylon," he explained, slipping easily out of his precise manner of speaking, into the Rastafarian patois"

Chinee, intimidated by the palatial surroundings, and made nervous by the man's precise way of speaking, stumbled over his reply.

"Er - my name's John Ho Graham, er - Father. My friends call me Chinee."

"Quite," responded Father Good. "Well, what are your intentions?"

"To take over the whole ganja trade from the criminal gangs, and use the proceeds to finance our revolution," Chinee told him, judging it to be in his best interests to be honest.

"How can we be certain that the Twelve Tribes of Israel and other Rastafarian groups will continue to be supplied with the quantities we need?" asked his interrogator.

"I give you my personal guarantee that your supplies will be maintained," promised Chinee. "I'm certain that Brett Johnson will want to retain Rastafarian goodwill. He has already said the same about Obeah."

"Hmmm. That remains to be seen," continued the measured tones. "Meanwhile, you may leave. Peace, dread."

Chinee responded to the Rasta salutation with the only patois phrase he knew. "Give thanks, Rasta," and left hurriedly, to be returned to Kingston by his original escort. He went round to

BANANA

his parents' home on Sunshine Crescent to pick up his passport and clothes, and spend the two nights before his flight. His West Indian father and Chinese mother were not sure that they were pleased to see this errant son, who had forsaken his middle class background for the dubious cause of the Left, but in the hope that he might change his ways, let him stay.

Chinee's flight was uneventful. At Heathrow the immigration officer showed no special interest in him. Although his passport was closely studied, as were those of everyone else on the flight, he was waved through with no further formality. In the customs hall he was equally in luck. The interest of a group of customs officers was focussed on a Jamaican whose suitcase seemed to be full of bottles of white rum. Chinee walked straight through. It was 7.30 in the evening when he emerged from the airport, too late to try to find his ganja distributor contact. He decided to find some cheap lodgings and try to sleep off his jet lag. A taxi took him to a bed and breakfast hotel near King's Cross station for a fare almost a tenth of what it cost to cross the Atlantic. In the hotel he crashed out for a full twelve hours.

Next morning he set out after an early breakfast to find Brett Johnson's cellmate. A flower seller outside the station pointed him in the right direction for Pentonville Road. His heart sank as he realised the length of it and the size of his task. The only clue he had was that Bucky Wilson lived in a flat in a converted house.

'That narrows the search down to a few hundred', he thought.

He spent the whole morning peering at nametags by the front doors of countless houses before he found what he was looking for. B. Wilson lived in a ground floor flat. He rang the bell next to the name. A flashily dressed black woman, in a too-

tight skirt and cleavage-revealing top, teetering on three-inch heels, came to the door.

"Yeah?" she asked.

"Does Bucky Wilson live here?" he asked in turn.

"Who wants to know?" she questioned him suspiciously. "Are you the filth?"

"Filth? – Oh, police. No. Tell him a friend of Brett Johnson wants to talk business,"

"He's out – don't come home most nights - but Ah'll tell him when Ah sees him. Don't come here again though. He hangs out in the snooker hall near King's Cross. Be there 'bout eight," she instructed, and shut the door in his face.

Just after eight, Chinee entered the vast, dingy hall. Half of the thirty-two tables were in use. Their shaded lights cast rectangular pools of brilliance in the darkness. On one side of the hall was a small bar where a group of, mainly, black men stood drinking and smoking. Chinee walked purposefully over to them, watched curiously by the men at the tables he passed.

"I'm looking for Bucky Wilson. Anybody know him?" he asked, glancing around the group.

"That depends on who you are and what you want," said one.

"If I mention Pentonville and Brett Johnson?" volunteered Chinee.

"That's good enough," replied the same man. "We can't talk here, though. Come an' play a game."

He collected a box of balls from the barman, picked up cues from a rack on the wall near their allotted table, and set up for a frame of snooker as the light above the table came on. He made the break, then handed his chalk to Chinee and asked,

"What's it all about?"

As Chinee, who had never even held a snooker cue before, gazed bemusedly at the confusion of coloured balls, he began to tell Bucky what sort of information Brett was looking for.

"I could find out, but why should I. What's in it for me?" the drug distributor wanted to know.

"It's in your interest. Most of the ganja smuggling methods have been sussed by customs, so your supplies must have been cut. We're setting up a new method, and we want you to handle distribution at this end."

"What's so diff'rent 'bout your way?" Bucky Wilson asked.

"Best if you don't know at this stage," replied Chinee. "Just find out what we need to know, and we'll fill you in on the details later."

That wasn't good enough for Bucky Wilson, but he thought he'd string the guy along for a while, and see what panned out.

"OK, shoot."

"We need to know exactly what happens to bananas after they reach Southampton", Chinee proceeded to tell Wilson, "how they're handled, where they're stored; for how long, how they're distributed, and where they're distributed."

Suspecting that this new outfit was proposing to use the already discredited method of shipping ganja in container walls that had landed him in jail, Bucky Wilson said, scathingly,

"I just done fi' years chokey, Man, takin' the rap for smugglin' dope in banana containers. Ain't goin' take 'nother fi' for the same thing."

Chinee realised that if he were going to get anywhere with this man, he would have to give him more information. "We're not going to use containers," he revealed. "Our ganja'll be hidden inside the bananas."

Bucky's interest was grabbed. He could smell big profits. He made his mind up quickly.

"Gimme a couple days to tap So'ton contacts. Be here 'bout this time," he instructed Chinee, turned his back, and returned to the bar, ignoring the game they had started.

Two days later, as good as his word, Bucky was back in the snooker hall when Chinee walked in. As a sign of goodwill, Chinee bought drinks for everybody at the bar. Again, he and Bucky went through the rigmarole of setting up a game. Bucky came straight to the point.

"Bananas come in ins'lated containers, packed in car'board boxes. They'se trucked to rip'nin' stores, then distribution depots. They'se graded, rotten fruit ditched, made up, an' check-weighed."

"Good. That's where we want to recover the ganja. It'll be in the over-ripe fruit that gets thrown out," said Chinee, with satisfaction.

"There's only one ship a week, an' the rip'nin' takes fo' to six days," added Bucky, helpfully. "Rip'nin' loss is five per cent."

"Fine," said Chinee. "Another one per cent won't be missed then. But we need to know which stores the Thompson bananas go to."

"Two reg'lar stores, supplyin' Covent Garden and distribu-tors in de south," remembered Bucky.

"Great! That's where your suppliers need to get people into the grading system, collecting ganja from the waste."

"No prob," replied the confident Bucky. "Mos' of de guys doin' de gradin's brothers. A ganja bonus is all dey need."

Pleased by the speed with which he had been able to track down Bucky Wilson, and impressed with the fellow's system

of contacts that allowed him to ferret out useful information, Chinee felt happy about leaving organisation of the UK end in his hands. Bucky would make arrangements with the graders and his old customers, and take his usual cut as middleman. Anxious to get back to Jamaica, Chinee fretted at having to wait out the full three weeks for his return flight. To pass the time he did some sightseeing and bought the usual souvenirs a tourist would take back, to at least give the appearance of being a tourist. Drug squad men keeping Bucky Wilson under surveillance also followed Chinee's every move.

KINGSTON
JUNE, 1973

The Scotland Yard Drug Squad was not alone in keeping an eye on John Ho Graham. News of his London trip, and the reason for it, had somehow leaked to the Matthews Lane Rasta mob. Dreadlocks were more in evidence than usual as he emerged from the customs hall at Norman Manley. A pair of them fell in beside him as he hurried towards the exit.

"Not another visit to The Citadel', he thought, resignedly.

No such luck! Outside, he was bundled into an old Ford Cortina, and made to lie on the floor. The car left with a screech of tyres, and headed off down the Palisadoes road at high speed. Its departure was observed by the Gad Marshall sidekick sent to check on Chinee's return. Immediately he got on the 'phone to the Left Wing leader and reported the snatch.

When the car stopped, a toe in Chinee's ribs persuaded him to his feet. He stumbled into the street in front of a decrepit, abandoned shop. The two Rastas grabbed him roughly by the arms and forced him inside. In a back room he was hauled before their villainous-looking, dread-locked leader, seated behind a table. Enlarged pupils stared at Chinee through a thick cloud of ganja smoke from a chalice pipe. The cruel mouth twisted and spat a gob of spittle towards him.

"Now, Chink. Yo' goin' tell I an' I what's goin' down. Who's makin' de runnin' in de ganja trade? What's de Lon'on set-up?" Chinee looked defiantly at his questioner, but was silent.

"OK, so yo' wan' try de Chinese way," the man facing him said, with an evil grin. "Strip 'im, an' get 'im on de table."

Two more men stepped forward to join the two holding Chinee. They ripped off his shirt and jeans. Struggling desperately, he was lifted by the four of them onto the table, where he was held by his arms and legs, spread-eagled, face up.

The Rasta leader stood up casually, and brought from his pocket a length of twine. Making a running loop at one end, he slipped it around Chinee's testicles. Slowly pulling on the other end, he gradually tightened the loop. As his victim felt the twine tighten, panic set in before the pain. From somewhere he found three times the strength, thrashing his limbs mightily as he tried to break the grips of his holders. A sudden jerk on the twine stopped his struggles dead, and he screamed in agony as it cut into his flesh. Fear of being made a eunuch overcame feelings of loyalty. He decided to tell the truth.

"Take that string off, and I'll tell you what you want to know," he managed to get out between clenched teeth.

His tormentor only loosened the loop, still holding the twine in view in case it was needed again.

"The Maoists —" was all Chinee managed to utter before there was a crash, and the door flew open.

Three men holding Kalashnikovs at the ready charged into the room. A concerted burst of automatic fire cut down the four men holding Chinee before they could go for their guns. Then the weapons were turned menacingly on the leader, who still held the end of the twine. He let it slip from his grasp and slowly raised his hands.

"Lift your gun with your finger and thumb, put it carefully on the floor and kick it over here," Gad Marshall told him. The Rasta gang leader did exactly as he was told, but in the act of kicking the gun along the floor, pulled out a flick-knife and held the point to Chinee's throat.

"Get away fro' de door, or de Chink dies. You - get up an' walk," he said to Chinee without looking at him. Chinee, hitherto paralysed by pain and shock, took a share in his own rescue. He grabbed the wrist of the hand holding the knife, and twisted it away from him. The shriek of pain from the gang leader was stifled as soon it began, by a bullet between the eyes, fired by Gad. His corpse slammed against the brain- and blood-spattered wall and collapsed in a heap.

"Get yo' clothes on, and let's get out o' here, befo' somebody else takes an interest in yo' body," Gad rapped out to Chinee.

Needing little prompting, the little Afro-Chinese put on his now buttonless shirt, and trousers so torn at the front, all that held them together was his belt. The group left the house through the back way, to avoid a gathering crowd of the curious, drawn by the sound of the shots as though by a magnet. Down the road, they piled into Gad's fairly new Oldsmobile and raced away, back to his headquarters for Chinee's de-briefing.

'No rusty old wreck for the Kingston lot', Chinee told himself, as he luxuriated in the back seat.

"That was a close call," were his first words. "Thanks, Gad. I'll never hear the expression, 'had by the balls' again without wincing."

There were looks of admiration from his fellow left-wingers at his matter-of-fact tone of voice after such a harrowing ordeal. Chinee filled them in on his London doings, but made it brief. The situation in the cockpit was of much more importance to him. He wanted to know what had happened to his friends from Montego Bay.

"There ain't been no contact fro' Wade Robinson since yo' went away, but we ain't heard nothin' on de grapevine about an attack, neither," Gad Marshall told him.

"I've got to get back as soon as I can. They need every man they can get." Chinee didn't issue a direct challenge, but didn't need to. He looked into each of the faces around him in turn. Gad's lieutenant and four of the young men volunteered on the spot, not wanting to be out-braved by this little man. Gad Marshall promised to put the word around that reinforcements were needed in the Cockpit.

Crammed into Gad Marshall's car, driven by his right hand man, the little band headed off straightaway on their long, roundabout trek. For safety they took the mountain route, out through Newcastle and Wakefield. The road was badly made. It crossed the winding Buff Bay River by ford in three places - there were no bridges. Soon after they started, a rainstorm on

the high peaks caused the river to rise. There was no problem crossing the first two fords, but at the third the river had swollen to five times its normal width. In the middle the water covered the car exhaust, and the engine spluttered to a halt. The wheels bogged down in the sandy bottom, and their combined efforts failed to shift it. To make matters worse, the rainstorm now reached them, and in seconds they were saturated. They were about to give up in despair and leave the car where it was, when about twenty boys appeared, as though from nowhere. Laying hold of the car wherever they could, they rocked it backwards and forwards, heaved it out of the sand, and shoved it in one long push out of the river. It was obviously a well-practised exercise. Not content with getting it out of the ford, they pushed it up the hill out of the valley, and down the next hill. Nothing could convince them that a push-start was impossible with an automatic gearbox. But the pushing had dried out the engine sufficiently for it to start when the driver tried the starter again.

There was a whoop of excitement as the engine fired. All the boys lined up at the driver's window with their hands out. As each one was given a coin, he went back and joined the end of the queue, until the men's small change ran out. An angry shout went up from the river bank. A group of menacing-looking men emerged from the surrounding trees, wielding machetes.

Not waiting to find out what they wanted, the driver put his foot down and left the scene at high speed. The engine coughed and spluttered occasionally as water found its way into the ignition system, but they were able to make it as far as the bridge over the White River at Ocho Rios before it coughed its last and stopped for good. No amount of coaxing would

persuade it to go again. Finally the battery died, and they had
to abandon the car.

From under the bridge came a sound of hammering. They
investigated. One man there was hollowing out a half-section
of cotton tree trunk with a chisel and mallet. Another was
fitting an outboard motor to a finished dugout boat made from
the other half of the tree. They stopped work and cringed in
fear as the armed men poured down the bank from the road
above. Chinee surprised the boat makers by asking them,

"What's your price for the boat?"

"Four hundred for de hull, an' six hundred for de motor,"
replied the man fitting the motor, "but it ain't for sale. It's an
order for a fisherman."

"That order's cancelled," Chinee informed him. "We're
taking the boat. You'll be paid for it later."

He borrowed a pencil and a notebook from the man and
scribbled out an IOU in the name of The Jamaican Revolutionary
Front. Spotting a can of petrol by the bridge wall, he appropri-
ated that as well, filled the tank and put the can in the bottom
of the boat. The five left-wingers, with no help from the boat-
builders, manhandled the heavy craft into the White River.
The motor was new. It was reluctant to start, but eventually it
did, emitting a cloud of blue smoke. They all scrambled aboard,
and puttered off towards the mouth of the river, a few hundred
yards away. The boat-builders waded across the river and ran
down the east bank to the point, to see which way they went.

For the benefit of any pursuit, Chinee headed due north,
through the gap in the reef, as though aiming for the nearest
point of Cuba. Only when the boat was out of sight of the
watchers did he turn west on a course parallel to the coast. He

explained to his companions that his intention was to try to land as close as possible to the overland access to the cockpit.

As dusk approached, the wind rose, and a worrying thought came to Chinee.

'If we don't get inside the reef in daylight, we're likely to be wrecked on it. Better start heading for shore and looking for a gap'.

He turned the boat towards land and headed south until a line of breaking surf indicated the presence of the reef. Turning west again, and following the reef, he issued instructions to his crew,

"Keep a lookout for a break in the line of surf, and hope that'll be a gap we can get through."

"How do you know it's the right one?" asked one of his apprehensive passengers.

"I don't," was the short reply, "but anywhere's better than risking a landing in the dark."

Almost immediately, one of the men at the left-hand side of the boat shot to his feet. The craft rocked dangerously, causing him to sit down abruptly. He gave an excited shout and pointed landwards.

"There's smooth water."

Chinee turned in through the narrow gap in the reef. The boat surged forward on the swell that funnelled through it. Suddenly they were in the still, calm water of the lagoon. Ahead, about two hundred yards away, lights were coming on in a cluster of low cabins. It looked like a beach club. Approaching, they could make out a sign:

SILVER SANDS BEACH CLUB

There was nobody about at that time in the evening but, anxious not to take any risks, Chinee elected to land further down the beach, out of sight of the cabins. He ran the bows onto the sand, and they all jumped out. The Kingston men were for leaving the boat there, but Chinee was adamant.

"Look, we should hide it. We don't want to leave any clues".

Reluctantly, under his direction, they hauled the dugout out of the water, manhandled it across the beach and hid it in a clump of bamboo. Only when he considered that it was safely out of sight was he satisfied that the party could set off to walk the few miles to the path over the cliffs into the Cockpit. He led the way, and kept a lookout for army observation posts. He spotted two long before they reached them. It was not difficult to avoid the posts, which were manned by men who, by this time, were thoroughly bored by the whole business, and not very vigilant.

RETURN TO THE COCKPIT

Back in the cockpit, the extra recruits were given an enthusiastic reception by Wade Robinson.

"We're pretty well stretched, with too many points to defend," he told them. "You men will give me a bit of flexibility."

He had stationed groups of defenders at each of the vulnerable points, and rotated most of them every six hours. On the ledge by the underground lake were two men. Forced to mount guard in the dark, they had the worst job. They were replaced every four hours. In the hide at the end of the gorge two more men provided backup in case attackers made it past the cavern. The strongest defences were deployed at the top of the cleft in the cliff, and near the flat rock, which were considered to be the only possible sites for helicopter landings. Six men were hidden in the trees at each of those places.

When Brett Johnson and Wade Robinson were able to take time off from reorganising their defences, Chinee brought them up to date on the situation at the British end of their enterprise.

"If Bucky Wilson's done his job of organising the distribution side, things are coming together. It'll soon be possible to start the first ganja run," he claimed.

"A great job, Chinee. It couldn't have been done better by a pro," enthused Brett.

"Nothing very professional about getting caught by the Rastas when I got back to Kingston," said Chinee, with feeling, and he went on to recount his painful experience with the twine.

His description of the torture was greeted with a mixture of hilarity and sucking-in of breath as they tried to imagine themselves in the same position.

"I don't suppose it's done a lot for your marriage prospects, Chinee," said Wade, showing mock sympathy, and suppressing a grin.

The rest of the group chuckled at Chinee's discomfiture. He took it all in good part, but said,

"I was surprised to be treated like that by those Rastas. In fact, that wasn't the first time I tangled with Rastamen. Just before I went to England I was kidnapped by Rastafarians,

and taken to their Citadel for questioning. They were very polite, and there was no threat of torture. All they wanted was reassurance about their ganja supplies."

"They'd be true Rastafarians," guessed Wade. "Smoking ganja's part of their culture. They see it as raising consciousness and opening the way to their god, Haile Selassie. So, to them it's sacred. They're only interested in smoking dope, listening to Reggae, and repatriation to Africa. The mob that tortured you are impostors, not true Rastas. They make themselves look sinister with the dreadlocks, and smoke ganja for effect, but they're common criminals."

Brett's response was spirited.

"I'm sceptical about that. My treatment by the Rastamen who handed me over to the Obeah Queen didn't impress me as a peaceful cultural pursuit. If they weren't criminals what were they?"

"One power the Rastamen put above their religion," conceded Wade, "and that's Obeah."

The rest of the group looked towards Moose, now a recognised authority on the cult since his revelations about Voodoo.

"Wade's right," he said, "they might worship Ras Tafari, but they'll go in mortal fear of Obeah, like any other uneducated Jamaican."

At that moment the clatter of a helicopter passing low overhead stopped all conversation. They looked at each other in apprehension. Was this the start of the long-expected attack?

THE WINDSOR CAVES
EARLIER THE SAME MORNING

Deep in the Caves, Chief Inspector Anderson felt the safety rope go slack. Tentatively he pulled on it. There was no resistance.

'So Steve's got through', he dared to think. 'Either that, or he's trapped and drowned somewhere in the flooded tunnel'.

Without revealing his negative thoughts the Chief Inspector ordered the underground party back to the surface. He went to the lieutenant's tent where he found him engrossed in writing a report. The startled man looked up, saw who his visitor was, and waited to hear something positive to put to his colonel.

"I think Andrews has got through, but it's not possible to be sure. Meanwhile, I don't like just hanging around, waiting for something to happen. I suggest we make a more detailed reconnaissance. Judging by Steve's experience in the cave, there's no mileage in trying to get men into the cockpit by that route. We need a better approach."

"I agree," said Lieutenant Butler. "We'd be asking for trouble. I assume they keep a watch on the other end. My men wouldn't last seconds. If Steve got through the cave alive, let alone into the cockpit, I'd be very surprised."

"Well, what else do you suggest?" asked the Chief.

"The only way in with a chance of success is by helicopter, but an assault by air with any sort of opposition isn't going to be easy," opined the lieutenant. "We're not even sure yet whether there are suitable landing sites. If for no other reason, I agree, we need to take a closer look at the place."

The lieutenant ordered his sergeant to accompany him in the helicopter, and the machine took off to make a more detailed survey. Three or four runs at five hundred feet were enough to convince the lieutenant that there was only one place where a helicopter landing was possible - on top of the flat rock where the towel had been spotted. Landing there was going to need some high order flying. Take-off would be even more difficult. The rock was uncomfortably close to the cliff, and crowded on its other sides by high trees. Satisfied that he now knew the problems, the lieutenant returned to camp looking very thoughtful.

"There's one possible landing place," he announced, "but it'll be very dangerous even if it's not opposed. Under fire, it'll be suicidal. We're going to need meticulous planning."

He described to the civilians the topography of the site, and the problems of landing a fully loaded helicopter on the rock. Using a stick and a patch of bare earth, he sketched the layout of the rock and its surroundings.

"It's not possible to drop straight down onto the rock," he said. "The cliff's too close. In any case, under fire, a vertical landing exposes us like sitting ducks. Instead we'll have to vector in just above the trees," he explained, drawing a straight line from the treetops to the rock in his sketch. "The first men in secure the landing site, and give covering fire for the helicopter to take off again. That should be easier with a lighter load."

"How many men can you carry at a time?" asked the Chief Inspector.

"With full equipment, only four," replied the lieutenant. "That's my main logistical problem. It's not many if the cockpit's well defended. There'll be no element of surprise."

The lieutenant called in his sergeant and three corporal section leaders and explained .the plan of campaign in great detail, down to the dispositions he wanted the first men in to take up.

"Sergeant," he said to the keen-looking man beside him. "I want you to go in with the first group, and secure the landing site, then give covering fire for later landings. I'm afraid you'll have to do the job with only three men - four, if we're lucky. Let's try that out now."

"Yes sir," was the brisk response. The sergeant turned to the most experienced of the section leaders. "Corporal, you and three of your best men with full gear, on board now."

As soon as the four soldiers were on board, with their backpacks and weapons, the sergeant joined them, sitting in the only space left, in the open doorway, with his legs dangling. He signalled the pilot to take off. The engine was roaring at full power before the helicopter was able to leave the ground. It lifted heavily about six feet, but no further. Taking it down again, the pilot shook his head. Climbing down from his seat, he reported to the lieutenant,

"Inside ground effect, I've got just enough lift to take off, but outside it, no chance. We'll have to reduce the load. There's only a matter of five or six per cent difference in lift with and without ground effect, so we're not talking about much of a weight reduction. What about getting rid of some fuel?"

"Good thinking," the lieutenant complimented the man. "Corporal, have half the petrol drained from the fuel tank."

The job was quickly done, and the helicopter attempted to take off again with its load of five passengers. This time the take-off was successful, if laboured. Lieutenant Butler waved

---

the sergeant on his way, and crossed his fingers in salute. The sergeant responded with the universal OK sign. The helicopter lifted over the cliff, and disappeared in the direction of the target. The next batch of four men, under the command of a corporal, got themselves ready for its return. They were glad that something was happening to relieve the boredom, but apprehensive about what might greet them when they got into the cockpit. They were well trained, but none of them had been under fire before.

COCKPIT ASSAULT

The helicopter came in sufficiently high over the northwest rim of the cockpit to give its pilot a view of his landing site over the tops of the surrounding trees. Keeping the rock in sight, he flew a straight-line, dipping trajectory towards it, almost clipping the treetops on his approach. A barrage of automatic and rifle fire met the craft as it hovered close to the ground. Not waiting for it to land, the sergeant ordered his men out. They leapt onto the rock and fanned out to take up defensive positions near the edge, firing as they went. Two of them were injured badly in the legs, but in spite of that, began to pour directed fire at the defenders' positions.

Without its load the helicopter rose rapidly, and returned for reinforcements. Within minutes it was back with the second contingent of men. Two Bren guns were quickly set up.

The deadly hail of high calibre rounds from the accurate, stable weapon diminished the return fire from the trees. There were already casualties among the defenders; one dead, and two with serious upper body bullet wounds. Wade Robinson was in a dilemma.

'Should I withdraw and try to escape with as many men as possible, or throw in everything against the landing?'

His mind was made up for him. Down the path from the clearing trotted ten men headed by Moose. They were armed with Kalashnikovs and hand-grenades. Deploying through the trees around the rock, they loosed off such a barrage of automatic fire that the attackers were forced to get their heads down. Moose had never seen grenades before, let alone used them, but pulled the pins and tossed two in quick succession. More by luck than judgement, one destroyed a Bren gun and created carnage around it. The other Bren was still firing, but its barrel was over-heating. In the act of changing it, the gunner was killed by a bullet from a sniper in a tree that gave him a good view of the whole top of the rock.

In the helicopter, now making its third run into the cockpit, Lieutenant Butler was dismayed by the scene. Instead of landing with his reinforcements, he signalled frantically to the pilot to abort the landing and head back to base. Returning to the ridge, he ordered the Bell 47 in with stretchers to evacuate the wounded.

The unwounded sergeant looked at the casualties and the much-depleted force around him, decided to live to fight another day, and raised his arms in surrender. He was taken prisoner but, along with his uninjured men, was allowed to load the worst casualties onto the makeshift stretcher platforms bolted to the skids of the Bell. Men with horrific shrapnel injuries were flown out first. Then those with the most serious bullet wounds, from both sides, were airlifted out.

Back at the ridge, a fearful Lieutenant Butler was on the radio, reporting yet another failure to headquarters. The colonel was furious.

"How many casualties?" he shouted. "What in Hell am I going to tell the Prime Minister - that his army's at the mercy of a bunch of badly organised amateurs?"

"I'm sorry, Sir, but you're wrong about them being badly organised. They seem to me to be pretty well organised. They're well armed, and there are more of them than any of us expected. We were hit by automatic fire that could only have come from Kalashnikovs. They must have Cuban backing."

"Of course they've got Cuban backing," yelled the Colonel. How else do you think Russian weapons find their way in?"

Anxious to shift the focus of the colonel's rage, the lieutenant passed the responsibility for any future decisions up the line, by asking, "What are your orders for further action, Sir?"

"Do nothing till you here from me," the Colonel said, in a quieter, but still forceful voice. "I have to discuss the situation with Mister Manley."

"Yes, Sir. I'll wait for your orders. Lieutenant Butler signing off."

Colonel Watson immediately telephoned the Prime Minister's office, and was summoned to a meeting that evening at Jamaica House. The Defence Minister was present. Mister Manley was not in a good mood. The two politicians were seated, the PM behind his desk, and the Minister in front of it, facing the door. The colonel was left standing, like a small boy before the headmaster.

BANANA

"Well, Colonel, explain yourself," began the Prime Minister.

For his benefit the colonel went over the latest events in the Cockpit saga. After listening in silence to the whole sorry story, the Minister, glancing across at Michael Manley as he did so, asked the colonel,

"What strategy have you got for winkling these scum out of their hideout? It can't be all that difficult. You know where they are, and they seem to have only small arms," he pointed out, with the infuriating simplistic logic of the politician. Bristling visibly, the colonel replied with a glare,

"The Cockpit Country's the most difficult terrain possible for an attacker. There's only one way into this particular valley that we know about, and that's under water. There's only one clear space big enough to land a helicopter, and that's on top of a rock exposed to a hundred and eighty-degree field of fire, with a high cliff behind it. That approach has already cost too many casualties, and puts my last combat helicopter at risk. Before I risk that any more, I need to be sure of replacements."

"As you know very well," responded the Minister, his hackles rising, there are two Bell 212 Iroquois on order, but we're not on the priority list of customers."

The squabbling men were silenced by the firm intervention of the Prime Minister.

"Let's not get side-tracked from the issue of the moment. Leaving aside helicopters, what resources do you think you need to take the valley? This matter must be cleared up quickly, before it gets out of hand. With the election coming up, and Seaga snapping at our heels, we can't afford to be seen dithering."

"At least half a battalion, trained and equipped for abseiling. They would have to cut their way overland through the jungle between cockpits and drop into the valley from the cliffs. I have a commando platoon with the right training. In a few days they could show the rest of the men the ropes."

His unconscious pun made even the dour Defence Minister chuckle.

"A diversionary attack through the caves, using divers, would split the defence," the colonel continued. "There's a sapper unit, trained in clearance diving that could be used. It might be suicidal, though. They're not really combat troops."

"Do it, and take command on the spot yourself," ordered the Prime Minister, and dismissed the colonel with a wave of the hand.

Colonel Watson stalked from the room, smarting from his treatment at the hands of the politicians. He felt close to rebellion himself, but the mood soon passed as he contemplated the task he had been set. As soon as he got back to his office, he set the wheels in motion. His first action was to recall Lieutenant Butler. Although the man had been a failure so far, he was more knowledgeable about the cockpit situation than anyone else he had available. Next, he got together the commanders of the commando and clearance platoons, and briefed them on his requirements. On a blackboard, the lieutenant sketched the important features of the terrain, and pointed out the difficulties of penetrating the valley.

"Are there any places where abseiling down the cliff would be possible?" asked the young commando lieutenant.

"I saw a few places where the trees weren't tight up to the cliff, but there's no access to them from above," the lieutenant told him. "The rim of the valley's very rugged and solid with jungle."

"What about the cave access?" asked the leader of the clearance team.

"Well, we know there's underwater access through the Windsor Caves. We think a hydrologist working with us managed to get through, but he hasn't been heard from since, and we've no idea how things are on the other side of the flooded section," replied the lieutenant.

"I'm for sending a couple of men through to find out," proposed the clearance diver. "Using oxygen re-breathing sets, there'll be no tell-tale bubbles. They could be in and out again without giving themselves away."

"I like the idea," broke in the colonel, who was anxious to do something constructive for the benefit of his reputation with the politicians. "What we need more than anything at the moment is reliable information. Get moving on it, lieutenant." Turning to his captains, he issued the briefest of instructions.

"See to it that half the battalion goes through intensive abseiling training over the next three days. Then deploy them on the fringes of the Cockpit Country, and start hacking paths through to the target valley."

IN THE COCKPIT

Although casualties had been fairly high amongst the group defending the rock against the helicopter landings, it was

BANANA *Ganja*

much worse for the attackers. Dead and wounded were strewn over the top of the rock, and others had fallen to the jungle floor below. When the last of them had been shipped out, the prisoners were taken along the path back to the clearing, and pushed into the same cabin as Steve Andrews. The tiny store shed was becoming crowded.

Steve had listened to the sounds of the battle with mixed feelings.

'Either I'll be freed soon, or I'll be even less popular here'. Now he knew the outcome.

"Welcome to my humble abode," he greeted the new prisoners.

He received only grunts in reply from the apprehensive soldiers. They were all able to sit, but there was no room to lie down, even if they did it by numbers. There were no latrine facilities. Their prison would become unbearable very quickly. Shortly before dusk, a guard opened the door just enough to push in a pail of rice n' peas, then hurriedly barred it again. After they'd eaten, they were all taken out to exercise and, much to Steve's relief, perform their bodily functions. They were then locked up for the night.

At first light a meeting of the left-wingers was called to assess the new situation. Gathered around the table in the main hut were the group from Montego Bay and two representatives from the Kingston contingent. The women were excluded. Amongst the younger elements there was still elation over the defeat of the helicopter attack. They were all for staying put and fighting it out with the security forces. Wiser counsels, among them Brett Johnson, advised them to pull out while it was still possible.

193

"The army's not going to take a defeat like that lightly," he predicted. "From now on the area's going to be crawling with troops, and sooner or later they're going to find a way in. When that happens, we should be far away."

"Huh," snorted Wade Robinson, who was inclined to side with the more reckless element anyway, but increasingly found himself in opposition to Brett's ideas, "there's no place on the island as safe as this. Where else could we go?"

Chinee reminded them about the secret training camp in the Blue Mountains he had learned about from Gad Marshall. "We could lie low there and reorganise," he pointed out. "Here, we're sitting ducks - and dead ducks before long."

Nods of agreement came from around the table. Wade was in a minority. Seeing that he had little support for holding out in the cockpit, he accepted the collective decision to move.

"Right," he said, taking the initiative, "if we're getting out, we should do it soon, before the army can mount another attack. What better time than now?"

Murmers of assent arose.

"What about the prisoners?" someone asked.

"Leave them behind," suggested another.

"Kill them first," was the opinion of the young fanatic who had set out to torture Steve Andrews.

"They go with us," said Brett, in a firm voice which brooked no argument. "They could be a valuable commodity."

Preparations were begun immediately for a mass exodus from the cockpit, by way of the climb up the cleft in the cliff. Everything portable was collected at the bottom of the climb, and hauled to the top by rope sling. Then the main body of defenders started the climb, and the first snag was hit. A few feet from the ground, Queenie froze. She had no head for heights. She refused to go any higher. Most of the group was held up behind her. Wade, climbing next, tried to coax her upwards.

"It's no good," she told him, panic in her voice. "I'm never going to make it. Help me down, Wade. I'll take my chances through the cave. If I can't climb, at least I can swim."

"If you're going through the cave, I'm going with you," he told her, allowing feelings of loyalty to overcome his instinct for self-preservation. He helped her past him, and lowered her into the hands of the men below. The group of prisoners was inserted into the string of climbers somewhere in the middle. Steve Andrews found himself in their lead, following Della. In his youth he had been told never to look down when climbing. Now he found no hardship in looking up. When the whole party had reached the cliff-top, they set off in single file down the path cut through the undergrowth. Steve had the good fortune to again be close to Della. Only one man separated them. They made good progress towards the northern fringe of the Cockpit, but were suddenly halted by nearby voices and sounds of slashing machetes. A group of soldiers, cutting another path, intersected their own just ahead. The shock of the meeting gave the men at the head of the line of left wingers the chance to open fire before the troops had time to unsling their weapons. Those in the lead were cut down where they stood. The rest of the soldiers, and all the rebels, dived for cover in the undergrowth.

Steve took advantage of the confusion. Grabbing Della by the wrist, he bounded over a fallen tree trunk, and dragged her down behind it. Out of sight of the path he wormed his way, on the ground, into a stand of bamboo. She followed. They listened to the sporadic firing with bated breath, expecting any second to be discovered and shot. Half an hour later the shots died away. The troops had withdrawn, back along their own path. Cautiously, Brett Johnson's force continued along the route to the dried-up falls, without the company of Steve and Della. The couple lay low until the sun was high in the sky, passing the time explaining to each other why they were there.

"I had the biggest shock of my life when I saw you at the cabin window," she said. "What on earth were you doing in the cockpit?"

"Playing the White Knight," he replied, without irony. "I knew from Inspector Anderson that you were in there. As the only one with underwater experience, I volunteered to come through the cave and try to get you out."

"That was very brave of you, but not very intelligent," she said, with a smile that softened the criticism. "I wasn't a prisoner."

"No, but you were in danger. We think your colleague's been killed. A radio operator was convinced he heard a death gurgle from him at the start of a transmission," Steve told her, an earnest note in his voice.

Della Brook went quiet for a while, digesting the information and wondering about its implications. Now she knew why she had not seen Wayne around the camp for a while. She had thought nothing of it - just assumed that he was on guard duty at one of the outposts. Suddenly, in spite of the heat of the day, she went cold all over.

"Please hold me," she implored Steve.

Wrapping his muscular arms around her, he held her in a comforting embrace, feeling the trembling of her body as she clasped him tightly round the waist. Sobs racked her at the thought of the gruesome death her partner, and friend, must have suffered. Gradually, her shoulders shook less. She was able to turn a tear-stained face up to him.

"I'm sorry," she managed to say. "I'm not being very professional, am I?"

"Think nothing of it," he told her.

If he could hold her that close, she could be unprofessional all the time. Gently disentangling herself from the embrace she found all too welcome, Della tried to drag her thoughts away from their protective cocoon and back to the job in hand. She was in a difficult dilemma.

'Should I opt for safety, and take advantage of my 'rescue' or should I try to link up again with the left-wingers? If I go for safety, eighteen months of difficult and dangerous work will be wasted. The alternative's even more dangerous. 'If I'm discovered by the rebels to be an impostor, they'll kill me, or I might get shot by my own side. I've just come pretty close to that. I don't really have a choice, though. After all, duty calls'.

To Steve, she said,

"Steve, I have an awful admission. I didn't really want to be rescued. I'm in the middle of a long-term operation which it would be a shame to jeopardise."

"But you don't mind putting yourself in jeopardy," he said, more as a statement than a question.

"It's not quite as simple as that," she replied, on the defensive. "This is a dangerous organisation. We need somebody on the inside, to keep track of what they're up to. Since Brett Johnson arrived it's even more important. If anybody can start a revolution, he can."

BANANA

"Does it have to be you?" he asked, still feeling protective.

"I'm afraid so," she said, with a wry smile, and planted a lingering kiss on his lips, which stopped any further protest.

"There's only one snag," Steve pointed out. "You don't know where they are."

"I have a rough idea where they're going to be. Somewhere near Nanny Town, in the Blue Mountains. I overheard Chinee - the little Afro-Chinese - telling a meeting about a training camp there. Having no glass in the cabin windows is very useful for a spy," she added.

The fact that the Blue Mountains were more than a hundred miles away didn't seem to bother her at all. It bothered Steve Andrews more than a little. He didn't want to leave her to her own devices, yet he didn't want to risk falling into the hands of the rebels again. His mind was made up for him. A platoon of soldiers trotted by, emerging from the path they had cut earlier. From beyond them came the slashing sounds of other paths being cut towards the edge of the cockpit. Another assault was imminent. Steve was about to make their presence known when there was a rustle in the undergrowth behind him. A barely audible voice said,

"Don't say a word, and don't move. Turn round slowly. OK, Della, I've got him covered."

Chinee himself stood there, holding a Kalashnikov as though he was prepared to use it, and knew how. He had been separated from the rest of the left-wing group in the confusion, and had also been hiding out in the jungle, biding his time until it was safe to move.

"Come on," he urged Della. "Let's get out of here. What shall we do with him?" gesturing towards Steve with the barrel of his gun.

"Let him go," she insisted, rapidly thinking up an excuse. "He saved me from being raped by the soldiers."

"No," Chinee said decisively, "too dangerous. We'll have to take him along."

Chinee gestured with the gun for Steve to move ahead of him, and they set off down the path to the dried-up falls. Lagging behind, out of earshot of Steve, he confided to Della that he had a boat stashed away at Silver Sands Bay.

"If we take that, we can avoid the roads, and go along the coast till we are as close as possible to the Blue Mountains, then walk the rest of the way," he said, confidently.

The suggestion fitted in well with Della's duty-dictated course of action. Steve Andrew's presence would complicate matters, but she could see no alternative that would keep him alive.

"Good," she agreed. "Let's do it." They forged on along the path, taking cover whenever they heard nearby the sounds of preparations for another assault on the cockpit. On these occasions Chinee kept his automatic rifle trained on Steve. He became more jumpy as they neared the end of the path, until Steve feared he was in imminent danger of being shot accidentally.

"For God's sake, stop pointing that thing at me," he complained. I give you my word I'll not try to escape."

He wanted to stay as close as possible to Della for as long as possible.

"I believe him," chipped in Della. "Do as he asks, Chinee."

Reluctantly, the little Afro-Chinese slung the assault rifle from his shoulder, and the ill-assorted group continued on their way to the edge of the Cockpit Country, with Steve in the lead

and Chinee bringing up the rear. Soon they reached the bed of the dry falls, and slithered down to the base of the cliffs. Chinee led the way cross-country, back to where he had hidden the boat. He heaved a sigh of relief to find it was still there.

Launching the boat was a major effort for just the three of them, but eventually, after much heaving and shoving, they were afloat. The outboard started first time, and Chinee pointed the bows toward the same gap in the reef he had so recently negotiated with such difficulty. This time passage through the reef was much easier. As soon as the boat was well clear of the coral he turned east and chugged at a steady pace, back the way he had come. They made good progress, and by nightfall were well past the large concentration of lights he assumed was Ocho Rios. Steve had been watching for the last half-hour an ominous build-up of billowing black clouds out to sea. A storm was brewing.

"We'd better make land soon," he warned, pointing to the approaching clouds.

Even as he spoke, the clouds seemed to erupt as sheet lightning flashed from cloud top to cloud top. The display was continuous, supplying an eerie light to the scene. Large waves raised by the storm out to sea began to rock the boat violently, threatening to overturn it.

"Head for shore," Steve shouted, trying to make himself heard above the sound of the rolling thunder now reaching them.

Chinee didn't need telling twice. He swung the rudder over to put the boat's stern to the waves, and steered for the land. Every second he expected the bottom to be torn out by a graunching impact on the reef, but there was no reef. At least, there was no reef where he expected to hit one. At Galina Point the reef was now part of the land, lifted above sea level by some past earthquake. The boat, in the grip of a giant wave, hurtled along like a surfboard, and was smashed into the coral bow-first. Its occupants were catapulted out. They found themselves struggling in a foaming sea, about to be dashed against the same wall of coral. Chinee, a poor swimmer, went down and never surfaced again. Della and Steve, fighting to stay on the surface, were caught by a second giant wave. It lifted them high, and flung them across the top of the ancient reef, tumbling them amongst the old coral heads. As the wave receded, they felt themselves dragged back towards the sea. Steve grabbed Della by the wrist with one hand and scrabbled grimly against the ripping action of the coral with the other.

The wave retreated, still dragging them along, but suddenly they were no longer being dragged across coral. They were in water, but no longer smashed about by waves. In the stark light shed by the continuous lightning flashes, Steve could see that they'd been deposited in a large rectangular hole cut in the reef. Judging from the strength of the swell coming from below, it was obvious to him that the hole was connected to the sea. He almost panicked.

'We've got to get out of here fast, before the next big one comes in' was his immediate thought.

Della was barely conscious after their battering drag across the coral, but Steve found strength born of desperation. He heaved her half out of the hole, climbed out himself, shouldered her limp body, and stumbled over the jagged surface until he had put a safe distance between him and the killer waves. Then he collapsed. So far he had felt no pain, but gradually began to feel sore all over. He was bleeding from dozens of

cuts and abrasions inflicted by the sharp coral. Della's face and hands were covered with blood, her clothes torn. She gagged, and vomited seawater. It was clear that she'd been close to drowning. She staggered to her feet, but was in such a sorry state she told Steve,

"I'm not fit to go on yet. I'll have to rest."

Steve needed no convincing. Della looked as though she had been whipped and badly beaten. His own condition was not much better. Above them, on a bluff overlooking the raised reef, he could see the lights of a house. With an arm around Della's waist, he half-walked her, half-carried her, until he could set her down on a broad terrace which faced the sea. The terrace separated a swimming pool from a low bungalow. Wrought iron bars over the lighted windows and door indicated a fear of intruders. Steve knocked hard on the door, but there was no response. Again he knocked, and went on knocking. Eventually, a woman's voice came from behind the door. In apprehensive tones it said,

"Who are you? What do you want?"

"Our boat's been wrecked on the rocks below here," Steve told her, a desperate note in his voice. "We're both cut, and bleeding badly. Please help us."

Inside the house, the woman called through to her disabled husband, who sat in his chair holding a pistol. He had heard the exchange through the door. He called back,

"Let them in, but come back in here and stand behind me."

He kept the pistol at the ready. His wife unlocked and unbolted the door and the steel gate, and opened it fractionally, ready to shut it again if necessary. The sight on her doorstep caused her to gasp with horror.

"Oh, you poor creatures. Bring her in - bring her in," she urged Steve, who by this time was on the point of collapse himself, but still found the strength to support Della into the house.

The lady, a middle-aged white woman with a kindly face, took charge immediately.

"First, let's get rid of those clothes and get you cleaned up," she said to Della, grasping her hand, and leading her off to the bathroom. "John will tell you where to wash, and where to find some dry clothes," she added, addressing Steve over her shoulder, then dropping her voice to a whisper she confided, "Don't mind John and his gun. He's paranoid about some coming revolution. He'd rather go and live in Haiti".

John Paige, a white man with the brown, leathery face of one who has spent a lifetime in the tropics, had put down his gun, but it was noticeable that he kept it handy on the arm of his chair.

"You can never be too careful in such an isolated spot as this," he said, by way of an apology. "I'm not very mobile, and Diana has to leave me on my own most days."

Steve introduced himself.

"I'm Steve Andrews, a lecturer in the Geology Department at the University."

"John Paige," the man held out his hand.

His relief was evident in the relaxed way he began to talk about himself.

I'm a retired sugar engineer. I worked at the refining plant on the big plantation at Caymanas. I bought this place cheaply because of its exposed position, but I'm beginning to regret it." He gestured towards the bedroom door. "Help yourself to any of the clothes in the wardrobe that fit you."

In the Paige's bedroom, Steve stripped off his blood-soaked rags, washed at the hand-basin, and put on the only things that would fit his large frame, some outsize khaki shorts and shirt. He had to settle for bare feet. Feeling something like human again, he returned to the sitting room. Della emerged from the bathroom at the same time, clad in a towelling wrap, with a hand-towel round her hair. Apart from her bruised face, she looked more like the Della he knew. The broad smile when she saw the comical khaki outfit was even more the Della he knew - and loved, he told himself.

BACK IN THE COCKPIT

Wade Robinson and Queenie made their way from the foot of the cliff escape route to the cave. For Queenie the water siphon also held terrors, but it was the lesser of two evils. On the ledge inside the cave she prepared herself mentally, taking deep breaths. When she was ready, she nodded to Wade and slipped into the water. They swam together to the spot above the cave entrance. At her signal they dived simultaneously. The torch he had picked up from the ledge illuminated the entrance. Pulling themselves down, they entered the cave and began an upside-down, all fours scramble along the roof. Shortly before they reached the end they were met by divers moving in the opposite direction. Before the torch was dashed from his hand, Wade caught a fleeting glimpse of the ominous-looking full-face mask of an oxygen re-breathing set. Hands grabbed him and Queenie, and they were unceremoniously dragged through the exit, into the Windsor Caves. They emerged, gasping for air, to find the light from a powerful lamp shining in their faces. Unseen hands hauled them out of the stream and thrust them against the wall of the cave. Their interrogation began on the spot. At first, neither spoke in response to questions about the cockpit.

"Are there any more coming through? How many people in the cockpit?"

Silence. The diver holding the lamp had taken off his mask. He slapped Queenie across her face. The noise of the slap echoed in the cave like a gunshot. She screamed. The man raised his hand again. Wade had seen enough.

"We are the only ones in the cave. The rest have left the cockpit over the cliffs," he confessed. "That's the truth," he added hurriedly as the diver looked about to strike again.

"I hope, for your sake, it is the truth," the lead diver said. "If not, you'll answer to me. Wayne Daniels was a good friend of mine. If I ever get hold of his killer - -."

He didn't utter the threat, but the implication was unmistakable.

"Take these two back to the entrance, and hand them over to the Chief Inspector," he instructed the back-up team. "Tell him we're going ahead with the assault but don't expect much resistance. It looks as though the birds have flown."

Motioning his team to follow, he replaced his mask and submerged again. This time he found his way through to the lake. Staying submerged, but switching off his lamp, he swam slowly towards the faint light penetrating the depths which, he assumed, came in through the exit. The prisoner was telling

the truth, he realised. The cavern containing the lake was deserted. There were no guards on the exit. There was nobody in the hutment camp downstream. Suspecting a trap, though, he set up a defensive position inside the largest hut and waited. He looked at his watch. In a few minutes the overland assault would begin.

'When the abseilers get into the cockpit it'll be soon enough to start searching the rest of the valley', he reasoned.

A fusillade of shots ringing out from the cliff-top signalled the start of the assault. The sounds were short-lived. Someone had won a decisive encounter. For a moment the jungle sounds ceased, but then resumed as though nothing had happened. Hours later, teams of troops finished hacking paths to the cliff edge in four different locations along the northern side of the cockpit. A fifth team waited at the top of the cleft where the left-wingers had installed ropes. In all five positions belays were set up in preparation for an abseiling assault. At a radio signal from Colonel Watson, five streams of men abseiled rapidly down the cliff face. Unaccountably, there was no opposition, even at the bottom of the cleft, which was obviously the defenders' own route. Regrouping at the bottom of the cliff, the troops began forcing their way through the dense undergrowth towards the centre of the cockpit, expecting opposition to materialise all the way. Nerves were jangling. Two groups struck the hutted clearing simultane-ously. A keyed-up soldier in one group opened fire on the other group, which returned the fire. Men died in both groups. The screams of badly wounded soldiers filled the cockpit. In the main hut the divers also opened fire, believing they were surrounded and under attack. Too late, the appalling truth

206

dawned on the attackers. All the fire, including that from the hut, was 'friendly'.

Up on the rim, awaiting news of the success of the operation, the colonel received the information of the heavy casualties with a sinking heart. 'Out-foxed again, by a bunch of amateurs. What do I tell the Prime Minister this time?' He radioed down instructions to evacuate the wounded and the bodies; search the whole cockpit for the fugitives, and withdraw all troops except for small guard detachments on the cave and cliff access points to prevent the return of the left-wingers.

GALINA POINT

John Paige was curious about the circumstances of the boat wreck. "How do you come to be outside the reef in a small boat, in the dark, in conditions like these?, risking your wife's life, he asked Steve."

Deciding not to contradict the assumption about his marital state, and wary about revealing the true nature of their exploits, Steve trotted out a cock-and-bull story.

"We were on a fishing trip, got caught way out at sea by a sudden storm, and lost our bearings in poor visibility. Stupidly, I didn't have a compass. We headed towards land by sheer luck - if you can call running into the rocks lucky. We need to get back to Ocho Rios as soon as possible," he added.

"Neither of you looks in any condition to do anything tonight," John Paige told him, in a voice full of concern. "You

can rest in our holiday accommodation while Diana repairs your clothes."

Steve and Della exchanged relieved glances. They both felt exhausted. There would be no advantage in leaving this safe haven before morning. What they needed most of all was sleep. Steve answered for both of them.

"That's very kind of you, Mr. Page. If it's no trouble to —"

"You are very welcome," interjected John Paige. "We don't have many visitors this time of year. Diana, will you show them through?"

His wife led them through to the holiday apartment, which occupied one wing of the L-shaped bungalow. Leaving them alone, she picked up their discarded clothes and went off to wash, dry and repair them. Seconds later she remembered their cuts, and returned with a box of sticking plasters and a bottle of antiseptic.

"I think you might need these," she said, handing them over with a smile.

Gratefully, Steve accepted them. Carefully, he removed the bathrobe from Della's sore body. Her arms and legs, in particular, were covered with coral cuts and darkening bruises. Gently, he dabbed antiseptic on each cut and covered it with a plaster. She winced as the fluid bit into her raw flesh but, oddly, found his tender attentions highly erotic. When the final plaster had been applied, she put her arms slowly around his neck, pulled his body close, and kissed him - a soft, lingering kiss on the lips, which conveyed her feelings. He winced.

"I love you, Steve Andrews," she breathed, as their lips parted, but she gasped at her thoughtlessness as she saw the blood oozing through the shirt. "Now, let me treat your cuts."

She made him take off the ridiculous shirt and shorts. Her gasp of surprise had nothing to do with the sight of his erect member, which had already made itself known when she kissed him. The cuts on his body were much worse than hers. When he had been dragged across the reef, trying to prevent her from being swept away, he couldn't protect himself. The coral had lacerated his chest from top to bottom. As well as the bleeding, the skin around the wounds looked inflamed. Even deeper feelings of love suffused her whole being, as the impact of what this man had done for her benefit struck home. She rested her hand briefly on his erect companion as though bestowing a benediction.

"Patience, my friend," she said, as she went to work with the antiseptic.

The burning pain as the antiseptic penetrated his cuts soon caused a droop in even that autonomous organ. Della smiled as she noticed the response. She pushed Steve towards the bed, made him lie down, and covered him with a sheet. Climbing into the other side of the bed, she slid down beside him and snuggled close.

"Turn your back to me," she suggested, wanting to avoid hurting his chest.

Spoon fashion, she snuggled up to him. Exhausted, they both fell into a deep sleep.

CHAPTER 11

SOUTHAMPTON
JUNE 1973

HM CUSTOMS

In the superintendent's office, Inspector Williams of the Scotland Yard drug squad was briefing his Customs colleagues on the movements of Bucky Wilson.

"As you know, this fellow's just done five years for distributing marijuana. It's not his first stretch for the same offence, and I don't suppose it'll be his last. He's been busy doing the rounds of his old contacts in the banana shipping business for the last couple of weeks, and —"

"Surely he won't try to pull the same trick with the banana containers," broke in his opposite number.

"Well, he's been seen twice meeting a Chinese-looking Jamaican in London. He's not known to us, but we can't be too

careful. Wilson's a slippery customer. I wouldn't put it past him to try the same scam again, on the grounds that lightning doesn't strike twice in the same place."

"OK, we'll keep an eye on the Jamaican imports, and especially the banana containers, but I must say, I'm sceptical," agreed the Customs Superintendent.

"I don't think it's quite that simple," went on Inspector Williams. "Wilson paid visits to ripening store foremen at two distribution depots. In my book, that suggests the dope's still present in the shipment after it's been transferred to the ripening chambers. So it's not in the container walls as it was before."

"So, where is it?" asked the Superintendent, beginning to show his exasperation.

"I don't know yet," confessed the inspector. "It must be in the individual boxes, but that's for your men to find out."

He gave orders for surveillance of all future Jamaican banana imports. The shipments were followed right through to the distributors, and the activities of their handlers watched. Joint Customs and Drug Squad teams were set up to provide twenty-four hour cover of the docks and the distributors' warehouses. Nothing suspicious happened. Bananas were delivered in insulated containers, and ripened for four to six days under ethylene gas. They were graded and check-weighed. Over-ripe ones were thrown into a skip and replaced. The rest were shipped out to wholesalers. The watchers were baffled. For three successive weeks, deliveries from the weekly Fyffes boat were tracked. Nothing out of the ordinary happened. That was not really surprising. They were not to know that no ganja had been shipped out of Kingston yet.

Ganja
BANANA

THOMPSON ESTATE
JUNE 1973

The first shipment of ganja had arrived from the processors that morning, packed in used fertiliser bags. Old George took three or four loaders at a time into the privacy of his hut and showed them how he wanted the bananas cut and the ganja plugs inserted. Back at the temporary storage racks they set about doctoring just one of the bananas in one hand of each bunch. The women worked quickly. In a matter of two hours they had dealt with the whole consignment. When they had finished, to any casual observer there was no sign of any tampering with the fruit. The banana bunches were left on the racks for the morning's task of hand-cutting and boxing. Next morning the cutters did their job as usual, and the women boxed and loaded the bananas, as usual, into the rail wagons for transport to Kingston.

At the packing sheds in the docks the purchaser from the Banana Board checked the quality of the fruit in a few randomly chosen boxes. He was satisfied with its appearance, failed to spot the doctored bananas, and passed the consignment for acceptance. Immediately, he telephoned the JAMCO representative in London to settle the 'Green Boat Price' for delivery to the ripening depots in the UK. A price agreed, he authorised packing into the containers reserved for the Thompson fruit, ready for loading into the temperature-controlled holds of the Fyffes banana boat waiting at the quay. They would be stored on board at 56 - 57 degrees Fahrenheit to hold ripening in check.

Two days before the consignments had begun arriving for

this particular sailing, men from the Jamaican Special Branch had carried out what was now their routine examination of the shipping containers to be used. They had no intention of allowing the drug runners to get away with another operation as big as the one five years before that had led, when it was discovered, to the jailing of one or two lesser lights in Kingston, and Bucky Wilson in the UK. Today, a TELEX had arrived from Southampton, asking for a special watch on the containers in case of a repeat performance. Chief Inspector Anderson put two men on surveillance in the docks. They did a second check on the containers, tapped the walls for more solid – sounding parts of the insulation, and examined the doors - nothing. Everybody going in and out of the containers during loading was kept under close observation - again, nothing.

When Chief Inspector Anderson received the negative report from his surveillance team, he responded in icy tones,

"For Christ's sake! They're not going to use the same method again. Look in the boxes."

From then on, one in ten of the boxes was opened and searched for drug packages before the consignment was allowed to be loaded. Nothing was found in the boxes from any of the producers. Chief Inspector Anderson received the news with mounting frustration. Once more he had nothing positive to report. He was glad his embarrassment couldn't be seen by the people in England as he telexed the Customs Office in Southampton:

DETAILED SEARCHES FOUND NO CANNABIS IN CARGO
OF FYFFES BOAT LEAVING 20 JUNE
BELIEVE SHIPMENT CLEAN: J.A.: KINGSTON: 19 JUNE

The news was received in Southampton with equal frustration. Bucky Wilson's activities had convinced the Drug Squad that some big operation involving the banana trade had been set up with Kingston, but how did it work? Inspector Williams had a gut feeling that the key was to be found at the distribution depots. With the collusion of the management, he infiltrated a man into the sorting shed at each of the two suspect depots. The agents were put into the gangs grading the bananas as they were taken out of the ripening chambers. The job followed a long-established routine. Boxes were taken out and opened, and the contents examined. Over-ripe bananas were removed from the hands and tossed into a waste skip. The boxes were then weighed, and any deficiency made up from other boxes. Nothing out of the ordinary happened to arouse suspicions. The story was the same for the deliveries the next week, and the following week. Inspector Williams called in his men to go over their experiences in detail.

"Explain again, exactly what happens from the time the bananas arrive to the time they're despatched to the wholesalers," he ordered.

Each man went into great detail about the handling process in his particular plant, describing how he had carefully, but surreptitiously, watched as many boxes as possible being opened, and their contents taken out for examination. Neither had seen any packages removed. Only the occasional rotting banana was taken out, and was thrown into a rubbish skip. The truth hit the inspector like a revelation.

"Of course, that's it," he shouted, in a rare burst of excitement. "Can't you see? The ganja must be hidden inside the bananas. Clever! What happens to the waste from the skips?"

The agents had to confess that they didn't know.

"Then find out," yelled the inspector.

It emerged that early every morning the waste fruit was taken away for incineration by a local contractor. But last thing every night, some of the sorters were staying behind after their shift to pick over the rejected fruit. Many of the over-ripe bananas yielded plugs of cannabis resin. When Inspector Williams was told this, he nodded in satisfaction at the outcome of his hunch. He withdrew his agents from the distribution depots and put them onto surveillance of the sorters after they had retrieved the drug consignments. They were small fry. He was after the big fish of the operation, on both sides of the pond. The trail led straight back to Bucky Wilson, and on to the major dealers he supplied. When the time was ripe they could all be picked up, and the ring smashed. But the time was not yet ripe. First the Jamaican end of the operation must be cracked. There was no point in cutting off the tail if the head was still functioning. It would simply grow a new tail. A TELEX was sent off to Kingston:

CANNABIS RESIN FOUND INSIDE BANANAS FROM
FYFFES BOAT
SOURCE OF BANANAS NOT KNOWN
CAN YOU DETERMINE ORIGIN?
D.W.: SOUTHAMPTON: 17 JULY, 1970

When the message was handed to Chief Inspector Anderson he experienced his first feeling of elation for weeks. The saga of failures to apprehend the still-missing Brett Johnson and his band had depressed him. He had been given a momentary lift

when Della Brook telephoned her information about Nanny Town, the day after she had been wrecked on the reef, but an air search of the area had revealed nothing - a too familiar story - and his depression had returned.

'Now I can at last get my teeth into some unconnected matter', he told himself, with renewed enthusiasm. 'It's obvious that the ganja isn't getting into the bananas at the docks, so the job must be done back at the estates. The problem is which estates?'

He gave orders for a thorough search of the cargo arriving for the next banana boat, including the bananas themselves. A lot of producers were upset at having their fruit hacked open. No ganja was found until the train from the Thompson estate was unloaded. Every second box was found to contain a banana with a plug of resin inserted into its core.

Colonel Thompson's response, when tackled about the use to which his product was being put, was almost to explode on the spot. His face turned red, then purple. He spluttered incoherently at first, but managed to get out,

"I'll have your badge, Inspector. You don't think I'm party to any of this, do you?"

"Chief Inspector, if you don't mind, - - - Sir," John Anderson replied, not bothering to disguise his contempt for the man. "The circumstances are somewhat incriminating, but I'm willing to suspend judgement until we establish the facts. The first thing we have to do is find out who's actually stuffing the bananas. Maybe then we'll learn who's behind it," he said, holding the colonel's eye with a steady gaze.

"Hrrmph," went the colonel, speechless for long seconds. "If you're adamant about this, we'd better get down to the packing shed." On the way they picked up the estate manager, who professed to be as mystified as the colonel. The Land Rover pulled up in the estate workers' compound with a screech of brakes, amid a cloud of dust. The colonel jumped out with a shout of,

"George, get your arse out here."

Old George shambled out of his hut with a fearful expression on his face, sensing that the trouble he had anticipated from the time he had agreed to this ganja business had arrived.

"Now, you old crow," roared the colonel. "What do you know about ganja in the bananas?"

"Ganja, Boss? Ah don't know nuthin' 'bout ganja," the cringing old man replied, afraid of his employer, but petrified by the thought of incurring the wrath of Obeah.

"Get the packers out here," Colonel Thompson told him, in a quieter, but more menacing voice. "Let's see if they sing a different tune."

The women packers had by this time gone back to the village, where they were engaged in their normal evening domestic activities. At the summons from the estate everything was dropped. The colonel was feared by everyone in the village, so it was a subdued procession of women that wound its way through the plantation to the packing shed.

"Line them up George," ordered the colonel.

When the scared women had shuffled into a ragged line, Colonel Thompson started asking them, individually, whether they were involved in stuffing the bananas with ganja.

"No sir," or "No Colonel," was the answer in almost every case.

One of the carriers, a tall, upright woman with the sturdy development of one used to carrying as many as four fifty pound bunches of bananas on her head, spoke up.

"Yes, Sir, we'se all doin'it, Sir. Orders from the Obeah Lady. We'se afraid not to"

Non-plussed, the Colonel turned in frustration to his Manager.

"What the Devil's she on about? Do they still believe this mumbo jumbo?"

"I'm afraid so, Colonel. It's a very strong force in the villages. Most of the absenteeism we get's because the Obeah Lady says it's not a good day to work."

Chief Inspector Anderson had so far said nothing, but he thought,

'At last things are beginning to fall into place. So Obeah's behind the ganja trade, but why? What's a primitive cult got to do with it? he thought, then aloud, said, "I could understand if it the Rastafarians were behind this, but the Obeah connection baffles me."

"I don't care who's behind it. I'll soon put a stop to it," muttered the Colonel. Raising his voice, he issued an ultimatum to the row of women. "I want to see you all back at work tomorrow. If you don't turn up, you'll be sacked. If you're caught with ganja, you'll be sacked."

The women, relieved at not losing their jobs on the spot, but afraid still of the Obeah reaction, began to drift back to the village, twittering in subdued voices. Colonel Thompson drove off towards the plantation house, leaving his manager to assist the Chief Inspector. John Anderson started by interrogating old George.

"Now we know what you've been up to, George, you can tell us when you expect your next ganja delivery."

"Tomorrow, Boss, after dark," replied the old man, anxious now to collaborate.

"Two men."

"How much ganja?"

"Two hundred pounds."

"Pheew.   Quite an operation," commented the Chief Inspector.

Next day ten Special Branch and police officers were concealed around the compound when an old Ford van drove in and stopped outside George's hut. When Moose and his companion got out they found themselves facing a ring of weapons. There was nothing for it but to surrender. They raised their hands and the policemen closed in. Handcuffed, they were led off to the plantation house, where they were paraded before Colonel Thompson. Under the house lights the Chief Inspector was startled to find that he vaguely recognised the big fellow. Racking his brains to recall a different context, he suddenly recalled the connection. He remembered mug shots of some of the missing students who were thought to have become left-wing activists.

'There's more here than meets the eye. This man could be one of the Montego Bay left-wingers we've been trying to track down in the Cockpit Country. What's he - what are they doing in the ganja trade?' Aloud, he said to the pair, "OK your game's up. Where's Brett Johnson?"

Taken by surprise by the unexpected line of questioning, Moose began, "He's not - -" then realised he had given himself away, and stopped.

He refused to answer any more questions. Colonel Thompson, who had been unusually quiet since the men were brought to the house, was puzzled by the line of questioning. Mention of

the Left Wing activist brought all his old fears rushing back. The revolutionaries were already at his door - actually in his house!

'You have to be ruthless with these people', he thought, remembering the efficacy of his methods in Malaysia.

"Give me a few minutes with the men," he requested. "I'll soon have them singing like birds."

"There's no need for that sort of thing," responded John Anderson, with undisguised distaste. "We know roughly where he is. It's just a matter of time before he's found and flushed out. The army's looking after that now."

Apprehension of Brett Johnson had become something of an obsession with him. This connection with the ganja trade made it even more important that the man was caught. As he motioned for the two prisoners to be taken away, and followed them outside, he noticed how well the house was fortified against attack. A germ of an idea began to form. He went back inside.

"Colonel, there is a way you can help to catch Johnson. This place is like a fortress. If we can hold the prisoners here, and spread the word they're here, maybe Johnson will be tempted to make a rescue attempt, and we can catch him in the open."

The Colonel, ever a man of action, liked the idea. It would be a chance to have a go at his favourite target, the Left, and be a good test of his defences.

"You're on", he said, hardly able to contain his eagerness. "You can put the prisoners in the cellar."

The Chief Inspector ordered them to be locked up, then sent a local man to a bar in Bog Walk with instructions to let slip that the captives had not been taken to Kingston, but were still at the Thomson estate. He then arranged to wait in the plantation house for developments. The Colonel, his estate manager, the estate engineer and his assistant manned the machine guns at the corners of the roof. Two men with rifles patrolled the walkways. For two days nothing happened.

High up in the Blue Mountains, like many an escaped slave before them, Brett Johnson, Wade Robinson and his band were holed up in the Stony River gorge. The 'training camp' turned out to be a series of man-made caves, hollowed out of the rock face on the west side of the gorge. It had the advantage of being remote, and invisible from the air, but reaching it involved a long climb. For that reason alone, the failure of Moose and his companion to return from the ganja delivery aroused no concern for more than twenty-four hours. Wade then began to fear the worst, speculating that his friends had run into trouble at the Thompson estate. His suspicions were confirmed by the arrival of a Rastaman with a message from the Obeah Queen. Through old George and his contacts she had been informed that two of the band were being held prisoner in the estate house. Another piece of unwelcome information was that the area around Nanny Town was crawling with army units. Wade expressed his concern to the rest of the band.

"Moose is my right-hand man. We should mount a rescue attempt before he's moved to Kingston."

Brett felt that he was responsible for the capture of the two men.

"It's too risky for a group to try to get through" he said. "I'd stand a better chance on my own. I know the estate, and the layout of the house. Let me try. Give me a day, and if I fail it's up to you."

Wade reluctantly agreed. Brett collected supplies, stuffed them in a haversack, picked up his Tokarev T33 pistol and set off down the gorge.

The Rasta was right. There were detachments of troops all over the area where he climbed out of the gorge. Keeping on the ground, using his elbows for locomotion, he wormed his way between two of the groups. They made enough noise for him to avoid them easily. He didn't feel safe enough to rise to his feet until he was over the next ridge. There were no paths there, but that meant that it was a fair assumption there were also no soldiers. The vegetation was dense, but not too dense to push his way through. He made good progress across country, moving downhill all the time. At the bottom of the next valley, in a clearing at the end of a track, he came across a collection of jeeps. They were unguarded. Sauntering over, he casually got into the nearest. The key was in the ignition. A quick check of the surroundings proved quite unnecessary. He was still alone. The jeep started immediately. Brett donned a fatigue cap left on the passenger seat, and bumped off down the track. His cap was a poor enough disguise, but his appearance aroused no suspicion in the groups of soldiers he passed. When he reached what passed for a road, but was really only a better class of track, he headed north, making for the coast road. He struck it at Hope Bay, and turned west.

'Now I need to decide whether to stick with the jeep, and risk being challenged, or abandon it and be slowed down', he thought, considering the options carefully. 'I'll go for speed and take the risk. The longer Moose is held, the worse it'll be for him', he decided, remembering the attitude of Colonel Thompson to left-wing revolutionaries.

Having made the decision, Brett drove on, turning off the coast road about two miles after Anotto Bay, and taking the road over the foothills to Bog Walk. There, he abandoned the vehicle outside the station and entered the Thompson plantation by his boyhood route. Deep amongst the bananas he settled down to wait for nightfall.

CHAPTER 12

NANNY TOWN
JUNE, 1973

Immediately on receipt of Della Brook's information about
the flight of the left-wingers to the Blue Mountains, the Chief
Inspector had passed it on to Colonel Watson. Army units were
despatched to the Nanny Town area. The prospects for finding
the fugitives in that terrain were almost as bad as in the Cockpit
Country. Helicopter searches were no more fruitful than they
had been there. No sign of the quarry could be seen from the air.
The only clue was Della Brook's information that there might
be a rebel training camp 'somewhere near the site of Nanny
Town'. That left a lot of trackless wilderness to be searched. The
operation was begun by concentrating forces at the site of the
old town. Platoons of troops then fanned out in every direction
the terrain allowed. It was a long, exhausting process.

A missing jeep was reported to the colonel. The long-suffering man gritted his teeth.

"Am I surrounded by incompetents?" he hissed, rolling his eyes heavenward.

He made a wager with himself.

'I'll bet my next leave the bird has flown - yet again'.

In spite of his private beliefs he felt that he had to continue the search of the area. Even if his main target had vanished, there was a good chance of rounding up the rest of the rebels. He gave orders to carry on the operation, but with redoubled vigilance. Troops moved out along the valleys and over the ridges. It was a slow process, requiring great caution, as the soldiers searched every likely spot, expecting all the time to be met by a hail of bullets.

As dusk approached, activity was suspended, and the men were ordered to bivouac on the spot. Sentries were posted, and the rest flopped to the ground, exhausted by the heat and the heavy work of pushing through the thick vegetation. Up in the Stoney River gorge, reports from outlying scouts warned Wade Robinson that the army noose was tightening. He called the fugitives together to discuss the new crisis.

"There are army units closing in from the north," he informed them. "We are much more vulnerable here than we were in the cockpit. As I see it, we have three options. We can fight it out, but it's only a matter of time before the gorge is taken, and we're all killed. We can surrender, in which case we'll have to stand trial and probably be executed."

He hesitated, and an anxious Queenie broke in.

"Well, come on Wade, what's the third option?"

"A long shot," he replied, "but when you consider the alternatives, it's worth trying. We could call in the help that was promised to Brett by Obeah."

"What sort of help?"

"I don't know. We'd have to leave it to the Obeah Queen." replied Wade.

"How do we contact her?" asked one of the men in the group.

"One of us has to get through the army lines, and make it as far as Lucky Valley. That's where Brett had his run-in with Obeah," Wade told him.

"I think a woman might stand the best chance of getting through. Let me go," volunteered Queenie.

Most of the rest agreed with her idea. One man was sceptical. He was Gad Marshall's sidekick; a one-time clerk at a Blue Mountain coffee plantation, who had lost his job after the plantation had been taken over by a multinational. His bitterness had taken him into the left-wing movement.

"There's one option we haven't considered. We could try to make it over the mountains to the south, away from the army. If we can reach the southern foothills, I know the area. It'll be easy to disperse and disappear from there into Kingston."

"That sounds OK in theory, but you'd have to cross the highest passes in the Blue Mountains, through trackless jungle," Wade objected. "It could take days, if you made it at all."

"I'm game to try," replied the man.

"Well, that's your democratic right," Wade conceded. "Anyone else want to try the mountain option?" he asked the rest of the group.

Only the remaining three of the Kingston volunteers who had joined Chinee on his return to the cockpit opted for the climb. Sheepishly, one said that it looked like the most direct route back to Kingston and the others nodded agreement. They had always felt like outsiders, and had never really integrated with the Montego Bay crowd. The four men stuffed what they could into backpacks, picked up their machetes, and moved slowly up the bottom of the gorge, hacking a path through the growth. Queenie, meanwhile, had put on the one dress she had managed to hang onto since her flight from Montego Bay, a clinging cotton number in a pastel shade of mauve. The few creases were soon ironed out by the warm thrust of her voluptuous figure and, at least in the lantern light, she looked as though she might just have stepped out of a High Street dress shop.

"My idea's to make my way, after dark, through the army cordon, and get to the nearest road. I don't think anybody'll be suspicious if I'm seen hitching a lift. I've done it often enough before to go into town."

About 2.00 am Queenie set off, picking her way along the rocky bottom of the gorge, using the boulders of the river bank as a path through the over-hanging trees. At the junction of the Stoney River with the Back Rio Grande she came across the first army patrol. She was alerted to their presence by the snores of sleeping soldiers. Freezing where she crouched, she waited. It wasn't long before she was able to sense the position of a sentry. When the man moved behind a rock to light a surreptitious cigarette, she glided past like a ghost. As the moon rose above the treetops, she was thankful for the dim light it cast. The going seemed to get rougher and rougher, but at least there were no more army patrols in the direction she was going.

'But which way is that?' she wondered, having no real sense of direction.

By daylight she was heading straight towards where the sun was rising.

'At least I know the sun rises in the east, so I'm going in the opposite direction to the one I want. If I try to leave the river, I'm bound to lose myself, but if I follow it downhill it must take me to the coast and the coast road'.

A few stumbling hours later, the river she was following joined another, broader stream, flowing right to left. She was on the wrong bank of the tributary to be able to follow the main stream downwards. There was nothing for it but to swim across to the other bank of what was, unknown to her, the Rio Grande.

She had not bargained for the strength of the current, boosted by the recent rains. Hard though she swam, she was swept along, into the Rio Grande, and found herself struggling in mid-stream, unable to make any headway towards the bank. In a panic, she looked wildly around her. By good fortune, a few yards away there was a floating branch. A supreme effort took her across to it. Although waterlogged it gave her enough support to allow her to rest and be carried along by the flow.

Eventually, Queenie realised that she was probably making better progress than she would on the bank, so continued drifting downstream, making no attempt to land. Eventually, round a bend in the river, she saw a settlement. Along the bank was a row of bamboo-log rafts. A man carrying a long pole was leading a white couple towards the raft at the end of the line.

"Help," she shouted. "Help me, please."

The startled people, not knowing at first where the voice was coming from, looked everywhere but the middle of the river.

"Help," she called again, desperation in her voice.

"There," called the girl, who was about to take a rafting trip with her husband. "By the floating branch," she said, pointing to where Queenie was now trying to swim towards the bank.

"Hang on, honey," the raftsman shouted, loosing the mooring rope of a raft, and leaping aboard.

Quickly, he poled across to meet her. By the time he had hauled her on board, the raft was gathering pace on its way down river, and there was no way he could get back to his base.

"Thanks," gasped Queenie. "You saved my life. I was exhausted."

"Oh, don't thank me," he said, grinning, and giving her an approving once over. "You only cost me a fare."

"What do you mean?" she asked, mystified.

"I get paid to ferry tourists down from Berrydale there, to Saint Margaret's Bay.

Understanding dawned. Queenie had heard about the Rio Grande rafting trips. By doubly good fortune, she had been rescued, and was going to be taken where she wanted to be.

"I've no money, but I will pay you," she promised, treating him to the most dazzling smile she could muster.

The smile, and the sight of the way the wet dress was now clinging to her body like a second skin, was enough payment for the raftsman.

"No problem, Miss," he said, so reluctant to take his eyes off her he failed to negotiate a bend, and ran the raft into the bank. I can always do an extra run."

"Just watch where you're going. I don't want to wind up in the river again," she ribbed him.

A puzzled expression appeared on his face as she reminded him where he had found her, and he pondered her presence in the river.

"How did you get in the river in the first place?" he asked her. "There's no —"

"It's a long story," she broke in, "and I'd rather not go into it now."

"Oh, OK," he grumbled, feigning hurt. "If that's how you want to be."

For the rest of the trip down to St. Margaret's they were both silent. By the time he helped her off the raft at the landing stage she had begun to feel guilty at her off-hand treatment of the man. Giving him a quick kiss on the cheek, she thanked him again for pulling her out of the river. Before he had time to think, she was heading for the road. Watching her trim figure until she rounded the corner, he touched the spot on his cheek, grinned, and put it all down to experience. After all, how often did he get to rescue damsels in distress?

There was much to-and-fro of traffic on the road between Berrydale and St. Margaret's; taxis and minibuses taking tourists up to the rafting centre, empty trucks coming the opposite way, and carrying rafts back to the start of their run. Queenie had no difficulty hitching a lift down to the town in an empty truck. The driver thought his lucky day had come.

"Hop in, honey," he invited her, leaning across to open the nearside door. Offering a hand, he helped her heave herself up onto the high bench seat. He ran his eyes over her with a leering grin as she made herself comfortable and smoothed her dress down over her thighs.

"Where's yo' headin', baby?" he asked, revving the engine, but making no attempt to move off.

He couldn't take his eyes off the body provocatively outlined by the thin, clinging material of her still-wet dress. A hand shot out and grasped her thigh. She firmly removed it.

"Yo' should get out o' those wet things. Let me help yo'," he suggested, and made a grab to rip open the buttoned front of the dress.

As his body came across her, she swung her left knee into his groin. He gasped, and let out an agonised shout. The hands that had clutched her now clutched their owner's injured crotch. The respite from his attentions allowed her to open the door, but as she tried to scramble out, he grabbed her by the hair. She let out a piercing scream, and raked the driver's forearm with her nails.

"Cut that out, yo' bitch," the driver yelled, and followed up with a blow across the side of the head that made her senses reel.

A passing army jeep screeched to a halt. Its occupants leapt out and ran to Queenie's aid. A blow from the rifle butt of one soldier dumped the truck driver senseless on his own seat, and the second soldier caught Queenie as she fell. She was carried to the jeep and propped in the corner of the back seat. Quickly, she gathered her wits.

"I've got to get to Bog Walk in a hurry," she gasped. "Can you give me a lift to the coast road?"

"We can do better than that, Miss," the jeep driver offered. "We can drop you there on our way to our Kingston headquarters."

The grateful Queenie settled back, and was lulled into an exhausted sleep by the rocking motion of the jeep over the rough roads. The irony of the hunters' help for the hunted had totally escaped her.

"Bog Walk, Miss."

The jeep driver's call woke Queenie with a start. For a moment she had no idea where she was or why she was there. Then it all came flooding back. Somehow she must contact Obeah and enlist its help for Wade and his band in the Blue Mountains. They could be in serious trouble by now, or even captured. Climbing stiffly from the jeep, she walked round and gave each of her rescuers a resounding kiss on the cheek.

"Thanks, fellers. You've no idea what a good deed you've done today," she told them, smiling as she thought of their chagrin if they only knew.

"That's OK, Miss," said the man who had wielded his rifle so effectively. All in a day's work".

The driver put the jeep in gear and roared off towards Kingston. Queenie looked around her. This was unfamiliar territory. Across the road was a row of shops.

'If anybody knows how to contact Obeah, the shopkeepers will', she reasoned.

She chose the shop with a display of vegetables outside, and went in. When her eyes had adjusted from the brightness of the sun to the gloom of the interior, she could see a plump figure sitting on a cane chair in the shade just inside the door. Coming straight to the point, she said, keeping her voice down,

"I need to talk to the Obeah Lady. It's urgent."

"Don't know no Obeah Lady," replied the woman, with a guarded, sullen expression, mindful of the Obeah threats to her friends who worked the Thompson plantation.

"Oh, come on," said Queenie. "Every woman knows her. Who do you go to when you've got a bad period?"

"Ah'm sayin' nothin'" was the stubborn reply. "Go an' see old George, the Thompson foreman."

Queenie was getting nowhere fast. Leaving the shop, she asked directions from a couple of loafers outside the station. They told her where to find the estate office, which was not far down the street. A clerk, busy writing in a ledger looked up enquiringly, but said nothing.

"I'm looking for a job on the plantation," Queenie announced.

The clerk, sizing her up quickly said, "I don't think there's any jobs, but you can try. Go and see the foreman."

He gave her directions, and she set off on foot into the plantation to see George - the man she was looking for.

"I'm not looking for a job," Queenie told George, when he started explaining that he had no jobs. "I know you've got Obeah connections, and I want you to take me to the Obeah Lady."

Although taken by surprise by her statement, he had enough presence of mind to feign ignorance. He was just about to deny all knowledge of Obeah when she followed up with the information,

"You'll be helping Brett Johnson."

Afraid before, he was now doubly so. Looking around furtively, he whispered,

"Come back in an hour. I've got to go to Spanish Town for food supplies. I'll drop you at Lucky Valley first. You can find the Obeah Lady there. But you're on your own."

At mid-day, Queenie returned, to find George waiting in a pick-up truck that looked almost as old as him. She climbed in, and off they went in a cloud of smoke. At Lucky Valley, George told her to get out, and pointed towards the path leading into the jungle at the top of the village. Without a word, he let in his clutch, and was off as fast as the old truck would go. Queenie made her way up the valley to the shack in the clearing. Smoke was rising through a hole in the roof. Inside, a handsome woman with a statuesque figure was bending over a pot, stirring the contents slowly with what looked like a human thighbone.

"So you want the help of Obeah?" the woman asked, without looking up. Startled by the question, the flustered Queenie replied,

"Yes, but how did you know?"

"Everybody who comes here wants the help of Obeah," was the answer.

The woman, up to this point, had still not looked up from her task, but now fixed Queenie with penetrating eyes. She felt that the eyes could read deeply into her innermost thoughts, and had this confirmed when the eyes narrowed and the Obeah Queen said,

"So Brett Johnson needs my help against the army?"

A cold shiver swept through Queenie. In her city life she had heard of the powers of Obeah, but had mentally dismissed the claims as so much mumbo-jumbo. Faced now with a demonstration of this woman's power, she was gripped by fear of the unknown, and felt a strong desire to get out of there as quickly as possible.

"Yes, his people are trapped in the Stoney River gorge," she blurted out. "Can you do anything to stop the army?"

"I know where his people are, and I know where he is," the Queen said, disdainfully. "Leave me."

The relieved Queenie shot out of the hut, and ran at breakneck pace back down the path to Lucky Valley. She didn't

stop running until she had put a good half-mile between herself and the shack.

That night, around every army bivouac, on every path leading southwards into the Blue Mountains, Obeah symbols of death appeared. The grisly concoctions of dog skulls, vulture feathers and chicken feet were placed at eye-level, so they could not fail to be seen by anyone heading up into the mountains. An hour before dawn, the slow, faint beat of a big drum sounded, seeming far away. The booming rhythm of the Maman drum built to a thunderous intensity, as though coming nearer, and nearer, before fading to become almost inaudible. As the alarmed soldiery leapt to their feet, the rhythm changed to a slow, relentless beat, which increased in intensity until their bodies felt the resonance. Then, to the south, east and west, Seconda drums superimposed their own rolling rhythm. Superstitious troops milled about in terror. Fears of Obeah, instilled in childhood, came welling to the surface. In panic they abandoned their camps, ignored the commands of their officers, and fled. Some men encountering the death symbols fell to the ground gibbering. Only the paths to the north were free of the awful images. Within minutes the bivouacs were clear, except for the few terrified, prostrate men. As though obeying a signal, the drums stopped simultaneously, and the only sounds, apart from the babbling of the terrified troops, were of bodies crashing through the undergrowth and jeeps starting up in the valleys below.

High in the Stoney River gorge, Wade Robinson heard the drums and grinned at the remaining members of his inner group.

"It looks as though she made it, boys. Here's to Queenie and the Obeah Queen," he proposed, knocking the top off the last

Red Stripe and drinking from the bottle, before passing it round for each to take a swig and raise it to a successful mission.

The rout of the army attackers wasn't the only fruit of Queenie's mission. Around the country, mysterious breakdowns of machinery occurred; a broken main conveyor belt at a bauxite plant; fractured blades in a power station steam turbine; mysterious, that is, until the rumour that Obeah was behind it all began to spread. The effect was electric. The collapse of a dam supplying water to a hydroelectric scheme applied the final twist. Obeah was blamed for that. Frightened workers in industrial jobs left their posts in droves, 'because Obeah doesn't want us to work'. The situation was quickly becoming serious, as production plummeted.

A special cabinet meeting was convened, at which the Prime Minister called for briefings on the various sectors involved. He understood, more than most, the parlous state of the economy, and the catastrophic effect a prolonged standstill of industry would have.

CHAPTER 13
THOMPSON ESTATE

Brett's memory served him well. The route he took through the plantation brought him to the chicken wire fence around the estate workers' compound. Dropping to the ground, he edged his way round the fence to the side of the compound facing the plantation house, taking care not to disturb anyone inside the workers' hut. The last thing he wanted was to involve any of the plantation men in this night's activity. Speed and silence were paramount. Besides, could he be sure that he wouldn't be betrayed by one of them? Since the discovery of the ganja plot, Brett Johnson was unlikely to be the most popular name on the lips of the cutters. Keeping in the shadows of the Malaysian palms surrounding the house, he moved round all four sides, trying to spot the guards' positions. He knew about the machine gun turrets and the walkway near the roof, but were there sentries anywhere else?

'The colonel's a past master at this business', he warned himself. 'Be very careful Brett'.

In two positions on the veranda that ran round three sides of the house, the brief glow of cigarettes betrayed the presence of guards outside the two side doors. There was no such evidence of guards outside the front door, or in any other position, but that was no proof that there were no other guards.

'The colonel's too old a hand to overlook such an obvious point', he reasoned, 'unless he's setting a trap. This isn't my night for falling into elementary traps'.

Ignoring the ground floor of the house, Brett concentrated his attention on the higher level. Around the eaves were substantial cast iron gutters to cope with the frequent tropical downpours. Equally robust pipes brought the rainwater down to drain channels. Another circular tour revealed a partially open second storey window at the side of the house.

'It might be covered by a fly screen - it's impossible to tell from here - but it looks like my only hope'

Brett's first problem was how to cross the moonlit open space between the house and the palm trees without being seen by the guards. Clouds were few and far between, but he waited impatiently for one to obscure the moon. When one did, the darkness produced was such a contrast that he was able to sprint across the space to the northwest corner of the house without detection. Safe in the shadows, he tested the strength of the drainpipe fixings. They seemed stable enough. Hand-over-hand, with his feet braced against the sides of the pipe, he hauled himself up. When he reached the eaves, he switched his hold to the gutter, and traversed left towards the open window.

There was a fly screen! He hung there, deciding what to do next. There was nothing for it but to kick in the screen, and hope there was nobody in the room. Hanging by his arms, with his left foot against the window frame, he tried an exploratory push with his toe - end. The mesh screen swung inwards - it wasn't secured. Breathing a sigh of relief, he lowered himself to the window ledge, and seconds later was inside the room. From a small bed with its head against the opposite wall came faint snores of someone in a deep sleep. In the dim light from the window he could just make out a black face against the pillow. He surmised that he was in a maid's room. Silently, he crossed to the door, opened it a crack, and cast a wary eye over the scene on the other side. The bedroom opened onto a long landing, with a balustrade overlooking a broad hall. The stairs, with open work banisters, descended from the centre of the landing. Stairs and landing were both deserted.

Brett slipped through the door and closed it quietly behind him. He padded along the landing and descended the flight of stairs, keeping to the ends of the wooden treads. Even so, an occasional loud creak made him freeze in his position. No alarm was raised. There was a guard inside the front door, he noted - a policeman armed with a holstered pistol. The man was dozing in a chair to one side of the door. He would have to be dealt with.

The layout of the house was as he remembered it from the days when he had delivered messages from Steve Andrews to the colonel, to inform him in advance where the next batch of drillings was to be made. The parlour and the colonel's library-cum-study were on one side of the hall, and a sitting room and dining room on the other. Behind the stairs were the kitchen and the pantry. There, also, was the trapdoor leading to the cellar, where he guessed his friends would be held.

'How do I get rid of the policeman?' Brett wondered. 'If he sees me skulking about, he'll raise the alarm, and I'm sunk. Maybe a direct approach would be best. He'll not expect to be attacked from inside the house'.

Brett walked down the rest of the stairs, sauntered across the hall as though he owned the place and, as the man raised his head sleepily, hit him with a chopping blow where his neck joined his shoulder. As the policeman slumped sideways, Brett caught him, lowered him to the floor and removed his pistol. The whole episode had taken less than half a minute. Still there was no sign of an alarm being raised. He ran across to the trapdoor. It wasn't locked. There was just a single bolt. Sliding it, and raising the trapdoor, he found a light switch on the wall below. The light revealed stone steps leading down to a bare stone floor. Stepping cautiously down the steps, he entered a large cellar extending under most of the house. In the corner on his right was a stack of wine racks. Near the far wall were Moose and his colleague, manacled to rings in the wall.

'Relics of slaving days, I suppose', Brett thought.

The two prisoners blinked in the unaccustomed light. When they recognised their visitor, their faces registered a mixture of relief and delight.

"Hey, Man, are we glad to see you?" were Moose's first words. "Get us out of here before that maniac colonel gets his way."

"Not so simple," cautioned Brett. "First I've got to get those manacles off."

"The colonel's got the key," said the other man, one of the lesser lights of the Montego Bay group. "I saw him pocket it when he locked us up."

"Then we'll have to find another way," was Brett's brisk response. He looked around for a suitable lever. In a corner was a branding iron - another inheritance from the plantation's slave labour past. Inserting the handle of the implement into the link attaching Moose's chain to its ring in the wall, he exerted all his strength and forced it open. He did the same with the other chain. Although each prisoner still had a manacle and a length of chain attached to his wrist, at least he was free to move. Brett led the pair up the steps, and raised the trapdoor just enough to peer into the hall. His view of the door was blocked by the stairs. Motioning the prisoners to wait, he crept to a position from which he could see the front door. The guard still lay unconscious by his chair. Signalling to Moose to help him, Brett propped the guard on the chair with his head lolling forward onto his chest, to all intents and purposes fast asleep at his post.

Brett and the freed prisoners were about to mount the stairs to leave by the route through the maid's bedroom, when a measured tread sounded from the floor above. Colonel Thompson was on one of his middle-of-the-night tours of his defences. As they heard the footsteps leave the walkway and head for the landing above, the three men scuttled for the cellar steps, and had replaced the trapdoor by the time the colonel reached the head of the stairs. His eye fell on the apparently sleeping guard as he reached the bottom. Outraged, he marched over and kicked the man's leg. Slowly, the guard toppled over, to sprawl on the floor at the feet of the open-mouthed colonel.

'The prisoners have escaped', was his first thought, but before raising the alarm, he rushed over to the trapdoor, raised it, switched on the light, and clattered down the steps to check.

By this time the two erstwhile prisoners were back in their places, the broken manacles hidden by their bodies. Brett was behind the wine racks, out of sight, but he made a slight noise that caused the colonel to move suspiciously over that way. He caught sight of Brett just as the others sprang to their feet. They pinioned his arms, and Brett emerged from his hiding place with a broad grin on his face.

"Good evening Colonel," he said. "Remember me?"

"No," blustered the Colonel, peering closely at Brett. "Who the Hell are you?"

"The 'brat from Kingston' you took on as assistant to the English hydrologist."

Slowly, the realisation dawned that this man was the very Brett Johnson they had set out to trap. That he was also the brat he had sponsored to work on the plantation stuck in Colonel Thompson's gullet.

"So this is how you repay my kindness?" said the Colonel bitterly.

"You were kind out of self-interest then. Now you've a chance to indulge your self-interest again. In exchange for free passage out of here, you will not be harmed," Brett told him.

"And if I refuse?" asked the Colonel, who was not lacking in courage.

"We'll have to fight our way out, with you as a hostage," he was told. "A needless lot of blood could be spilt, including yours."

The Colonel looked disparagingly at the weapons available to the three left-wingers - Brett's pistol and the revolver taken from the knocked-out guard.

"You don't think they're going to get you past my defences do you?" he asked.

"With your help, yes", he was told in a determined voice.

"What do you mean?" the truculent Colonel demanded.

"What I mean," explained Brett patiently, "is that you are going to stand down your gunmen, order them into the cellar, and lock them in. If you don't, you will be in the lead when we attack your machine gun positions."

Weighing up the possibilities and plumping for valiant discretion, the Colonel decided, for the time being at any rate, to comply with his captor's demands. He led the way up the stairs and on a tour of the walkways to the fortified turrets at the corners of the house. At each position he ordered the man on guard to abandon his gun and follow him. The small procession wended its way down to the trapdoor. The guards were herded down the steps, and the trap door bolted. Colonel Thompson, too valuable an asset to be disposed of yet, was not left behind. Instead, he was instructed to open a side door, and order the guard there to come inside. As the man entered, a pistol was stuck in his ribs. He lay down his rifle without protest, and was, in turn, pushed down the cellar steps. The trap door was re-bolted.

Meanwhile, the time had arrived for changing the guard, an event Brett had not bargained for, but the Colonel was relying on. The sergeant in charge of Chief Inspector Anderson's men had roused them for their spell of guard duty. When he found the first of the gun-posts was unmanned, he raised the alarm. The sound of running footsteps reverberated through the house. Brett's small party took advantage of the ensuing chaos to burst through the door and make a run for the trees, dragging the Colonel in their wake. Before they reached the cover of the palms, one of the machine guns at a front corner had been

re-manned, and began spraying fire across the open space. Fortunately for the fugitives, the gunner was a policeman in-experienced with the weapon. His fire was aimed too low, and raked the ground well behind the escaping group.

Once out of sight of the house, the group stopped to deal with the Colonel, who was now a liability. His wrists and ankles were tied with his own shoelaces, and he was gagged with his own handkerchief. Before his speech was cut off he managed to recover sufficient of his breath to gasp out,

"You've not seen the last of me, Johnson. If it's the last thing I do, I'll see you pay for this. If you don't hang, it's through no fault of mine."

Brett Johnson merely gave him a disparaging look in reply. He was left propped against a palm, struggling against his bonds. The trio of left-wingers melted into the plantation with Brett leading them over the familiar terrain. It was not long before Colonel Thompson managed to free himself. His shouts brought reinforcements - his own men and police - with the Chief Inspector not far behind.

"They headed towards Bog Walk," the Colonel reported. "Get after them."

Immediately, the police and those of the Colonel's men not locked in the cellar, set off towards the village - the wrong direction as it transpired. The fugitives had doubled back, and were travelling east, aiming across country in the hope of later picking up transport to take them back to the Blue Mountains. After his men had milled around in the plantation without success, the Chief Inspector called off the search. He guessed that his quarry must by then be miles away.

'Am I doomed to be out-foxed by this man?' he muttered

beneath his breath, a feeling of frustration bordering on desperation overcoming him.

Returning to the plantation house, the Chief telephoned army headquarters to report the latest setback to Colonel Watson, his voice betraying his mortification at yet another loss of face. He felt less embarrassed when he was informed that half a battalion had failed just as badly in the Blue Mountains as he had in the Cockpit Country. Colonel Watson was fuming as he described the effects of the Obeah drums and death symbols.

"I would never have believed that the Obeah mumbo-jumbo could have such an effect," he marvelled. "Some of my troops were reduced to gibbering idiots. Now the Prime Minister tells me that walkouts are bringing industry to a standstill - Obeah again! It looks as though there's some connection between the left wing revolt and the rise in Obeah activity."

"That's all we need," said John Anderson, with a resigned shake of his head. "Can you think of a more unholy alliance? Please keep me posted, Colonel, and it would be as well for your people to keep a lookout for Johnson's return to the mountains. I suspect he's heading that way."

"Thanks, Chief Inspector. I'll act on your information. Meanwhile, goodbye, and good luck," he said abruptly, slamming down the telephone as Lieutenant Butler came in with his latest assessment of the situation.

John Anderson looked quizzically at his receiver before replacing it. He was more accustomed to handing out such treatment than receiving it. Still, Brett Johnson had begun to get to him also - long ago, it seemed. As his reason for stationing men at the plantation house had disappeared, and was now on his way to - who knew where? - Chief Inspector

Anderson ordered his men back to Kingston. The sergeant was instructed to keep them on standby, in case of further developments outside the remit of the army. He retired to his home to catch up on some decent sleep. He told himself he was getting too old for this cat-and-mouse game.

SOUTHAMPTON
JULY, 1973

As Superintendent Baker passed through his secretary's office, and was about to unlock his own door, the TELEX machine in the corner chattered into life. He had only dropped in to check his mail before going off for a rare day out to Wimbledon. For the first time in the club ballot, he had drawn Centre Court tickets for the men's semi-finals day. Nothing's going to interfere with that, he told himself, dreading his wife's reaction if he allowed official duties to spoil an experience she had coveted for years. Nevertheless, he felt obliged to read the TELEX in case it was something important. The message coming off the machine was an important one; good news on the West Indies marijuana link at last. It read:

SOURCE OF STUFFED BANANAS LOCATED. SUPPLIERS
IDENTIFIED AS LEFT WING POLITICAL ACTIVISTS, BUT
NOT ALL APPREHENDED. DO NOTHING YET AT UK
END. WILL ADVISE FURTHER.
J A: KINGSTON: 6 JULY, 1973
COPIED TO WILLIAMS AT SCOTLAND YARD

With a sigh of relief that no instant action was necessary, Superintendent Baker went happily off to pick up his wife and enjoy the tennis. That morning, the weekly Fyffes boat docked. As was now routine, Customs Officers had the whole unloading and distribution process under surveillance. Bananas from the Thompson estate were followed from the docks to the ripening stores, through the unpacking and grading phase, to the reject bins and the incineration plant. The pattern was the same as before. Bucky Wilson turned up at the plant the next day with a Bedford van, and handed over a package in exchange for ten heavy-looking boxes. He drove the van to the back of a snooker club near Kings Cross, where seven of the boxes were unloaded and carried inside. The other three boxes were delivered to two pubs and a night-club, where this time Bucky received small packages in return.

The destination of the boxes left at the snooker club was a mystery to the surveillance team. To the Special Branch Inspector heading the observation it seemed unlikely that the ganja was simply stored there. He thought it more likely that there were pushers among the club clientele, and the club was a distribution centre for smaller quantities of the drug. In spite of the negative result, his report confirmed one of the last links in the chain. Arrests could be made at any time. All that was necessary now, to wipe out this particular drugs operation, was word from the Kingston end that the principals there had all been identified and located. Simultaneous crackdowns would then be the order of the day. Nothing much could be done about the minor producers at one end, or the users at the other, but at least, two sets of middlemen and the pushers would be taken out.

'No doubt the gaps they leave will soon be filled by others, and the game will start all over again', Inspector Williams thought, on hearing the news, 'but there'll be one less supply route, and a raft of low life removed from the scene'.

KINGSTON, JAMAICA
THE SAME DAY

On the far side of the Atlantic things didn't look so rosy. Brett Johnson had escaped the net yet again, and Chief Inspector Anderson was beginning to despair of ever landing the man. The intervention of Obeah was bad news.

'If the effects on the army are half as bad as Colonel Watson described, what about the effect on my men? With luck, they won't be put to the test, if the army can be licked into shape to do its job', he mused, but consoled himself with the thought, 'But they're a tough bunch, so I guess I can rely on them in a tight spot'.

He was about to finish off his frugal breakfast with toast and mango jam, when a call came through from the Prime Minister's office.

"Can you attend a ten-o-clock meeting with the PM, the Industry Minister and Colonel Watson?"

"Of course," he replied.

"Good, we'll send a car," and the private secretary rang off without further ceremony.

At 9.30 an official car drew up outside. The chauffeur was standing by the open rear door by the time the Chief Inspector reached the pavement. He settled in the back seat, and was whisked off to Mr Manley's office. On the way he tried to second-guess what the Prime Minister wanted, and rehearsed the answers to hypothetical questions. With a sinking feeling, he anticipated that the meeting would have some connection with Brett Johnson.

Sure enough, as soon as the PM entered the office, he ushered the other three men to the table where a large-scale map of the island was laid out.

"Colonel," the Prime Minister said, "for the benefit of these gentlemen, give us a summary of what you told me last night."

Colonel Watson cleared his throat, and began speaking in measured tones, with an apparent calmness he didn't feel.

"All over the east of the island, people in factories and construction projects are walking out," jabbing his finger as he spoke at Spanish Town, Kingston and Port Antonio. "They're saying they are afraid to work because of Obeah. That's bad enough, but what concerns me more is that they're forming themselves into mobs, chanting anti-government slogans, and calling for Brett Johnson. I don't —"

"There does seem to be an unholy alliance between Obeah and the left wing," broke in the Industry Minister.

"Yes", agreed the Colonel. "I found that out to my cost in the Blue Mountains. My men were turned back from an assault on a left wing stronghold in the Stoney River gorge by Obeah drums and death symbols. Their morale's at an all-time low."

249

"The question is, what can we do about it?" asked the Prime Minister. "What's your view, Chief Inspector?"

"I'm not very optimistic, Sir. I've been trying to lay hands on Johnson for months now. He's like a will-o-the-wisp, popping up all over the place and disappearing again. Last night he managed to free two of his friends who were being held as bait in the cellars of Thompson's plantation house. The only consolation I can offer is that he probably hasn't been able to re-join his comrades in the mountains."

"Good," put in the Prime Minister. "If he's isolated, he can't do much harm, but we've got to prevent him collecting more followers. I'm inclined to call a state of emergency. That will allow me to make strikes illegal and put a ban on Obeah activities."

"Obeah's been made illegal before - in the last century - and all the law achieved was to drive it underground," cautioned the Chief Inspector. "As far as I know, it's still illegal."

"That's as may be" replied Mr Manley, "but it won't do any harm to resuscitate the law as a reminder."

"You can make as many laws against Obeah as you like. Enforcement's going to be the problem," stated the colonel. "I'm sure the Chief Inspector will agree that the police force's too small for the job. Even the army would be spread thin on the ground, particularly if it has to implement a state of emergency."

John Anderson merely nodded his agreement. His thoughts were back with the events of the previous night. He was racking his brain to come up with ideas for tracking down the elusive Johnson, to no avail. The Industry Minister concurred with Colonel Watson's views.

"There's not much we can do about the mumbo-jumbo itself," he said, "but it's going to take a state of emergency to force the workers back against the threat of Obeah. If industry's at a standstill for more than a few days, the economy will take a nosedive. It's already in a pretty precarious state."

"That settles it," said the Prime Minister. "This afternoon I'm going to introduce a Parliamentary Motion for an emergency debate. I'll have a word with Seaga beforehand. There shouldn't be any Opposition problems if he knows the facts of the matter."

A state of emergency was declared that evening, without a division. It made little difference. The malign force of Obeah was stronger than anybody had anticipated. A few hard left groups exploiting the situation put up fierce resistance, using weapons that appeared as if by magic, but the majority of the workers simply melted away; some into their shanty towns, some into nearby villages. Wherever they went, it was not back to work. By withdrawing units from their positions in the Blue Mountain foothills, the army was able to concentrate sufficient firepower to subdue some of the revolting workers' groups, but that allowed the band in the Stoney River gorge a respite. They gathered a few reinforcements, and were able to re-supply with food and ammunition. Brett Johnson was still missing, however. This situation was quite acceptable to Wade Robinson, who had never taken to the idea of playing second fiddle. As far as he was concerned, the man could stay away for good.

The man in his thoughts was not all that far away. He and his companions, after narrowly avoiding the few army patrols that remained in the area, had decided to lie low for a while.

Seeing the Obeah death symbols guarding paths leading up into the mountains brought a grim smile to Brett's face.

'It looks as though the Queen's keeping her promise', he thought, remembering his ordeal at her hands, and the subsequent understanding. 'Perhaps she can be persuaded to help us to disappear for a few days'.

He put the idea to his two companions. Having heard his account of the encounter, neither Moose nor his friend was keen to go through the same experiences, but Brett could be very persuasive if necessary. Soon they were heading across country in the general direction of Lucky Valley. Heading straight through the village, Brett led them along the familiar path up to the clearing where the ceremony had taken place, and beyond to the hut where he had been made the Obeah Queen's sexual plaything. He began to feel soreness just at the thought. The hut was completely empty. There was no sign that it had ever been occupied by Obeah.

'Surely I didn't imagine everything. It was all too vivid and painful. This hut was full of Obeah paraphernalia that I'd no idea existed. I couldn't possibly have imagined it. The woman was real enough, and so was the fear and the pain', he reasoned, keeping his thoughts to himself. 'This place is probably one used for major ceremonies, and she has some other place'.

To the others he turned a baffled face.

"This is the place alright, but the bird seems to have flown," he told them. "Our only hope is to go back to the village and try to find the Rastafarians who kidnapped me."

The scene in the bar was a spine-tingling example of déjà vue. Four Rastafarians were playing cards and smoking at a table - whether the same four, he couldn't be sure. At any rate, with the backing of Moose and his friend, he was not apprehensive about approaching them. Going directly up to them, with the other two in close attendance, he asked,

"Remember me?"

"Yeah, Man," said one. "So,what?

The four shoved back their chairs and rose, ready to attack, or defend.

"No need to be alarmed," Brett told them, but he was prepared for whatever action was necessary. "I'm not here for revenge. I need to see the Obeah Queen."

"Not possible, Man," the evident leader of the four told him. "The Queen sees nobody. She'll only accept petitions through Obeah."

"She'll see me," predicted Brett, with a show of confidence he didn't feel. "Either you take us to her, or we make our own way."

His bluff cut no ice with the Rasta, who was perfectly well aware that there was no way that anybody could find the Queen without the Rastafarians' assistance. He looked speculatively at Moose, who flexed his massive shoulders and glared at the four. Any thought of violence was suppressed, and the man agreed, with obvious reluctance, to escort them. The other Rastas were never far behind. A short walk to the fringe of the village brought them to a small, modern bungalow. The Rasta's knock was answered by a conventionally dressed, but statuesque woman whom Brett was sure was the recently elevated Obeah Queen. The contrast of the atmosphere of normality generated by her present clothing and surroundings with the ambience of the Queening ceremony was startling. She offered a hand to Brett, which he shook self-consciously.

"Come in," she invited Brett and his men. "You are expected. Please sit."

They sat in the chairs indicated, set in a semicircle in front of a large, ornate desk.

"You seem surprised to see me without Obeah regalia," she began. "If I wore that stuff all the time it would clear my hotel of guests. "My superstitious followers expect it though."

Still with his mind boggling at the transformation to this efficient looking businesswoman, Brett nevertheless began to doubt the powers of Obeah to extend the effects it had initiated.

"I'm grateful for what you did to halt the army's advance in the mountains," he said, "but as well as protecting my people in there, I want to start a left-wing rebellion throughout Jamaica when my preparations are finished."

"Obviously you've been out of touch with events. Your revolution's already under way. All over the island, workers are walking out under the instructions of Obeah. Some have arms, and are attacking the security forces," she told the astonished Brett.

Aghast, he had great difficulty in controlling his anger, but managed to speak in a relatively calm voice.

"Don't you understand that a rebellion needs co-ordination, and central direction?" he asked her in exasperation. "All these little independent risings are like pinpricks to the army. They're doomed to failure. They'll be isolated and picked off like ripe mangoes. The actions are too soon and too scattered."

The woman stared at him with rising anger.

"You must realise that Obeah's a blunt instrument," she replied. It works through fear - of the unknown - and rumour.

There's no way rumour can be confined to one place. You asked for my help. You got your rebellion. You must accept the consequences."

Stunned by the news, and nonplussed by her attitude, he rose to leave. Moving towards the door, and followed by the others, he was not surprised to find the way blocked by the Rastafarians. From behind him came the voice of the Obeah Queen.

"You surely don't think you can be allowed to leave, knowing what you now know about me and Obeah. Kill them," she instructed the Rastamen.

The Rastas moved to carry out her instruction. Drawing their knives, they came at Brett. He side-stepped the stabbing blow of the man in the lead, grasped the wrist of his knife arm with his right hand, and gave it an outward twisting wrench. There was a sickening crack, accompanied by an agonised scream as the man's elbow dislocated. Moose picked up a chair, and wielding it like a flail, smashed the weapons out of the hands of the two who attacked him. Discarding the chair, he grabbed them by the dreadlocks and brought their heads together with such force they rebounded. Neither took any further interest in the proceedings. The fourth Rasta fared better. He succeeded in thrusting his knife between the ribs of Moose's partner, who collapsed and lay dying as his life-blood spread rapidly over his shirtfront. Moose bellowed with rage and flung himself forward. The attacker took one look at the advancing giant and fled for the door, which he slammed behind him. Moose was delayed long enough for the man to escape through the front door of the house. He sprinted through the village as though pursued by the Devil himself, and disappeared into the trees on the far side.

BANANA

Brett turned to deal with the Obeah Queen. She had vanished. A search of the rest of the bungalow was fruitless. So now, he had another, more implacable enemy, allied with the powers of darkness and the unseen. He could not repress a shudder at what might have happened in the Queening ceremony, and what could still happen. In the drawer of the desk he found car keys. They fitted the Volkswagon beetle parked in front of the bungalow. With the passenger seat pushed as far back as it would go Moose was just able to cram his bulk into the vehicle. As Brett was familiarising himself with the controls, Obeah drums began to sound from all sides. She had lost no time.

"For Christ's sake, Brett", shouted Moose. "She's stirred them up already. Step on it, and let's get out o' here."

Brett did as he was advised. With a squeal of tyres the little car shot down the road towards Prospect and Bog Walk. He had nothing more in his mind than the need to put as many miles as possible between them and the centre of Obeah power. When he reached the A1 at Bog Walk he turned right, for no rational reason, and headed for Ocho Rios. A few miles from the town he encountered the tail of a slow-moving army convoy. Minutes later the convoy stopped and troops began to set up a roadblock. The Volkswagon was waved back. There was no alternative but to turn and go the opposite way. Brett reversed into a lane entrance, turned back, and had travelled no more than half a mile when the engine spluttered and stopped. The petrol gauge showed empty. The two men abandoned the car and struck across country, aiming to circle round the road block and make their way on foot to Ocho Rios, where Brett reckoned they would have a better chance of lying low for a while.

They had not gone far when the rattle of machine gun fire, punctuated by the crack of rifle shots, announced a battle ahead. They had just crossed a minor road running roughly east to west. About a mile away, to their left front, they could see billows of black smoke rising.

"That looks as though it could be coming from the Ameral bauxite plant," speculated Moose, who was familiar with the geography of the area.

"And my guess is, the workers have revolted, and they're under siege," Brett replied. Let's get closer and see what's happening."

Cautiously they crept through the forest, keeping a lookout for army units. Now the small arms fire was interspersed with the thud of mortar explosions. The defenders were being subjected to an unmerciful bombardment.

CHAPTER 14

GALINA POINT

Steve and Della awoke from a deep sleep when Mrs Paige knocked on the door. Waiting for Steve's sleepy, "come in," she entered bearing a laden tray. A full 'English' breakfast was put before the ravenous pair. There were eggs, bacon, sausage, tomato and lashings of toast, with butter and marmalade. A large pot of tea topped it off.

"Mrs Paige, we're very grateful," Steve told her. "Here we are, people you don't even know, and you're treating us like royalty."

"Think nothing of it," said the good lady, dismissing his concern. "You come to us, battered and half-drowned. What do you expect us to do? I couldn't live with myself if I'd turned you away, and my husband wouldn't have been very pleased, either. Just enjoy your breakfast, and then I'll drive you down to Ocho Rios. You can catch a bus there."

"The least I can do is wash the dishes before we leave," offered Della.

"That would be appreciated," Mrs Paige replied. "Maria hasn't turned up again today - she's my maid - supposed to help me with the bed-and-breakfast guests and my domestic chores. That's two days running. She'll come back with some cock-and-bull story about the Obeah lady telling her not to work."

"Surely Obeah isn't that strong, is it?" asked Steve.

"Very powerful in these country areas, especially among the farmers and labourers," Mrs Paige told him, "but I never know whether to believe her when she trots out the Obeah excuse. I suspect 'Obeah holidays' are as frequent as the Catholics' saints' days."

At that moment, Mr Paige called them through into the main part of the bungalow, sounding very worried. He had been listening to the radio. Quickly, he told them,

"There's an uprising of industrial workers across the country, and particularly at the bauxite plants run by the big three foreign companies. They seem to be well armed, and the situation's so serious, the army's been called in. The Prime Minister's declared a state of emergency. There are rumours, according to local correspondents, that Obeah's behind it".

"No wonder your maid hasn't turned up," said Steve to Mrs Paige. "She's probably scared witless."

"So that's the reason," she replied, turning to her husband, who was reaching for his pistol.

"I know how anti-Obeah you are, John, but I think it's all a lot of gobbledegook. There's no good to be done by blowing your top."

She ushered Della and Steve back into their room, where their uneaten breakfast was getting cold. Della took the opportunity for a private word with Steve.

"I've got to get back to the Montego Bay Group," she said quietly. "I'm not doing my job here, enjoyable though it's been. It's not the best time to take a holiday."

"After what you've been through, I think you're entitled to a holiday," Steve told her, as he caught hold of her round the waist and kissed her tenderly on the lips. There was nothing she would have liked better than to respond, but she pulled away gently, and said,

"Please, Steve. I have a job to do. I must try to contact my boss. If we can get to Ocho Rios, I should be able to get in touch with him through the police there."

Mrs Paige came back into the room.

"I'm afraid I won't be able to take you into town after all. My husband thinks that, with the fighting going on, it'll be too dangerous. I'm sorry, you'll have to make your own way," she added, in a worried tone.

"Never mind, Mrs P", Steve told her. "That's what we assumed we'd have to do anyway. We'd better be off now. Thanks again for your help. Goodbye."

Della took Mrs. Paige by both hands, looked into her eyes, and said quietly, "Thank you, Mrs Paige. You've no idea how close to collapse I was when you took us in. I'll always be grateful to you. Goodbye."

"Go on with you, my dear. Anybody would have done the same. Goodbye and good luck to both of you."

Waving as they went, they walked up the drive and set off on foot along the Ocho Rios road. Minutes later they flagged down an empty minibus with the destination Ocho Rios on the front. The driver said he could take them to the outskirts of Ocho Rios, but no further, because of the fighting on the other side of town. Sure enough, they were stopped on the outskirts at a roadblock manned by soldiers. The lance corporal in charge came over. He had been with the unit operating in the Cockpit country, and recognised Steve.

"You're Dr Andrews, the hydrologist, aren't you? We thought you'd bought it in the caves," he said, a note of wonder in his voice.

Steve wasted no time in explanations. Nodding, he said, "We need to get through to see your Colonel or Chief Inspector Anderson."

"I don't think they're in Ocho Rios," replied the Lance Corporal, taking off his helmet and scratching his head. "Lieutenant Butler's OC here," he said helpfully.

"Good, we know the lieutenant. Can you take us to him?"

They were waved to a nearby jeep, and were soon on their way through town. On the far side of Ocho Rios, an occasional 'crump' of a mortar bomb or a hand-grenade, and the rattle of machine gun fire were signs that the fighting was not far away. The bauxite plant was out of sight behind a tree-covered ridge, the only indication of its presence being an ugly red effluent stain, spreading into the sea from the nearby river mouth.

'The company's contribution to the local ecology', thought Steve, bitterly, the hydrologist in him taking the pollution almost as a personal insult.

Another environmental contribution now caught his eye. A drifting cloud of black smoke billowed above the trees. Something vulnerable had stopped a direct hit. The

jeep turned off the road without warning, onto a track rutted by heavy trucks, and bumped its way along to the edge of a huge quarry. On the rim of the quarry a group of soldiers had set up a communications post, protected by a machine gun nest. Lieutenant Butler was there, directing operations, and nearby was Chief Inspector Anderson. A second white man and a black police sergeant were lying near the edge of the quarry, observing the scene through binoculars. Steve and Della joined them.

Startled, John Anderson turned to the new arrivals. His face lit up at the sight of the agent he had given up for lost until he received the call the previous night.

"Della, am I glad to see you. The thought of two agents lost was unbearable. You'd better let me have a report on your activities as soon as possible - which won't be yet," he exclaimed, as a burst of automatic fire came their way.

Everybody ducked. When they raised their heads again, the eyes of Chief Inspector Anderson and Steve Andrews met.

"Dr Andrews, I presume," the Chief said with a grin. "Welcome back, Steve. I'm grateful to you for restoring Della to us."

"It's only temporary," Steve warned him. "She's got a bee in her bonnet about getting back undercover."

"That's something we need to discuss," said John Anderson, turning a severe gaze on Della.

Just then the white man still watching the quarry rolled on to his side.

"I know that voice," he said. "Steve, me old hydrological oppo. How's your belly for spots?"

Steve greeted his old geologist friend enthusiastically, wringing his hand warmly as he scrambled to his feet.

"Jack Bevington. You old reprobate. What are you doing mixed up in a shindig like this?"

"I only work here," his old friend said with mock sadness. "I got driven out with the rest of the management this morning when the men went on the rampage. I don't know what's got into them."

"An unholy mix of left-wing politics and fear of Obeah," chipped in John Anderson. "A powder keg just waiting to explode."

"Well, let's hope the lieutenant and his men can do something about it," was Jack Bevington's response. "Then we can get together for a jar, Steve."

"I'll look forward to that. There's a lot to catch up on. "The last I heard, you were working in the States."

"In Missouri, for the same company, Ameral. I'm a sort of peripatetic geologist, going around their sites troubleshooting, and at the same time doing a bit of bauxite prospecting."

"I'll bet you didn't bargain for this sort of trouble," Steve said, indicating the battle still raging in the plant below.

"No, nor this," replied Jack, as a company Land Rover careered down the track and came to a halt nearby with a screech of brakes.

Out clambered an enormous bull of a man. His thick, ridged neck, and sun-reddened skin labelled him as the archetypal red-neck. He had been the quarry boss at the biggest Ameral plant in Missouri, where the workers lived in fear of his violent

BANANA

methods. To his mind, anybody to the left of J F Kennedy was a Commie, and he wasn't sure about him. When signs of labour unrest in the Jamaican operation surfaced, he was the company's automatic choice to be sent in to sort things out. The liberal-minded Jack Bevington had already crossed swords with the fellow, over his rough treatment of men complaining about conditions in the quarry. Now, though, the man's target was the lieutenant.

"Are you crazy," he bawled, jabbing a finger towards the burning building below. "Look what your idiots are doin' to mah plant. They-all should be down there rootin' out them nigger rebels han'-to-han', 'stead of lobbin' mortars random fashion."

The grating Southern speech and the man's reference to his black brethren as niggers didn't go down well with the lieutenant. He ostentatiously took his pistol from its holster and held it dangling from his hand, evidently prepared to use it if necessary.

"Your only concern's for your precious plant. Mine's for the safety of my men," he said, angrily. "It would be suicide to send them in without softening up the rebels first."

"That plant gives employment to yo' folk. It's only jus' economic now, what with yo' Gov'ment levy on bauxite expo'ts. Now that Commie bastard Manley's got in, he'll force us to smelt here. Then there'll be a levy on aluminium an' all, he said, expressing his disgust by spitting near the lieutenant's feet. Now yo' git yo' asses down there, an' stop wreckin' mah plant," he shouted, fully expecting to be obeyed by the lieutenant.

Lieutenant Butler turned his back on the bullying quarry boss, and calmly ordered his men to step up the mortar bombardment of the positions of the rebels below. The redneck stormed off,

hurled himself into the driving seat of the Land Rover, crashed his gears in his haste, and hurtled off down the track. Minutes later, the vehicle appeared at the quarry entrance. It raced across towards the working face, drawing fire from the rebels occupying the hopper, crusher and screening buildings as it went. A bullet scored a direct hit on a rear tyre, and the Land Rover slewed to a halt near the giant excavator. Grabbing a pump-action shotgun from the back seat, the redneck leapt out. Firing random shots towards the rebels as he went, he ran for the ladder to the cab of the excavator. Scrambling up, he wrenched open the door and flung himself at the controls. He jabbed at the starter button, and the leviathan roared into life. Expertly manipulating the levers, he brought the giant boom of the machine round to rest its bucket string at the top of the conveyor taking ore to the crushing plant - stationary since the start of the uprising.

There was no doubting his courage. Switching off the excavator motors, he climbed out of the cab, and stumbled his way up the boom catwalk, temporarily protected from shots aimed from below by the string of huge buckets. A figure carrying an automatic rifle appeared in the conveyor entrance to the crushing plant. Red-neck dropped to one knee and blasted him backwards with a single shot, then disappeared from the view of the onlookers, into the plant. The watchers included Brett and Moose, who had arrived at the top of the working face of the quarry just in time to see the action at the top of the crusher conveyor.

"That maniac's got to be stopped," Brett said to Moose, casting around urgently for some means to descend the quarry face.

His eyes lit on the many yards of cable connecting the charges set ready for the next blasting operation. Ripping out several lengths, he knotted them together, tied one end round the nearest tree, and flung the other down the quarry face. He grasped the improvised rope, and was about to ease himself over the edge when Moose put a restraining hand on his shoulder. "No, leave this to me.

Taking the knotted cable in his enormous hands, he lowered himself hand-over-hand down the rock-face. As soon as he reached the bottom, Brett followed, but Moose didn't wait for his friend. He sprinted for the conveyor, hauled himself on to it, and was racing up towards the top of the crushing plant before Brett could stop him. Reaching the gloomy interior of the crushing shed, he found himself above the jaws of the gigantic crusher, now stationary. The body of the shot man lay nearby, a gaping wound in the side of his head. On the far side of the landing, Redneck was lying prone on the decking, exchanging shots with unseen defenders at a lower level in the next building. Leaping over the mouth of the crusher, Moose launched himself at the back of the quarry boss, who heard the attack coming, but wasn't quick enough to turn to face it. Moose's powerful right arm encircled the thick neck and forced the head back, while his left hand tried to wrestle the shotgun from the two-handed grip of the man as he hit back over his head to try to dislodge his assailant.

The two big men were equally matched for strength. Moose felt his neck-hold slipping as the muscular shoulders hunched and the bullet head strained forward. He was forced to release his hold on the gun. As he did so, the man made a supreme effort, throwing him off and rolling clear. He rose, holding the shotgun by the barrel and, wielding it like a club, lunged for Moose. Moose side stepped, but caught a glancing blow on the side of the head that momentarily stunned him. Instinctively, he grabbed the gun and, as he fell, took his attacker with him , raising his feet and pitching the man into the jaw-crusher, still holding his shotgun. Redneck staggered to his feet, straddling the jaws, and aimed the gun at the groggy Moose, who was himself just rising to his knees. Brett arrived on the scene, took it in instantly, and pressed the 'on' button of the crusher at the same time as the gun was triggered. Moose was blasted backwards by a shot taken full in the chest. His death was accompanied by the screams of the man disappearing inch-by-inch into the maw of the giant crusher.

Brett turned away, sickened by the result of his spur-of-the moment action. He saw that he could do nothing for his friend. There seemed to be a lull in the fighting outside. Cautiously, he peered across the quarry from the position from which the killer of Moose had been shooting. There was no sign of the men who had been defending the next building. No more shots or mortar bombs were coming in from the quarry rim. There was a deathly silence, almost palpable after the din of the conflict. Over at the quarry entrance, military vehicles were collecting, ready for a final assault on the buildings. The defenders had re-grouped in the building that housed the silos of crushed and graded ore. Brett could see that their continued resistance would be futile. How could he and they escape?

He had seen the giant excavator in operation when Moose's killer had used it to gain access to the top of the crushing plant.

'If I can find out how to drive the thing, I can use it to climb out of here', he concluded. Pausing only for a last, sad look at

his newly made, and lost, friend, he ran down the conveyor belt to the excavator, stumbling over the lumps of shattered ore as he went. As he leapt on to the boom, and sprinted along it, he drew fire from the troops on the far quarry rim, but the distance was too great for accuracy. Inside the cab he was protected, and the firing stopped. Poring over the controls, he was baffled at their complexity. There were so many levers! There was a plaque in front of him that he presumed described their functions.

'Hmm. I need an instruction book to follow this', he thought. 'It'll have to be trial and error. I don't have time to work it out. At least I can tell which is the start switch'.

He threw the switch, and the monster roared into life. Gingerly he tried small movements of the various levers, and watched their effects on the boom. Soon he was fairly confident that he could swing, raise and lower it. Control of the vehicle's movement was a different matter. Each of the gargantuan tracks was operated independently, with its own forward and reverse gears. By the time he had made any sense of how to synchronise them in order to reverse away from the conveyor, he had half-demolished it. Even then, the machine zigzagged drunkenly backwards towards the quarry face. Before he reached it, he realised that he would have to choose a spot where the face was lower. Stopping one track, he allowed the machine to swivel so that he could drive it forwards, and be better able to see where he was going. Raising the boom to its full elevation, be brought it up close to the face. It just about reached the rim of the quarry.

Switching off the engines, Brett glanced back to check that the rebel defenders had realised what he was doing. A band of figures running in his direction from the silos was sufficient indication that they had. They were not the only ones who realised. As he hauled himself up the steeply inclined boom catwalk, a fusillade of shots rang out, from the far quarry rim and from the troops advancing from the entrance. Brett was panting from exertion, but unhurt, as he scrambled from the end of the boom, onto the cleared strip at the edge of the quarry. Losing no time, he ducked low and sprinted across into the cover of the trees, accompanied by the zing of bullets. It was a close call, and he thought the chances of the rebel band emulating him were slim.

'If I'm to get out of this in one piece, I haven't time to stop and find out', he told himself, and reluctantly set off to put as much distance as possible between himself and the quarry. It was soon obvious that his progress over the broken, jungle-clad terrain was too slow, and he was forced back onto the cleared strip next to the quarry edge. There, he was out of sight of the troops below, but in full view of those with Lieutenant Butler on the far side. Again he was lucky that the distance made the moving target difficult to hit. Unscathed, he headed for the quarry entrance road, now clear of troops, who were otherwise engaged inside the quarry.

Back on the quarry rim, Della was trying to persuade her boss that her duty was to go back under cover with the left-wingers in the Blue Mountains.

"I'm still in their confidence, and I can still give you useful information on their intentions," she told the Chief Inspector. "There shouldn't be any radio communication problems like those in the Cockpit Country."

Reluctant to risk his agent again with the embattled band in the Stoney River gorge, the Chief Inspector began to give his reasons.

BANANA

"I don't —"

He was interrupted by the lieutenant, who was standing nearby, listening to the conversation.

"Excuse me butting in, Sir. It wouldn't be wise for Miss Brook to try to rejoin the band up the Stoney River. Obeah's stepped up its activity in the area, and we're getting reports - unconfirmed yet - of some of our men being zombified. Half the troops are terrified, and on the point of mutiny. The rest can't wait to get their hands on the Obeahmen and the rebels they think are behind them. It wouldn't be safe for anybody thought to be connected with the left-wingers."

"That settles it," the Chief Inspector told Della. "I want you to report to HQ for other duties. I'm heading back to Kingston myself for a meeting. You can catch a lift in my car."

"If I'm no further use to you, I ought to be getting back to my job," chipped in Steve Andrews. Any chance of me coming with you?"

"That goes for me, too," said the hitherto silent geologist. "I need to give a firsthand report to Ameral headquarters. If you can squeeze me in, I'd appreciate a lift."

The motley collection piled into the Chief Inspector's car, and bumped off down the track to the coast road, leaving the lieutenant to organise pursuit of Brett Johnson.

CHAPTER 15
LUCKY VALLEY

Shortly after disappearing from her bungalow, the Obeah Queen re-appeared, in full regalia, in her hut near the jungle clearing above Lucky Valley, surrounded by its previous contents. Squatting before her altar of skulls, she contemplated the recent events in a cold fury. It was obvious to her that the left-wing rebellion she had espoused was likely to fail.

'Too little, too soon', she thought. 'I've got to prevent a government backlash, or Obeah will be destroyed as well'.

She came to a decision. Minutes later the Obeah talking drum began to boom out a message. It was taken up and relayed by other drums in the surrounding hills. After nightfall, flaming torches began to appear around the clearing containing the massive tree stump. Whirling figures sprang into view. Obeahmen and women in their threatening, horrific costumes

gyrated in their dance of death. 'Possessed', they spun faster
and faster to the accelerating drum beat until, with a heart-
stopping screech, the Queen bounded into their midst. At
her appearance the drums stopped. The grotesque dancers
prostrated themselves in a circle around her, with faces in the
dust, and outstretched arms pointing towards her. This time
she was not naked. She wore a vulture-feather head-dress, and
a dogskin cape with feather epaulettes. Her face was hidden
by a hideous horned dog-mask. In her hand she carried a long
staff tipped with a flaming human skull. Turning consecutively
to north, east, south and west, she gestured with the staff, each
time calling in a strange, ululating language. After the final call
there was dead silence for a minute. Then, to the muted beat of
a drum, from the four points of the compass, small processions
entered the clearing. Each consisted of four Rastafarians bearing
an empty coffin, two others escorting a soldier with his hands
tied behind his back, and an Obeahman prancing along behind,
swishing a sisal whip. The processions came to a halt at posts set
in the ground, forming a cross with the Queen at its centre.

The petrified soldiers' hands were freed, and they were
stripped naked. Each man was bound to one of the four stakes,
facing the Queen, with their hands behind the stakes, and ropes
around their necks and ankles.

'This time, no half measures', the Queen muttered to
herself.

She moved around from man to man, blowing into the face
of each a small cloud of zombie dust, poured from a gourd onto
the palm of her hand. The dust was a concoction based on the
dried and powdered carcasses of poisonous land and sea reptiles,
puffer fish livers and deadly leaves of tropical plants, designed

to induce a state of suspended animation resembling death. Its action was more extreme than the puffer fish poison administered alone. To ensure that the dust was inhaled, as it was blown into the face of each man, the guard behind him took away the hand that had prevented him from breathing, so that he was forced to gasp for air. Eyes popping with suffocation-induced terror, the prisoners had no option but to take the deadly dust deep into their lungs. Immediately after the dust had been inhaled, the antidote, consisting of a suspension of ground tropical leaves, animal and human bones, in a mixture of sea water and alcohol, was applied by the coffin bearers. Handfuls of the vile-smelling green liquid were poured from gourds and rubbed into the skins of the unfortunate soldiers to prevent sudden death. When the skin-rubbing phase was complete, the victims were cut down and placed in their coffins. The rough wooden coffins were set in a square around the Queen, now seated on her tree-stump dais, and the Rastamen stood sentinel at the corners of the square.

The solitary drum began to beat out a slow, insistent rhythm, gradually increasing in loudness. Obeahmen formed a circle around the coffins and moved in a strictly co-ordinated, stiff-legged dance. With hands held above their heads, palms up, their routine was; four bent-kneed steps forward, a two-legged hop back. On and on they went, round and round, in ecstasy-inducing repetition.

At the first sign of dawn the drum rhythm was increased to a frenzied beat. From the mouths of the dancers came spine-chilling screams, and they fell exhausted to the ground. The Rastafarians lifted the lids off the coffins, removed the 'corpses' and bound them again to their stakes. The Obeahmen with the

sisal whips, who had stood motionless during the whole of the proceedings so far, stepped forward and lashed the bodies systematically all over. When the zombified men showed signs of reviving under the lashes, they were force-fed a paste of datura stramonium, the so-called zombie cucumber, and salt solution, intended to revive them, but maintain the state of living death.

The four men were then marched round the clearing, supported by pairs of Rastas, until they were able to walk by themselves. They were taken down to the village, shoved in the back of an old Bedford van, driven east, and released where they could do most harm, near the hamlet of Durham, where they had been picked up. Troops besieging the Stoney River gorge were concentrated there. That's where they would be known. When they were found wandering, with staring eyes, able to see, but unable to speak, a wave of fear and alarm spread through the army units. The dread name Obeah was whispered. Many of the lower ranks refused to go near the paths that were guarded by Obeah death symbols. A full-scale mutiny appeared to be on the cards. A signal was sent back to the commanding officer in Kingston, who immediately requested a meeting with the Prime Minister.

OCHO RIOS

Chief Inspector Anderson's car had just turned onto the coast road when a call on the car radio informed the driver that Brett Johnson had been spotted running along the quarry entrance road. Lieutenant Butler was requesting interception by any police cars in the area. John Anderson snatched the handset, acknowledged the message, and ordered the driver to turn into the road. It was deserted.

"Another wild goose chase," muttered the Chief. "Stop here, and help me to search the bushes," he told his driver.

The two policemen got out, to be confronted immediately by a determined-looking Brett Johnson, wielding a pistol. With a wave of the gun, he motioned for the other passengers to get out. At the sight of Della Brook he registered no surprise.

"So, my suspicions were justified," he said in a voice so low it reached only her ears. "A pity you're as treacherous as you're attractive," he hissed, remembering the vision on the rock and the episode that followed, when it seemed their feelings were mutual.

She looked him straight in the eye and said, also in a whisper, half defiantly and half regretfully,

"I had my job to do, Brett. At another time, in different circumstances, things could have been different."

"Get back in the car," he ordered her. "You're coming with me," and said to the rest of the group, who were still standing by the side of the road, covered by his gun, "I want free passage to the airport at Montego Bay, and a 'plane fuelled up. This woman's betrayed me once. If I see any sign of pursuit I'll not hesitate to kill her."

His germ of an idea was to fly to Cuba. If he could persuade Della that her future lay with him, so much the better. The last thing he wanted to do was kill her.

"Into the driving seat, and drive like hell," he instructed her, throwing himself in the passenger seat, and holding the gun to her head. Della turned the car in the entrance road and set off in a cloud of dust towards the coast road. As it turned left and vanished, an army jeep appeared from the direction of the quarry. The chief inspector leapt out in the road and flagged it down. Recognising him, the driver stopped.

"What are your orders?" the Chief Superintendent asked the corporal who was the only passenger. "To intercept Brett Johnson," the soldier replied. "I've been told to check that road blocks have been set up on all the roads out of Ocho Rios."

"He's heading west, in a police vehicle," John Anderson told him, "but he's got a hostage. He shouldn't be stopped."

"Jump in," said the corporal, urgently. "It's probably too late."

The four men piled into the back of the jeep, and it roared off in the direction the fugitive had taken. It was too late! A bare third of a mile along the coast road, where it crossed Dunn's River, the road was blocked by army trucks. Della brought the car she was driving skidding to a halt, broadside on, only just avoiding a collision. Brett made her get out on his side and, pointing the pistol at her head, and grabbing her by the wrist, forced her to the side of the road. There was a path down to the river below. Dragging Della behind him, he almost fell down the steep path, while the soldiers looked on helplessly, their weapons cocked but afraid to fire them in case they hit the girl. The path ended at the riverbank. There was no alternative but to take to the river. Although shallow, it was fast moving. Wading downstream would be the easier option, Brett decided. Pulling Della along in his wake, he headed downstream. Behind

him, the soldiers, uncertain whether to leave their roadblock, stood in confusion as the pursuing jeep pulled up.

"They've taken to the river - heading downstream," yelled the lance corporal in charge.

Out of the jeep leapt the chief inspector, the geologist and Steve Andrews. Steve wasted no time. He tore across to the path, tumbled down it and pitched face-first into the water.

"Let them go," advised Jack Bevington. "The river here falls down a limestone escarpment, six hundred feet high, in a whole series of step-like terraces. You can climb down - tourists go up and down all the time - but it's a lot easier driving down to the beach. We can get to where the falls hit the beach as soon as they do."

The corporal gave orders for a guard to be placed at the top of the path, and then he and his passengers got back in the jeep and drove off at speed down the beach road. Meanwhile, Steve had found his feet in the swift-flowing river and set off in pursuit of Brett Johnson and Della, who had by then disappeared behind overhanging vegetation, towards the falls. He made much quicker progress than Brett, encumbered by Della, and caught up with them on the brink of the first step in the fall. Brett, hearing his splashing approach, swung round to face him, with the pistol pointing at Steve's chest.

"I don't want to have to shoot an old friend," he said, calmly, "but if you give me no choice, I promise you I will."

For a moment, he had taken his eyes off Della. She coura-geously lunged for his gun arm, and succeeded in deflecting the gun away from Steve, who hurled himself at the man he now saw as a rival. Grasping Brett's arm, he attempted to wrestle the weapon away. Brett released Della's wrist and brought his

left fist crashing against Steve's temple. The blow felled Steve, who nevertheless took Brett down with him. They both slipped over the edge of step of the falls, into the pool a few feet below. Their momentum took them over the lip of the next step, to fall yet again over the edge. The force of the impact with the rocky bottom knocked the gun from Brett's grasp, and the ducking restored Steve's reeling senses. He fought like a tiger against a man who was much more at home in the water. When Brett fought free and staggered off down the limestone terraces, Steve launched himself recklessly after him. Once more they grappled, sometimes one on top, sometimes the other, both emerging half-drowned, only to fall over an edge into the next pool as they struggled. On and on they fought, down and down, until they tumbled down the final cascade, into the shallow pool on the beach. Steve was held down until he stopped struggling, too exhausted to fight on. Brett Johnson, himself at the end of his strength, released him and staggered off down the beach, following the river on its path into the sea. He had waded out, waist deep and started to swim with a feeble stroke by the time the chasing group in the jeep arrived on the scene.

The corporal and his driver splashed in after Brett, but as both were poor swimmers they were reluctant to follow out of their depth. They returned to the beach, where they had left their weapons, and began taking pot shots at the small target of Brett Johnson's head, moving slowly towards the gap in the reef created by the river flow. Eventually the head disappeared. Had Brett Johnson met his end, or was he simply hidden by the surf breaking over the reef? They couldn't tell.

Della, scrambling down the waterfall terraces in the wake of the battling men, caught her breath in alarm as she saw Steve floating face down in the pool at the bottom of the falls. She hadn't the strength to haul his big body clear of the water, but dragged him far enough into the shallows to get his head and shoulders onto the beach. Rolling him onto his side, she pummelled his back to make him disgorge the water in his lungs. Although water poured from his mouth, he still showed no sign of breathing. Feeling the beginnings of panic, she found herself asking the question,

'What do I do now? What did my hostess training tell me to do in a case of drowning?'

Her training came to her aid. Pushing Steve onto his back, she tilted his head back, made sure his tongue was not blocking his throat, held his nose closed and began mouth-to-mouth resuscitation. Placing her mouth over his, she blew into it until his chest rose, then stopped, and pressed down hard on his chest. Again and again she repeated the pattern, to no avail.

When John Anderson arrived, he took in the scene, and rushed to Della's assistance. He began pressing down on Steve's breastbone between her mouth-to-mouth breaths. To their relief Steve vomited more water, his whole body convulsed, and he began to fight for breath, coughing water and spluttering. His eyes opened in a blank stare at first, then gradually focussed on the anxious face above him. He managed a wan smile. Della smiled back. All she could think to say was,

"I love you, Steve Andrews."

The Chief Inspector pulled the 'body' clear of the water, and now feeling that he was in the way, retreated in embarrassment. Steve, with Della's assistance, climbed groggily to his feet, and weaved his way on rubbery legs to the jeep, where he flopped thankfully on the rear seat. He had never in his life felt

such weakness. It had its compensations though! Della fussed over him like a mother hen, until, that is, the reaction set in. As the adrenaline drained from her system, she began to tremble, and almost fainted. John Anderson, turning from watching Brett Johnson escaping yet again, saw what was happening and caught Della before she fell. He pushed her in beside Steve, who was beginning to revive already, and encircled her with a protective arm.

"You, young lady, are going to take ten days' sick leave before you report back for duty," the Chief told his undercover agent. "A spot of leave wouldn't do you any harm, either," he said to the hydrologist. "I'm sure the University could spare you for ten days. There are plenty of places on the island where you could find some peace and quiet," he added, with a fatherly twinkle in his eye.

Della and Steve looked at each other, and the idea dawned in their minds simultaneously.

"Mrs. Paige's," they said, in unison, and burst out laughing.

The corporal and his driver were standing by, looking thoroughly bemused.

"Corporal, will you take us back to Galina Point before you go about your business?" Steve Andrews asked him.

"Whatever you say, Sir," replied the corporal, glad to make a positive contribution to something. He issued instructions to the driver, who straightaway started his engine, rammed the vehicle into gear, and roared off down the beach. Ten minutes later he deposited them at the front gate to the Paige's bungalow.

KINGSTON
LATE THE SAME DAY

Chief Inspector Anderson arrived late for his meeting with the Prime Minister. Mr. Manley was already deep in conversation with Colonel Watson and Commander King. As the head of the Special Branch was ushered into the cabinet room, the PM was saying, with a grim face,

"This is the most serious crisis facing the country since the sugar crop failure. If we don't do something soon about this twin threat from Obeah and the Maoists, we're going to rue the day Johnson was ever allowed to land."

Waving the latecomer impatiently to a seat, he was about to ask about progress on the Left-wing front when the Chief Inspector forestalled him.

"The news about Brett Johnson is that he escaped us again, but he was last seen swimming out to sea in a weakened condition. He disappeared from sight, out beyond the reef at Dunn's River beach. With a bit of luck, it could be the last we see of him."

"Didn't anybody follow him, Man?" asked the incredulous Prime Minister.

"No strong enough swimmers, and no boats nearby," the Chief Inspector replied, his face reddening with embarrassment.

"Well, never mind that for the moment," Mr Manley snapped. "What I want to know is what's being done about his followers. Even if he's gone, he's left a dangerous legacy."

"We are making some progress there, Prime Minister," put in Colonel Watson. "I've reports that the rebellion at the Ocho

Rios Ameral plant has been snuffed out, and most of the rebels killed. Our problem now's the spread to other industrial sites."

"Fuelled by the Obeah connection," commented John Anderson. "That's the key."

"Yes," agreed the colonel. "The only reason we can't dislodge the left-wingers from the Stoney River gorge is my men are running scared of Obeah. Not surprising, when they see their friends turned into zombies."

The Prime Minister looked at him sceptically. "You don't really believe all that guff," he exclaimed.

Feeling more and more on the defensive, Colonel Watson replied,

"Well, I haven't seen them myself yet, but according to the report of a very reliable officer, four men in a zombified state have been picked up in the same area near the gorge where they disappeared twenty-four hours before. Their skins are green, they're covered in whiplash weals, they've got staring eyes, and they can't speak. Oh, and they walk as though they're moving through molasses, my lieutenant says."

"Hmmph," snorted the incredulous PM. "In that case, what do you propose to do about it?"

"Drop an elite force at the top of the gorge - soldiers who haven't been in contact with Obeah yet,"- the colonel answered, trying to keep his tone civil in face of the anger he felt at the attitude of the Prime Minister. "Attack 'em in the rear."

"Fine," agreed the Prime Minister, recognising the suppressed anger, and moderating his approach. "But that does nothing about Obeah."

Commander King, silent until now, voiced his opinion. "There's no way you're going to eradicate Obeah. It's been tried before. All that happens is that it goes deeper underground. What we need to do is cut off its head. Yesterday I had a contact from an undercover source who's managed to infiltrate Obeah, and is actually posing as a minor Obeahman. He's had to lie low because of army activity in the area, but managed to get a radio message out. A new Obeah leader - 'Queen' they call her - was 'accepted' recently at a ceremony in the Lucky Valley area. Why don't you send another elite section in to capture her, and then make an example of her?"

"Good thinking," agreed Tiger King. "To the ignorant, Obeah priests are invincible. They can't be killed. If we could eliminate this Queen, and publicise the fact, it would set Obeah back out of sight."

"Do it," commanded the Prime Minister.

As the men rose to leave, Colonel Watson raised a restraining hand. "One more thing," he said. "These rebels seem to be exceptionally well armed - mainly with Russian weapons. I suppose they're coming in through Cuba?" he asked, turning to Tom King.

"There's no doubt about that," replied the Commander. "We stop a lot, but you know the north coast. It's easy to land small shipments at any number of sites. What really baffles me is where they raise the finance."

"Easily answered," John Anderson told him. "Castro will finance any left wing rebellion".

"A bloody unholy trinity!" exclaimed Tom King. "Obeah, Communists, and Rastas".

The meeting broke up, and the men went their various ways; the colonel to organise his elite force, the Secret Service and Special Branch chiefs together to compare notes on the Left Wing and Obeah.

Next day a task force of fifty airborne troops was dropped in relays by helicopter on the pass at the top of the Stoney River gorge. They swept down the rocky gorge, trapping the small band of defenders in their caves. Most of the rebels were quickly wiped out. Only a group of ten, holed up in a cave whose entrance was protected by a jumble of large rocks, managed to hold out for any length of time. They were well supplied with small arms and ammunition, and had plenty of food and water. Hand-grenades lobbed over the rocks couldn't be directed into the cave entrance, so failed to dislodge the defenders. The situation was stalemate, calling for desperate measures if it was not to drag on for days.

The captain leading the airborne force ordered an abseiling attack down the cliff above the cave entrance. Two men on parallel ropes descended to right and left of the cave, to positions where they could, by bracing their feet against the cliff-face, lean out and throw their grenades deep inside. The few occupants not killed or injured by this new tactic immediately surrendered. Casualties among the airborne force were light, a few flesh wounds and a couple of broken ankles sustained in scrambling for cover amongst the rocks. The victorious force, carrying its injured, and driving its explosion-dazed prisoners ahead of it, picked its way down the gorge to Durham. On the way they destroyed the Obeah death symbols they came across. They were met in the village by Colonel Watson, who congratulated them on their success, but lost no time in dispatching them to Lucky Valley.

Captain Ross's orders were to comb the area for Obeahmen, hold them prisoner, and destroy any Obeah paraphernalia found. As one squad of troops, under the command of a

sergeant, entered the clearing in the jungle above Lucky Valley, a hidden drum struck up an ominous, staccato beat. After a few seconds it stopped, and the beat switched to another drum nearby. In turn, a relay of drums encircling the clearing took up the menacing rhythm. The men exchanged apprehensive glances, which turned to raw fear when all the drums, as though at a conductor's signal, began to boom out sounds that struck them like body blows. Seeing the effect on his men, the sergeant, just as fearful himself, rapped out an order, and led them at a run down the path that, unknown to him, ended at the Obeah Queen's hut. She, in full regalia, sat cross-legged in front of the pile of skulls, facing the door. Her face was covered with a dogs-head mask, and she was swathed in her feathered cape. Draped across her shoulders was the serpent symbol of the dark power of Obeah. She muttered incantations in some unintelligible language as she stirred the contents of an iron pot sitting on a hot charcoal fire. When thick vapour began to rise from the pot, she tossed in a pinch of another ingredient. With a 'whoomph' the vapour ignited to give an incandescent light that temporarily blinded the intruding soldiers.

Gradually the blinding light subsided, and sight returned to the men. The scene that met their eyes was still well illuminated. The Queen had become a human torch. Her cloak and mask were blazing furiously. A blood-curdling shriek was turned into a continuous scream as her hands tore at the flaming mask. It was no good. Her own flesh was on fire. There was a sudden, nerve-tingling silence as the flames cut off the air supply to her lungs, and the screams and drumbeats stopped simultaneously. The shocked soldiers looked on in open-mouthed awe as the burning body collapsed into an unrecognisable heap before them.

The sergeant was the first to recover his composure. Shakily he gave instructions for the flames to be doused, then reported back by radio to Captain Ross. His description of the events in the hut, and identification of the body as female were sufficient to convince the captain that the Obeah Queen was no more, but his superiors insisted on seeing the evidence themselves. He was instructed to put a guard on the hut and its approaches. Colonel Watson arrived on the scene with Captain Ross to find a scared-looking sergeant standing in the doorway of the hut.

"The body's vanished, Sir" he reported, almost not believing his own words.

The charred remains had been spirited away right under the noses of the guards. To add to their fear of the unknown, a drum nearby began a sombre beat, which was taken up instantly by others further away, relaying its message into the distance. The message conveyed was at first one of death, but gradually the first drum's beat took on a triumphal note. 'The Queen is dead, but the Queen lives' it seemed to say. All around, and away into the distance, louder and louder, the insistent beat built to a crescendo. Then, suddenly, silence reigned.

"This is appalling," Colonel Watson said quietly to his captain. "The last thing we want is to reinforce the idea of Obeah immortality. Get me a radio link to the Prime Minister, fast."

He reported the latest developments to Mr Manley, who was not impressed with the bungling that had allowed the body to be removed. There was still rebel activity in several industrial centres, and still a chance that the rebellion would spread. The Prime Minister had followed up his declaration of a state of emergency by taking the precaution of mobilising all available troops. Any spread of a belief in the power of Obeah,

and the invincibility of its Queen, would be a threat to the government's own power. The threat would have to be countered. He decided on a direct broadcast to the nation. That night the regular radio programme schedule was interrupted by a Prime Ministerial statement, which was preceded by the National Anthem.

"Fellow Jamaicans, we are facing a national crisis. Our industry is being brought to a standstill by a left-wing rebellion, fomented and armed by Cuba, and backed by Obeah. Your Government has the situation well under control. The rebel leader is believed to have drowned, trying to escape capture by swimming out to sea. The rebel band that took over the Ameral bauxite plant has been defeated, and many of them killed. Other plants are under siege by the army, and in a short time I expect to announce that the rebels there have also been eliminated. Today, the Obeah Queen burned to death in a fire started by one of her own magic rites. So much for the myth of Obeah immunity to death! The cult is a sham, and its practitioners are merchants of fear and mumbo jumbo. I advise you to ignore Obeah threats and rumours, and ask you to support the Government against the Maoist subversives. Thank you, and good night."

SOUTHAMPTON
AUGUST, 1973

The TELEX machine in the HM Customs superintendent's office chattered out the message:

ORIGIN OF GANJA BANANAS TRACED TO
THOMPSON ESTATE.
LEFT WING SUBVERSIVES RESPONSIBLE. MIDDLEMEN
ELIMINATED. NOW ALL CLEAR FOR UK ACTION. J.A.
KINGSTON, 9 AUGUST, 1973

Receipt of this message triggered a joint Customs/Drugs Squad operation to round up Bucky Wilson and the other UK links in the chain, who had all been under surveillance for weeks. Film evidence of every part of the collection, transport and distribution system had been amassed, and every link from the prime mover to the dealers identified. Simultaneous dawn raids in Southampton and London turned up a motley crew of surprised and bewildered criminals. The re-arrest of Bucky Wilson gave Inspector Williams the most satisfaction.

"Welcome home, Bucky," he greeted the drug distributor as he was escorted into the interview room. "This time you'll be a guest of Her Majesty for a good ten years, but you're lucky at that. If it was left to me, you'd be locked up for good."

The criminal looked murderously at the Inspector, but said only,

"I want my brief."

He was well used to 'helping the police with their enquiries', and had every intention of providing as little help as possible.

"I suppose you want the same shyster who defended you last time," prompted Inspector Williams. "You know the form – you're allowed one 'phone call."

When the solicitor arrived, Bucky was charged with importing and distributing cannabis resin, on the basis of film

evidence. He was advised to say nothing, but his silence did him little good. Next morning he appeared before a special magistrates' hearing, and was remanded in custody to await trial in Crown Court. The dealers with previous convictions were also remanded in custody, and the rest of the drugs supply chain given bail, on condition that they reported weekly to their local police stations.

CHAPTER 16
RETURN TO GALINA POINT

Steve knocked on the door of the Paige's bungalow. It was opened tentatively by Mrs Paige. Her face lit up with a smile of delight when she recognised the young couple. "Dr. Andrews and Miss Della, how lovely to see you again! Come in - come in," she welcomed them and waved them inside. With some embarrassment, Steve realised that, all along, the good lady had known they were unmarried. Shepherding them into her sitting room, where they were greeted like old friends by John Paige, she insisted that they sat, and offered them tea. Gratefully, they accepted, and she bustled off to prepare it. Out came her best Royal Worcester china and a well-stocked biscuit barrel. Once satisfied that they were comfortable, and well supplied with tea and biscuits, she sat down herself, and beamed at them in turn.

"Well, it is good to see you both looking so much better," she said. "I was so concerned when you turned up in such a sorry state."

"We are very grateful for what you did," Della told her, and one reason we're here is to thank you again. But the main reason is to ask you whether we can possibly stay in your holiday accommodation for a few days. Of course, we expect to pay."

"Of course you can, my dear. It's not being used at the moment, and we'll be more than pleased to have you," Mrs. Paige told her. "Consider it yours for as long as you like. It is supposed to be self-catering accommodation, but I'll be happy to cook meals for you. You can eat with us if you like. My husband and I would both welcome the company."

She looked at them, instantly read the body language between them, and said, in a voice full of understanding,

"What an old fool I am. Of course, you want to be by yourselves. Your part of the bungalow is completely separate, so you can do whatever you like, when you like, but even so, we would like to see you occasionally."

Gratefully, Steve gave Mrs. Paige a hug.

"Just one more thing, do you mind if we have a swim?" he asked. "It would be nice to freshen up."

"You can swim anytime in the pool. We don't use it nowadays," she told them. "Or, if you're a bit more adventurous, there's the sea pool cut through the reef."

So that's what it was! The eyes of the couple met as they remembered all too well their traumatic experiences the night they were wrecked on the point, on that stormy night not so long ago, and Chinee went down with the boat. Now there was no wind. The sea was flat calm.

"I'd rather swim in the sea pool. It sounds exciting," said Della, grasping Steve's arm, and pulling him through the door into the extension. "We can be more private there," she whispered, when out of hearing range, not wishing to upset their hostess.

They made their way round to the rear of the bungalow, across the terrace, and down to the ancient reef. Gingerly, they picked their way between the razor-sharp old coral heads. By this time the sun was nearing the horizon. To their left, and illuminated from below, a bank of low cloud glowed red, orange and yellow, the colour mix changing from minute to minute as sunset approached swiftly. At the edge of the pool cut in the rock, Della quickly stripped off her clothes. At last her reason for wanting privacy dawned on Steve. Both of them had only the clothes they were wearing - no swimsuits. While she stepped slowly down the ladder into the water, facing him, and he took in the stunning lines of her body, he shed his own clothes. His arousal was plain to see. Embarrassed, he leapt into the water.

Della, spotting his condition, dived off the ladder and headed playfully towards him underwater. Opening her eyes at the bottom of her dive, she looked straight into the eyeless sockets of a bloated, yellow-black face. Chinee had not gone down with the boat! In the eerie evening light streaming in from the outlet to the sea, he was a horrific sight. She let out a scream which would have been piercing had it not been under water, and promptly fainted.

Steve, anticipating some sort of horseplay, ducked his head and looked around below him. Instantly he took in the scene. Della was floating just below him, evidently lifeless. Next to her was a fully clothed body. Duck diving, he linked his hands under her arms and kicked hard for the ladder. With a supreme effort, he climbed the rusting rungs, hauled her up one-handed, and laid her out on the hard rock. His reaction had been so quick that, although she had swallowed water, none had penetrated her lungs. Seconds later she was spluttering and gasping.

"A corpse. Down there. I think it's Chinee," she managed to get out.

"I know. I saw it. But I think we'll have to leave it where it is. Getting you out was as much as I could manage," he told her. "Come on," he said, handing Della her clothes. Let's get you to bed."

He helped her to pull the dress over her wet body, picked her up and carried her back to the bungalow, oblivious to the sharp coral under his feet, and unconcerned at his own nakedness. Back in their bungalow annex, he laid her down, and sat on the side of the bed. Her eyes fell on the inflamed scars of the barely-healed cuts on his chest, sustained when he was dragged across the coral on that stormy night that now seemed so long ago. Tears welled in her eyes as the realisation struck her that this man she loved had once again saved her life. She flung her arms around his neck and clung to him. If only such a moment could be frozen in time, she thought she would be happy to forego the rest of her life.

Steve Andrews winced as she pressed against his lacerated chest, but did nothing to move her and ease the pain. To have won the love of this special woman was all that mattered to him. He hardly dared contemplate what could have happened to her at the hands of Brett Johnson.

'If there's any justice, he thought, the arrogant sod's shark bait now'.

The object of his thoughts was nothing of the kind. After the fight down the falls he was almost too weak to swim, but immersion in the sea gradually restored his strength. Half an hour later he was swimming powerfully along the outer edge of the reef towards Ocho Rios. He had no plan except perhaps to go ashore and disappear into one of the resort complexes. Any such idea was banished when a coastguard patrol boat rounded the headland. He snatched a deep breath and dived. Clutching a fan coral anchored to the reef face to hold him down, his hope, tinged with pessimism, was that he hadn't been spotted. His pessimism was well founded. The specific remit of the coastguards was to find him, or his body. Binoculars were trained on him even as he dived. When he shot to the surface with bursting lungs, automatic weapons had substituted the binoculars. He was hauled on board roughly. Feigning exhaustion he collapsed in the well of the boat. More used to dealing with heavily armed Cuban gunrunners than unarmed fugitives, the four man crew let him lie.

The officer in charge radioed base and asked to be put through to Chief Inspector Anderson. When John Anderson came on the air, he couldn't keep a note of triumph out of his voice.

"Chief Inspector, Coastguard here. We've got your man. Where do you want him?"

The reply came over the loudspeaker.

"Take him to the police station in Ocho Rios. Tell them to hold him 'til I get back to take him to Kingston. I'm on my way to Galina Point to check up on Dr Andrews and Miss Brook."

"Understood, over and out."

Officer Thomas had no idea who John Anderson was talking

about. Brett Johnson had. He had listened to the whole exchange. Mention of the two names galvanised him into action. He sprang at the nearest man, held him in a neck lock and snatched his sidearm. Cocking it he pointed it at the man's temple and ordered,

"Throw your weapons in the sea. You," pointing to the officer, "tie them up, including this one, and make a good job of it".

The guns went overboard and the officer used a coil of rope on the deck to truss his colleagues. In minutes they were sitting back to back in the well, tied up and tied together.

"Now head for Galina Point, wherever that is", was Brett Johnson's next instruction.

The officer looked at the chart and saw that Galina Point was not far along the coast to the east. He revved the idling engine, engaged it and headed that way. Fifteen minutes later the boat was abreast of a solitary bungalow on a bluff overlooking the promontory.

"There it is. What —?"

Whatever the officer was bout to ask was cut short by a pistol blow to the side of his head. Brett Johnson caught him as he fell, dragged him to the well, and tied him up with the others. He threw the anchor over the side and waited until it caught before spying out the land. There was only the one residence on the Point.

'That must be where they're staying'.

He tucked the pistol into his belt, slipped over the side and swam the short distance to the raised reef. Reaching up, he hauled himself up the three feet or so on to the coral. Picking his way carefully across the uneven surface, he approached the bungalow on its windowless side. To avoid what appeared

to be the living quarters he crept round the landward side. Facing him was what looked like an annex. It was the annex where, unknown to him, Steve and Della were now sleeping. He dropped on all fours as he neared it. Raising his head cautiously he peered in at the windows from which the storm shutters had been hooked back. The kitchen was empty. The sitting room was empty. The bedroom - judging by the faint snores, was occupied. Peering between the slats of the half-open louvres he saw, turned towards him, a face he recognised. Steve Andrews was on the near side of the bed. The hump under the sheet behind him must be Della Brook. An overwhelming feeling of jealousy, frustration and anger swamped his rational being. He smashed down the louvre screen and climbed over the still. The startled sleepers shot up in bed. Their nakedness infuriated Brett Johnson even more. He covered them with the coastguard's pistol.

"Get up" he snarled, glaring at Steve. "Get over there in the corner. "You," he motioned with the pistol to Della, "come here".

Cringing, she grabbed the sheet to wrap around her and did as he ordered, moving to his side. His intention had been to kill Steve Andrews, who he now saw as a deadly rival, but his rage subsided as he contemplated the vulnerable man standing in the corner, hiding his nakedness. The old days in the banana plantation came flooding back into his mind. He contented himself with firing a warning shot into the wall beside Steve.

The profound silence following the loud report was broken as the connecting door to the annex crashed open. John Paige stood there, leaning heavily on a crutch, his pistol at the ready. Taking in the scene rapidly, he fired once. The heavy calibre bullet took Brett Johnson in the middle of his back and flung him towards Steve. Shot through the heart, he died as he fell. John Paige, unwittingly, was responsible for the beginning of the end of the revolution he feared.

Chief Inspector Anderson heard the shots as the army jeep carrying him pulled into the drive at Galina Point. With the corporal and driver behind him, he leapt out and tore across to the outer door of the annex as fast as his thickset legs would take him. The lock burst from its seating under the impact of his burly frame. Inside, he found a tableau frozen in time. Shocked, speechless people stared at a body lying face down in a spreading pool of blood.

'Too late again', he thought, in resignation. 'That must be Brett Johnson'.

He was the first to find his voice. His question was addressed to Della.

"Brett Johnson, I assume?" he asked, gesturing towards the body.

Still aghast at what had happened, and not trusting herself to speak, she nodded. Steve Andrews collected his wits with an effort and, determined to protect John Paige, explained what had happened.

"He shot at me and missed. Mr. Paige dropped him before he could fire again."

Steve moved to Della's side and wrapped a comforting arm

around her. John Anderson had every sympathy with the sugar engineer, and had no intention of apportioning blame.

"I understand. There will be a full police inquiry, of course, and I'll need statements from all of you, but they can wait," he said, his keen gaze taking in all his listeners in turn.

He looked directly at Steve and Della.

"Will you be staying here?" he asked.

Steve looked down at the upturned face of Della with unmistakable love in his eyes, and his raised eyebrows asked an unspoken question. She shuddered and shook her head. Nothing would persuade her to sleep in this room again.

"No," said Steve decisively. "You'll find us at the Casa Monte hotel, Chief Inspector. Ask for the honeymoon suite".

Della smiled up at him. She had no quarrel with that idea.

ACKNOWLEDGEMENTS

Rob Kerby, late of the Royal Australian Air Force, is thanked for his help with the technical information on helicopters available to the Jamaican Army in the early seventies.

Enjoyed this book?

Find out more about the author,
and a whole range of exciting titles at
www.discoveredauthors.co.uk

Discover our other imprints:

DA Diamonds traditional mainstream publishing

DA Revivals republishing out-of-print titles

Four O'Clock Press assisted publishing

Horizon Press business and corporate materials